D0678788

THE
DOGS OF
SNOQUALMIE

THE
DOGS OF
SNOQUALMIE

CALVIN MILLER

PUBLISHING GROUP

Nashville, Tennessee

© 2006 by Calvin Miller
All rights reserved
Printed in the United States of America

13-digit ISBN: 978-0-8054-4347-9
10-digit ISBN: 0-8054-4347-9

Published by B & H Publishing Group,
Nashville, Tennessee

Dewey Decimal Classification: F
Subject Headings: CULTURE CONFLICT—FICTION
                  WOLVES—FICTION
                  CLERGY—FICTION

06 07 08 09 10   10 9 8 7 6 5 4 3 2 1

To Barbara

PROLOGUE

The old priest could tell the wolf was hungry. On this misty morning, high in the foothills of majestic Mount Rainier, the priest had shot a rabbit and laid it on a rotting tree stump. It was intended as an offering for the wolf, whose prowling after prey was so unsuccessful his ribs all but protruded through his fur. "Good friend, *canis lupus,* father of dogs and the last of your kind to dare to live on the edges of a city. We have a job to do, you in your disappearing wilderness and I in an empty city of disappearing compassion."

The animal's powerful jaws ripped into the fur of the yet-warm rabbit. And the warmth of the dead rabbit gave up its warmth to the living. "Pardon the pun, my friend, but you certainly wolfed that down. *Veni canis lupus, amicus.*"

He laid the rabbit-killing fire-stick against a tree and turned his back on its killing power. This was the last dinner he would provide for the beast that seemed to want only what he wanted: a warm meal and a warm place to lie down before the snows came again. But even a beast cannot easily abandon a good friend.

The wolf turned toward the old man and approached him. When his broad muzzle was near enough, the rabbit-shooter reached out and touched him on the nose. The cold, wet nose fell against his warm hand, and the sandpapery tongue wrapped its enormous length nearly around the old priest's hand and wrist.

"I've never liked killing things, but in your case, I felt obliged to remember that the same mighty soul who made rabbits made you to prefer them. There is a plan set in motion now; and you who have found yourself alone, and separate from the pack must live alone. I can't give you much sympathy for your loneliness, for it is my calling too. And people will wonder where you've come from, and they will wonder where I have come from. Neither of us need answer, for where we are going is more important than where we've come from. For now, let us assume the roles that emerge from the question marks. I am shortly to become a psychotic, and you are shortly to be hunted in the forest. The world is a simple place as far as we're concerned. The cast is a simple trinity; there is God, I'm Peter, and, if I'm not mistaken, you are Kinta. Since you understand nothing that I am saying to you, it is pointless to tell you that the fire-sticks with the big barrels are called shotguns and will cause you no real trouble at a great distance. It's the skinny barrels with the heavy scopes that will pose your worst threat. Be careful."

The old man sat down on a large log and took a black outfit out of a sack. He took off his white coveralls and stood for a moment, thin and naked in the cold mist. Then he put on the black garment of a priest, complete with a clerical collar and a heavy neck chain that ended in a Celtic cross. "How do I look, old friend?" he asked his lanky companion.

The wolf looked baffled by the ranting of the man who had provided his dinner. But he understood nothing the rabbit-server said. He cocked his head and strained in such an effort at comprehension that the man laughed. "You look as though you are impersonating a human being by trying so hard to understand. But never mind. In Seattle everybody's impersonating somebody."

He took the giant head in his hands. "Be careful, Kinta!"

He turned to walk away, and the wolf followed him. He turned back and shouted, "None of that, now! Back into the forest! Keep to the shadows. I find my mind eroding. I'll soon be free of the wit required to shoot rabbits. So, off with you!" He stomped his foot on the ground and clapped his hands menacingly, and the animal turned back into the misty morning and was swallowed by fog.

Before the morning was over, the old man had no idea who he was nor what forest had been the womb of his psychosis. By late afternoon his mind kept no company with his body as he walked on toward the city.

Besides the wolf and the demented priest, there are only two other pertinent characters at this novel's beginning. One was a soul prejudiced against those he couldn't understand, despising them primarily because they were so unlike himself. Like the wolf, he too was a predator—a night stalker preying on those whose lives offended him. Unlike the wolf, he didn't kill to eat, but in a way, he did kill to live. There was a woman—her name was Victoria Billingsley—whom this unnamed man neither understood nor admired. None except she and the wolf need be named this early in the tale.

Kinta was hungry, and his need to leave the starving edges of the disappearing forest was great. Victoria was successful, and her success nagged the night stalker and fed his prejudices to the point of fever. And so he sat in a bar one Saturday night and ogled the woman as she laughed capriciously in the midst of her friends and hated her all the more for laughing when he so despised her. His hatred toward her blazed, and he followed her home from a bar where they had met. He drove his own car at a comfortable distance behind hers, so that she never suspected she was being followed.

The night seemed normal to Victoria as she prepared for bed. She listened to AC/DC on her Bose system and thought how her life was a blissful routine and smiled. But routines were not much of a security blanket in the uncertain world she called home. She felt the rip of terror in her gut as she heard the shattering of her glass patio doors. Immediately after the glass was shattered, someone hit the breaker panel, and all light died in the house. Fear, as she had never known it, gathered its clammy fingers about her heart, and her lungs froze for want of oxygen.

Two blue-green eyes gathered the last reflections of stingy illumination, and she heard a gurgle from the throat of something inhuman and hungry.

And that same April night in the same city, a priest fell asleep on the steps of a psychiatric hospital.

And so the tale begins.

CHAPTER 1

"Psychiatrists live off the fat of people who want to hire a listener without any intention of getting well. That's you, Levi. Why waste your money and my time?" Dr. Paul Shapiro was usually blunt with all his clients. Still, he preferred thinking of himself as honest rather than blunt. But Levi needed blunt. Blunt was, in his opinion, the only language the psychologically addicted understood. Had Levi been as honest as his doctor, he would have admitted he was addicted to his own ravings. He never got any better even when his doctor grew more blunt. So as Dr. Shapiro saw things, Levi needed blunt. All other forms of communication were lost on him. Besides it was Sunday afternoon, on the second of the month, and the doctor was violating his no-Sunday-therapy rule in merely agreeing to see Mr. Twist. But Levi was a pushy guy and had phoned the psychiatrist to see him for what he considered "an emergency!"

Levi Twist was the handsome icon of Pacific Woods. While he was well past fifty, he looked to be in his early thirties. This was due to his daily workout at the company's recreational and aerobics center. He pumped iron. His neck was thick, his arms crowded his shirt sleeves, and his waist pulled his boxy chest down to a lean and enviable picture of power.

But more than his body, it was his face that made him appear forever young. His dark hair and beard framed his wide-set eyes and sparkling white teeth with irresistible intrigue. A widower, he was quite popular at the best bachelor hangouts in central Seattle, often appearing in those chic bachelor tabloids that pack the door racks of singles bars.

Dr. Shapiro had been trying to get Levi Twist off his client list for more than two years. He had recommended a grief therapy group that Levi had attended then quit after two sessions because he "found himself in a group of people who were addicted to talking about themselves." Dr. Shapiro made it clear to Levi that "bores are those who insist on talking about themselves when you have a craving to talk about yourself." But Levi missed the force of his proverb, and as usual, found no way to apply it to himself. He just felt that grief therapy groups were not his thing.

"Levi, it's been five years since the death of your wife. You should be sufficiently free of her memory to begin other kinds of relationships."

Silence.

Then Levi's eyes clouded up, a tear or two systematically spilling out from the heavy lashes.

"I guess I'm just a one-woman man," he said. It was part of a self-pity tape Levi repeatedly played. "Will you renew my prescription?"

"No, I will not. This has gone on long enough. Drugs are not the answer. You don't need them, and I'm not going to give them to you any longer."

"Just like that you're saying no more uppers for me?"

"Just like that," Dr. Shapiro repeated.

"So, Doctor, you think you know what's best for me better than I do."

"I think you're close to dependency. I think you drink too much. I think you need to get honest about your grief . . . or your lack of it. I think it's not your wife's death that's bothering you. There's another pathology that's eating at you, and you don't want to discuss it. Whatever it is, it's so toxic that you're eaten alive by it—something dark that you don't want to face. I'm through wasting my time with you. You have a marked antipathy toward women in the corporate system. You're an antifeminist who can't control your rage. You need help but not for grief."

Levi stiffened. "It's women and gays who keep things riled up in America's corporate structure," he said and rose from his chair. It would be incorrect to say he stood. He never only stood. He always rose. A set of unseen hydraulics lifted him up till he towered impressively over the shattered world he wanted to terrorize. Psychotic or not, he was god of every world in which he stood. He was lord of the corporate world. He was president and CEO of Pacific Woods. He needed no fanfare to announce that he was king. He said it all by standing.

Dr. Shapiro also stood. He motioned Levi toward the door.

Levi balled up his hand into a fist. The size of the fist, knuckle-edged with white intention, caused Dr. Shapiro to step back.

Then Levi relaxed his fist and threw a parting shot. "You'll never understand what it means to lose your wife. You've still got Rhonda."

He turned and walked through the door and tried to slam it, but the heavy hinges slowed the slam to a felted close. He punched the sluggish door as he left the room.

Levi's anger terrified two people. Della Singleton, Dr. Shapiro's assistant, who had been dating Levi Twist off and on in a casual but deepening relationship, was always amazed at the force of Levi's anger. She wasn't at work on that Sunday afternoon, so she missed Levi's tantrum. Still, she saw him as a man at the mercy of his own rage. She pitied him for his unrelenting grief over his wife. But his fury always left her uneasy.

The other recipient of terror at Levi's anger was Levi Twist himself. He had run out of drugs and was prone to blame his runaway temper on that deficiency. As he drove to his lovely rural home on Snoqualmie River Road, he realized Dr. Shapiro was right. He did drink too much. The psychiatrist's assessment became a reminder of how hard it was going to be to get by without his next feel-good prescription. Levi knew how much he had used his overdone grief just to keep the drugs coming his way. There was only one answer to that, so he poured himself a glass of amber consolation and gulped it down—sipping held too small a cure for his mood. As he finished his drink, his eyes fell on a huge portrait of his deceased mate.

"Maybe Dr. Shapiro is right, my dear," he said to the photograph. "Maybe it *is* time to get honest. I have grieved your death long enough. I never missed your simpering dependency. Had I married the devil, I would have been as happy. I never loved you. But having been gracious enough to die, you were my ticket to the pharmacist. Now you're not even good for that. From hell to hell, you showed the way. You were my private purgatory while you lived— you're still my private purgatory."

He picked up the photo of his lost mate, frowning at it. Then he grinned at it and threw the photo across the room, shattering its case against the wall.

He walked across the room and planted his right foot on the shards of glass, grinding the slivers into her face. Then he poured himself another drink and picked up the demolished picture of his wife. "Bye now," he smirked at the damaged face and threw the picture in the garbage.

Then he picked up a more recent photo. It was a picture of his psychiatrist's assistant.

"Hello, Miz Singleton! You're the very picture of my way back to self-esteem."

CHAPTER 2

L ife is sometimes haunted even when the sun is shining," said Emma Silone. Gary Jarvis knew she was right. As long as he had been an inspector for the Seattle Police Department, he had never run into a murder so bizarre. "Madam—you are right—this is grisly!" he was answering her, and yet he was talking to the thin air. His sluggish mind could make no sense of the carnage before him. He gazed down at what was left of a woman whose neck and lower jaw were largely torn away. The half face that stared back at him was hard to study for long. Its missing parts turned his stomach. Apart from the fact that her neck and face had been decimated, there seemed to be no other marks on her body. He found this most puzzling. He looked at the victim one last time and zipped the body bag shut over the half face.

The old woman had quit crying, but her eyes were still red from all that the day had brought her.

"Now, Mrs. Silone, I want you to try one more time to remember anything that might be of help to us. This horrible crime happened just on the other side of the six-inch wall that separates your condo from hers. You must have heard something. There must have been some kind of noise in the neighborhood."

"Nope, no noise. I didn't hear a thing," she replied. But Gary, noting how she leaned forward and cupped her ear to hear him, realized she must have some hearing deficiency. "Victoria was a woman who lived a very quiet life. I never heard much out of her. But I did so like her, Officer. She was always very pleasant. She was most refined, and yet she was very athletic. She loved classical music and professional sports of all kinds—mostly football, but she liked baseball too. I often wished she stayed home more, but she never did. I can't tell you the number of times I have signed for her parcels. She did get a lot of those. She had a high-paying job, very professional, so she got a lot of those special, next-day FedEx letters. Her life seemed to have a beautiful quality about it. Victoria Billingsley. Even her name has a wonderful ring about it. It's elegant, don't you think, Officer?"

"Yes, I suppose," mused Inspector Jarvis quietly, almost to himself.

"Funny, though, for all the elegance of her name she was not too refined to subscribe to *Playboy* magazine," she said.

"Boy?" he asked.

"Boy what?"

"*Playboy,* not *Playgirl?*"

"Well, what's the difference?" asked Emma Silone.

"Well, they appeal to different kinds of people."

"Well, it's the same one my husband likes, so it must be *Playboy.*"

"That's odd. That's usually a man's magazine," said Gary. "Did she ever have men over to her house?"

"She never had anybody over that I remember. She lived alone."

It was easy for Gary to believe that Emma Silone heard nothing when the crime was committed, for she was obviously not hearing much of what the inspector was saying even now. She had discovered the crime after realizing that she had not seen her young, single neighbor for more than a day and had used her own key to enter the victim's side of the duplex.

"It must have been a horrible way to die, but at least it would have been fast. You know, Officer, my husband's been trying to kill me with Big Macs."

The young inspector tried to shrug off the heaviness of the crime he had come to investigate. He was not sure of the odyssey that the old woman's mind was about to begin.

"Yeah, my ex tried to kill me with Weight Watcher recipes, but I survived. You probably will too." Gary smiled, thinking she was trying to be funny. He was only trying to reply in kind, but a cursory study of her old gray eyes told him immediately that she was being most serious.

"Officer, mark my words. You'll be making a return call here at this condo. Next time it will be for me. When you come for my dead body, just check the trash can for Big Mac wrappers. You'll find at least one smudged with strychnine."

"Ah. And where is your husband now?"

"On a business trip. But when he comes back, he'll come home from work with a poisoned Big Mac and try to do me in. Ever since my stroke, he's been trying to get rid of me."

Gary could see for the first time that Emma Silone was not well. Some kind of mental illness had left her trying to row through the rough waters of life with only one oar in the water. "Sometimes life's not much of an alternative to death, lady," he said. He made the statement looking down at the body bag containing the victim. He touched it lightly with the right toe of his scuffed shoe. He was not in a mood that permitted him time to work through the old woman's paranoid delusions.

Three men from forensics had been working around Gary Jarvis' interrogation of the old woman. Once they attended to the photography and dusted for fingerprints, they loaded the black bag into a white van. The cherry-picker lights strobed suddenly to life. The inspector and the old woman watched them drive away.

Gary thanked the woman for her help, adding, "We may have to ask you a few more questions later." She nodded and looked vacant. She seemed to know what he said. He nodded and smiled and walked to his car.

For a moment he leaned against the car and looked down the tree-flanked margins of Snoqualmie River Road. It was as pretty a day as he could remember in Seattle. But its beauty had been marred by the half face he had just zippered into the heavy plastic bag. Who could have done that to a woman? Who could have killed with such savagery? It had to be an animal; no human would kill in such a manner. He reached his stubby index finger down though his tangled thatch of coal-black hair and scratched his scalp.

He pulled a ballpoint pen out of his inside coat pocket and studied the tip until he clicked the point into view. He then

finished filling out the report sheet. It was Monday morning, April 3. Victoria Billingsley had been dead at least since
the first. Gary hastily scratched "4-3-06" into the report. He
threw the clipboard into the interior of the unmarked police
car then opened the door and followed his clipboard inside.

He looked out the window, marveling at the sunshine as
he twisted the ignition key. The engine jumped to life. The
young detective began driving slowly, as though the velocity
of his car alone might destroy the sanctity of the sunlight.
He needed to feel the sun on his skin after witnessing the
horror at the condo.

It was always with some difficulty that Inspector Jarvis
folded himself into his car, for he was the stocky, low-to-
the-ground type. No sedan welcomed him in, and none
really made him feel comfortable once he was in. He was
handsome in a no-nonsense sort of way. His deep-set eyes
were black and so piercing he looked as though he could
hypnotize the devil into confession. His chin was obstinate
enough to compel the truth out of all but the most reluctant. Still, thinking about the woman in the body bag, he
felt hopeless.

He felt this way when he began each case. Where was he
to start looking for clues? What was he to make of it all? Was
he to look for a psychopath who needed to be jacketed or an
animal that was doubtlessly rabid and dangerous? Nothing
came to him.

He stopped for lunch at an Irish deli and ordered a high-
cholesterol sandwich he usually did not permit himself. His
first bite was eager and large. The corned beef and kraut-
mortared cheese were delicious. He dipped another cor-

ner of the sandwich in the cabbage broth and held it in his mouth, savoring the taste. He looked out the window, trying not to think of the half face that he had just seen in that bag, but found himself methodically poring over the crime for a long time. He was trying to remember any clue that he might have missed. Surely there was an insight that would turn on some light in his dull mind. Nothing came.

After lunch, he drove back to headquarters. He was in no mood to talk as he threaded his way though the maze of desks in the office's secretarial pool. When he was almost through the great steno sea, Malc McClendon, usually called "Mouth" McClendon, yelled across the host of heads focused on ranks of blinking computer screens. "Hey! What kind of dogs are they keeping up on River Road, pal? Whatever happened to kennel-and-leash laws?"

Malc called everybody "Pal." Like most people who call everybody "Pal," he really had very few friends. Gary waved him off and walked on into his own office. He sat down at his desk and adjusted the picture of his ex-wife he still kept there. He spent ten minutes going through the mail and threw away three while-you-were-out memos. When the unkempt sheaf of papers were all filed or trashed, he finally smiled down in pride on the clean and vacant surface of his desk. He picked up the phone and dialed Forensics. "Yeah," the coroner answered, somewhat abruptly.

"Gary here. About Victoria Billingsley—are you sure it was an animal, Al?"

"Not yet. But it must have been. Much of her facial flesh is completely missing. It's like whoever or whatever attacked her ate it."

"Don't curdle my blood, man. That's horrible!" Gary winced.

"To be real honest, we may not be able to pick up enough of a saliva trace to tell what kind of animal it was. The body had lain there so long before being discovered that the meat was pretty dry. I'm not convinced at this point that it was an animal. It could have been a sicko with a barbecue fork. We could have another Jeffrey Dahmer on our hands."

Again Gary swallowed hard. Even though he had been in the business for years, he never liked hearing any victim referred to as "meat."

"But by tomorrow morning, we will have the pathology report back on the tissues. Then we'll know for sure if it was an animal and if it's rabid."

"That will help. At least we can alert the neighbors as to the dangers of another attack in the same neighborhood." Gary made some final chitchat and hung up. He gave the rest of the afternoon to reports and office chores. He put up with the perfunctory work of headquarters. It was a kind of penance he endured just so he could pursue the wonderful work of being a criminal investigator. He loved being a detective as much as he hated the red tape that barnacled itself to his fascinating career.

At about 4:30 he decided to quit early and go home. Since his divorce, home was defined as a lonely studio apartment. The sterile space was presided over by a large wedding picture of him and his ex. He both hated and loved the haunted photo. He despised keeping the picture, but he had never been able to walk in the apartment without looking at it and quickly looking away from it. Back then he had been a churchgoing man, in love and with some real reasons to live. The divorce had left him with almost nothing. He owned a few pots and pans and the paraphernalia of his lost dreams: a bridal garter, a white Bible, and a stack of Gary-Melody wedding napkins. He also had wound up with the aquarium, consisting of a half-dozen frightened fish who, like himself, always seemed to be looking for a place to hide.

He picked up the remote and punched the television to life. He watched the evening news and ate a peanut butter sandwich and half a piece of cold pizza that he refused to re-microwave because he had nuked it once before. He drank a beer, napped for twenty-five minutes, then decided to drive out to the scene of the crime for a second think-through.

When he finally reached the duplex, he paused, rehearsing all he had been through earlier in the day.

He finally got out of his car just as Emma Silone suddenly appeared in her doorway. He walked up to her stoop.

"Hello, Mr. Jarvis!" she said cheerily.

"Mrs. Silone, have you seen a big dog anywhere in the neighborhood the last few days?" Gary decided the word *dog* would be less offensive and a more understandable term to Emma Silone than *rabid animal.*

"Have I seen a what, Inspector?" She hadn't heard him, but the question was irrelevant. There was only the slightest chance she had seen a dog and no chance at all she had heard one. Gary smiled back, thanked her, waved, and left. Even as he drove off, the half face in the body bag stalked his searching mind. The carnage did look like something an animal would do. He preferred thinking it was an animal. The name of Jeffrey Dahmer once again surfaced in his mind, but he dismissed it. The barest consideration that such a thing might have been done by one human being to another chilled him to the bone. The faster he drove, the more his dark mood fled. He hurtled down the I-5, washed by the late evening sun.

Gary thought of all the wild and unrelated segments that he needed to pull together—the horrible murder, the last days of his marriage to Melody. He thought of the haunted photo. The sunset was gorgeous. If there was a God, maybe he was on his side. Maybe there was a new and solid something forming at the center of his tangled, empty life.

He pulled up to his home, his reverie turning to the murder site. He pulled out a pen and his notepad and wrote the time and date—7:15 p.m. on April 3 on the I-5.

It wasn't till he got out of his car that he noticed something stuck on the side of his shoe. It was apparently a bit of animal feces—maybe dog. He hadn't noticed it when he walked through the shallow lawn at the Billingsley residence. He would have to return later and see if the lawn was indeed the source.

CHAPTER 3

Yahoo!"

Eric Compton's yawp could be heard through the glass wall of his semi-private office enclosure. It rang out over the steno pool that buzzed in the center of the circle of elegant glass offices. Every head swiveled toward his outcry. Though they were all accustomed to his outbursts, this one was louder than usual. His secretary shared his exuberance. So did Renée Thomkins, the corporate accountant in the office next to his. The oversize yawp told Renée immediately that Eric had closed the deal on the forestry project. Pacific Woods would celebrate. Levi Twist would be ecstatic. The environmentalists and naturalists would retaliate, of course, with marches and other things, like chaining themselves to trees and lying down in front of bulldozers. Still, it was done. A cheer rose from the secretarial pool.

"Hey! So you really pulled it off?" Renée asked as she ran into Eric's office. "Congrats! This is a big day for you."

"Big day? Very big! After years of sweat, Tuesday, April 4 is my day. Man, is the lumbering workforce going to love me!" Eric beamed, sticking out his chest and pointing to himself.

"And, man! Are the environmentalists going to hate you!" Renée said, sticking her own index finger into Eric's chest. Eric imitated a punctured tire and allowed his overinflated chest to deflate at the punch of Renée's finger.

Though they both laughed, Eric knew Renée was right. Next morning's paper in Seattle would carry the story and maybe his picture as the media "bad guy." There would likely also be a picture of the "poor spotted owl" whose future extinction would now be his entire fault. The next few days there would be letters to the editor condemning him and putting his job under further threat.

Eric Compton had long ago rented a secured suite in an apartment complex across town. There he knew he and his car would not be subject to harm. During the legal work of trying to sew up his many lumbering deals, he had already faced many environmentalist picket lines. These lines gathered daily around the Pacific Woods building. His name had been in the news so often that it was a household name in Seattle. He was seen as both the darling of the lumber industry and the demon of the environmentalist movement. Now those categories of love and hate would be drawn in even sharper contrast. He finished his coffee and gathered some file folders together for corporate review. At ten o'clock he met Renée Thomkins again in the deserted boardroom where they sat down at an empty corner of the long conference table. Renée's secretary brought in two fresh cups of coffee and set them on two coasters.

In a way it seemed odd that the two of them had become such close friends and yet had never been attracted to each other. Eric was five inches taller than Renée. They both had dark brown hair, but Renée's was a shade or so darker. Eric's face was square. Renée's face was thin, and her darker-than-average complexion made her outstandingly beautiful. Their widely separate lifestyles caused them not to spend much time together after hours, but they were very close friends at work.

As the corporate accountant, Renée reminded Eric that his legal maneuvers were eating into the budget. Dunn, Cable, Belz, and Woods was prestigious from its years of successful litigations. But Renée still ran a tight blue line through all corporate expenses. Still, Eric was a corporate favorite in the law firm. He was a sharp young attorney, and his reputation was becoming legendary. He was viewed by most who knew him as obsessive and hyper-tense, if not feverish. Now that he had pulled off the South River Project, his corporate stature would take a great leap in favor of legendary status. Eric Compton was not totally at peace with himself since he did a lot of hiking and camping and was a real lover of the outdoors. He always felt a little bad that he was helping Pacific Woods destroy a lot of the wilderness he so adored. He was, however, becoming rich and successful at his occupation—so successful they might even hang his picture in the boardroom. Renée had even sent out a comic memo ordering a few ingots of bronze in case they decided to erect a statue in honor of Eric.

Their heads tilted together over the corner of the boardroom table as they worked out the most reasonable way to handle the press. For the most part, Public Relations would deal with the media, but it was possible that either Renée or

Eric or both might be summoned for statements. And there was a real likelihood that Eric would be hounded by picketing tree huggers all over town. Nonetheless, the deal was done. Let the environmentalists scream. It would strengthen their lungs. They could find some other negative thing to protest. Nothing could be called back. Compton's corporate coup had been in the courts for almost twenty-seven months. The ordeal had eaten nearly half of Eric's entire six-year career with the company. But now it was over, and he was the corporate hero of the hour.

Eric felt great just in knowing what this would do to his reputation in the corporate world. It was *Fortune* magazine stuff. His career was leapfrogging over his Harvard Law School reputation in seven-league boots. When their official conversation was over, Renée asked, "Well, commander, what's your next maneuver?"

"Well, I can't say it out loud. . . . Aw, what the heck, I guess I can trust you. Renée, I've been footsying with George Callahan. I'm going to buy the whole grove for PW," said Eric, abbreviating Pacific Woods. "Boy, will DCB and W love me for it!"

"You're going to buy the whole Callahan Grove?" She was dumbfounded.

"I've been secretly litigating the small separate owners. There's a woman in the way. She owns 10,000 acres of those trees, and you can bet she's going to hold on and scream. She's a real envirospook. Still, I'll get her sooner or later, Rennie."

Renée didn't doubt it. She knew it would probably be later, much later—several court battles later—but she didn't doubt it.

They were about to leave their extended coffee break when Eric tossed a parting comment over his shoulder. "Hey! Did you read in the morning paper about the weekend 'dog murder' out on Snoqualmie River Road?"

"Oh yeah!" said Renée. "I meant to tell you about her earlier, but in all the excitement that you created around here this morning, I forgot to mention it. Eric, I knew that woman. Not well, but I knew her. Victoria Billingsley. I saw her every once in awhile out at My Kind."

"My Kind?" asked Eric.

"It's a gay hangout off the 405 in Bellevue."

"No foolin'. Must make you feel funny knowing a chick you knew was so brutally killed."

"It makes my skin crawl."

"Well, this bad stuff seems to be happening late at night in Bellevue." Eric rubbed his chin and took a sip of his now-cold coffee. "To tell you the truth, this whole thing with the Billingsley chick *is* just plain weird. A dog murder. Her face was partly gone. It's enough to make Jack the Ripper look like St. Francis. What kind of dog would be big enough to kill that viciously?"

"That Snoqualmie area is pretty high-rent, isn't it?" asked Renée. She knew Eric was familiar with housing values and the residential zoning codes for the entire city plus its surroundings.

"It is. Was this Victoria Billingsley a wealthy chick?" asked Eric.

"Wealthy enough. She was climbing the corporate ladder faster than you're scaling the walls of our law firm." Renée stopped and looked guilty over the time they were taking for private conversation. "Well, Eric, to the business at hand. The grand mogul, Levi, is going to expect a lot out of you today. Are your ducks in a row for the board meeting?"

Eric nodded.

The conversation was running out of both interest and impetus. They agreed they needed to get back together that afternoon. But first they both needed to study the remaining unpaid legal fees on the South River Project. Eric wagged off the coffee cups that Renée's secretary had brought in.

Minutes later, he was almost out the door when Renée stopped him. "Levi Twist says he's been tracking a lone wolf—a timber wolf, I think—on the edge of the Callahan Grove. Could be one of those the Feds released in western Idaho that somehow migrated over this way. However he got here, he must be the only wolf in Washington. Levi says he'll bag it one of these days."

"Bag it?"

"That's right. He says he's gonna have it mounted between two spotted owls and give it to the Northwest Environmentalist's Women's Society."

"The tree huggers?"

"That's right."

"A wolf, huh?"

"A big one. Says he kills calves and sheep. The farmers are on Levi's side. Levi thinks the wolf is rabid. And Levi ought to know rabid."

They both grinned.

CHAPTER 4

Dr. Paul Shapiro heard the horror-story buzz on the murder of Victoria Billingsley.

"So near your home!" said Della Singleton. "So ghastly. So otherworldly—werewolves on Snoqualmie Road!"

Dr. Shapiro didn't want to talk about it anymore at the moment.

"How's the old priest?" he said.

"Nobody feels sorry for a man of God who doesn't act like a man of God," the psychiatrist's assistant said. Dr. Shapiro shrugged off her judgment. "You can't believe how this priest rattles, Doctor," the assistant went on. "Where did he come from? Who referred him to our clinic? How could any cleric talk the way he does?"

She paused. "Paul, it's obvious that the man is sick, but who do I send his bills to? How did he get admitted without any paperwork?"

"Della, I told you. Saturday night he showed up in emergency having some kind of violent seizures in an old black suit with a clerical collar, babbling about how I had to help him get to the Virgin of Stockholm. The man needs help. There's still a state law that if they show up in emergency, we have to help them. The county won't take him for the same reasons we don't want him. He's penniless. But they did tell me that they would try to take him at a state facility by the end of April and they'd reimburse us at that time, OK? This is only the fourth, so we've still got twenty-six days to put up with him. I guess we'll just have to make the best of it."

"But he gets so violent. I don't know if we're really equipped to handle him," she protested.

"First of all, Della, he's sick. Second, as Don Quixote said, 'We are all men of God.'" In the process of his lecturing at medical conferences and conventions, Paul Shapiro had fallen into the habit of formally numbering his answers to even the simplest of questions.

Della hated the habit. She felt it stuffed arrogance into all his remarks. She mimicked his officiousness in her reply. "First," Della retorted, "what comes out of a man when he's sick is what was in him before he got sick. So this priest must have been the parish lulu, Sigmund." She enjoyed watching the psychiatrist grin, which he did every time she called him Sigmund, though he despised being connected with Freud as much as she loved needling him with the name. "Second, Don Quixote said, 'We are all the children of God,' not 'men of God.'"

Dr. Shapiro disliked being corrected by his nurse.

"Anyway," she continued, "the seizures have stopped. Not just the violent ones, the small tremors as well."

Dr. Shapiro picked up the orphan-priest's over-stapled medical report from the nearby Formica counter. He studied its contents, his eyes narrowing to slits as he scrutinized the turning pages. Finally he settled an elbow on the counter and looked at Della over the top of his glasses. He couldn't help but be struck by her beauty.

"The priest, is he drowsy—at all drowsy?" he asked.

"Drowsy?" asked his assistant.

"Drowsy, yes drowsy!" He was clearly irritated that Della seemed to be stalling her answer. It bothered him that he had ever thought her alluring. How quickly she could change from alluring to offensive.

"Well, I wouldn't say drowsy," she droned, putting plenty of space between her words, further irritating Dr. Shapiro. She often baited the trap of irritation for him, and he snapped predictably at the bait. She felt the deliciousness of what she knew would be a short-tempered reply.

"Well, then, what would you say?" he cut in sharply.

Della smiled. He looked annoyed.

"More like dreaming or absent or somewhere in between the two."

"Is he talking?"

"He answers questions but not much more. He set his television outside the room. No plugs in those things you know—he just pulled the cord right out of the wall. He could've just asked for a disconnect. Housekeeping is furious. It's no great expense, but it will have to be repaired. Know what he did last night?" She continued without giving Dr. Shapiro any time to guess. "He poured iced tea in his urine sample bottle! The folks in the lab were at first confused by the outcome of the test. Later, they were furious." Shapiro smiled then laughed. Della laughed as well then turned the conversation back to the murder. "That Billingsley woman who was murdered—she didn't live too far from you, did she?"

"Two or three miles down Snoqualmie Road," Paul answered. "My wife is scared to death. A pall has settled over our neighborhood, Della. If it is an animal, I sure hope they catch it soon. I drive by that condo every morning on my way to I-5. The place looks peaceful."

Della shuddered as she remembered how the newspaper described the killing. "The police are only partly sure it is a dog."

Paul also shuddered. "The victim lived in the same condo unit as Emma Silone."

"The 'Big Mac' paranoid?"

Shapiro smiled. "Yes, the Big Macaphobic."

He turned their conversation to the priest, and Della stopped him. "Everybody says he's worse after your sessions than any other time of the week. After psychoanalysis, he orders people out of his room—even when they only come to make the bed. They have to watch him take his pills or he throws them out."

The doctor studied the priest's charts and then turned to leave. "Della, be nice to him, understand? And get that across to the others too."

"Yes sir," she said, adding, "It's just that nothing much has changed since he got here. He just keeps asking everyone if they know the Virgin of Stockholm."

The phrase seemed to freeze Dr. Shapiro for a moment, then he walked briskly out of the office and down the hall. He turned into a neatly organized room, smiling as he opened the door. The priest greeted the psychiatrist in so courtly a manner that it was hard for the doctor to believe all that his assistant had just told him.

"Good morning, Father Peter," he smiled.

The priest was sitting with both feet dangling off the bed. One of the feet had a stocking on it. His hospital gown was gaping in the back, and his thin hair looked as if it had been combed with a washrag. His gray eyes looked straight ahead, seeing nothing. The eyes, pale as the fourth horseman of the Apocalypse, bored a hole through every object they met, including the psychiatrist. The face was high-cheeked, bony, and without stubble. He never shaved, and yet he was so smooth-skinned he appeared to be whiskerless. He was, in a way, nice looking. His forward and vacant gaze gave every evidence that he had not heard his doctor, who cleared his throat and repeated the greeting. "Ahem! Father Peter! Good morning!" He paused. "If you didn't want the TV, you could have asked to have it taken out."

"I took it out myself! Nothing on anyway but preachers and basketball games. Have you ever wondered how future historians are going to comment on our day? When they reach into the nuclear rubble and pull out a recording of an average day of TV viewing, what will they say of us? However they assess our culture, they'll probably get down on their knees and thank the post-Holocaust Jehovah, whatever they call him then, that there was a World War III."

"Nurse Della said you were quiet and answering in mono-syllables," Dr. Shapiro interrupted the priest's ramblings, offering him a chance to take an interest in therapy.

"I am and do to her," said Father Peter.

"She also said your seizures have stopped."

"Uh huh, she's right about that too."

"Are you having any luck in locating the Virgin of Stockholm?"

"No, nobody in this clinic ever heard of her. I met a man down the hall who fought at Waterloo 190 years ago, but in spite of his longevity, he had never even heard of the Virgin." The old priest studied the ceiling in a disconsolate manner and then blurted, "Doctor, I must find her. Please, will you help me? I must find her."

"Della says that you ask everyone you meet if they know this Virgin of Stockholm."

"Della doesn't seem concerned about my problem. Do I have to report things to Della?"

"Not if you don't want to."

"I don't."

"Peter, is the medicine making you drowsy? I mean, we have to find a balance between stopping those seizures and keeping you alert."

"Who says I want to be alert?"

"I want you to be."

"Why? Don't you like me?"

"Yes, but that's not the point. You have to get well, and you have to live in the real world."

"Who says!"

"I do. The world does."

"Off to a devil's hell with the world!"

With those words Father Peter began to look far away. He rose, moving to a section of the carpet where the tufting had lately been depressed by the television stand. He appeared a kind of prophet. Still, his gaping hospital gown and one-sock mystique rendered him a comic doomsayer. A light seemed to grow behind his glazed eyes as he raised a thin, bony finger into the air, his hand alabaster white as it rose out of his sleeve. He swayed. "He came unto his own, and his own received him not. Lo, he comes with clouds descending and the four beasts and twenty-four elders cry, 'He is worthy,' and the sea gives up the dead that are in it. And lo, the Virgin of Stockholm will come upon the Queen of Sanich and there will be thunder over the Orcas. Come thou Great Virgin and heal our sins!"

Dr. Shapiro smiled. "OK, Peter, let's start over. Try to remember your past, anything from your past."

"I have no past. I have come from the high altar of the other realm."

"Let's talk about the other realm."

"We talked about that yesterday."

"Let's do it again."

"OK, but I could drop back into seizures." The priest's voice trailed off to nearly nothing before he again began to look wild-eyed. He cried, "Behold the great whore of Revelation is rising with red lips and a beckoning finger. Woe unto you scribes, pharisees, psychiatrists." Peter began to shake all over. He climbed up on his chair and pointed down at the therapist. "You make clean the outside of the cup, but inwardly you are full of Sigmund!"

Dr. Shapiro grimaced and then asked, "Who is the Virgin of Stockholm, Father? Have you ever met her?"

"If I don't have to tell Della, why do I have to tell you?"

"Do you wanna get well or not?"

"I think I like being sick. I don't have any responsible image to fuss about. I can say what I want to and nobody cares. Because I am mentally ill, I can miss Mass and the Pope himself doesn't hold me accountable."

"Are you a Catholic priest, or are you some other kind of priest? Are you a priest at all? I have this feeling you're a genuine phony. I think you're not a priest. No parish has reported a missing priest. I think you're not as sick as you want me to think. Why can't you remember your past? Why don't you have a past? Who are you? How did you wind up at the door of my clinic? Think back. Think hard, Father Peter. You must remember something."

Father Peter bowed then held his hands above his head like a crown and spun on his feet. His bathrobe swirled further than his body, flying open to reveal a thin, old body.

Dr. Shapiro was both angry and amused at his odd antics. The doctor's session ended as his patient pirouetted and collided with the lamp table. The old priest stumbled to the wall and fell to the floor. He stared catatonically into space. The glazed eyes were open but unseeing. It seemed to the psychiatrist that when he was in these states he was indeed a creature from another world. It was like having ET as a patient, only he never seemed to want to phone home, wherever home was.

Dr. Shapiro knew he would remain in the catatonic state for some time. He folded the plastic cover of his clipboard over the sheaf of notes and left the room. He passed Della at the assistants' station and handed her the board.

"Well, how's our star patient?" asked Della.

"Oh, he's still trying to find the Virgin of Stockholm," replied Dr. Shapiro. "He knocked a lamp off the table. It's broken, I think."

"How did he do it?"

"Ballet."

"Well, I'll be," Della laughed.

"I'd give anything to know what goes on behind those vacant eyes of his when they're glazed like that. Have Henry Demond and one of the orderlies help him back in bed."

"Yes, sir! I'll get right on that, sir."

"Della, I'll see you tomorrow."

"OK, boss. Tell Rhonda to keep her doors locked," Della warned.

Dr. Shapiro didn't smile—her comment brought him back to reality. Something sinister stalked the suburbs. Perhaps it was empty fear. Perhaps not.

"Yes," he said, "I'll tell her to keep the doors locked."

Dr. Shapiro left the office. Della made an intercom order to take care of the priest, who remained on the floor in a trance. He was slumped against the wall, waiting for the Virgin of Stockholm to come and help him back into bed.

Paul Shapiro was uneasy for the rest of the afternoon although he couldn't exactly know why. It was only as he got into bed that his brain surrendered to the unnamed thing that kept prodding him into doubt all afternoon. The psychotic priest's right arm was covered with scars—especially his forearm. And then higher on the same arm was a tattoo.

He could see it now as clearly as he had in the afternoon. It was a blue-lined tattoo of an animal, a dog or a wolf. On his left arm was a second tattoo, a woman. What woman? Who could say? Maybe the Virgin of Stockholm.

His mind only left pondering the Virgin of Stockholm to settle on Victoria Billingsley. The Virgin had no face. Neither did the woman who was murdered in his neighborhood.

CHAPTER 5

On Tuesday night the skies between Mt. Rainier and Puget Sound dumped three inches of rain on Seattle. It seemed the rain would never stop, but by noon on Wednesday it did.

The great bulldozers in the Lee West Construction Camp sat silent in a sea of mud. The machines were as yellow as the emerging sun that spit gold through the hazy, leafy shadows of late afternoon. A wolf ventured into the lonely clearing. The lanky animal sniffed the vertical head-plate of one of the steel hulks. It still smelled of those workers who had come to cut the trees. The wolf circled the huge iron machines and sniffed at a pool of thick, black, sticky oil; it seemed the dark blood of the bleeding steel monsters had come to destroy his forest. The wolf's fur was slick and matted with rain. The muddy earth stuck to the pads of his broad paws. In the old days wolves never ventured so close to the city. Now the city had come to his world.

The forest was dying. It was falling before the shrill whine of chain saws. After the saws came the bulldozers, pushing out the amputated trunks. The hazy forest, whose mysterious shadows were nature's gift to the pack, was all but gone. The yellow machines scraped the forest floor until shrubs and grass were gone as well. Now the lanky predator circled one of the machines and sniffed a can punched with greasy top-holes. He seemed to recognize the stale odor that filled those cans left by the construction workers.

What the animal couldn't articulate he seemed to understand. Civilization is hard on wild things.

The city's encroachment that once terrified the wolf now only menaced him. On clear nights when there was no rain, he could hear the construction workers laughing and the piercing sounds of their grating music roaring like sour discord across the earth they scraped. He was a proud animal whose fear of civilization had made him increasingly aggressive. He was an animal who fought because he was cornered. Wherever he tried to run, there were people. They were not only trying to destroy his forest, they were out to destroy him. They hunted and killed in his world. The other animals were mostly gone. They had been killed or driven farther and farther into the forest. The advancing world jabbed at him with fear, but it also made him brave. He knew he must run from the hunters, for only if he ran could he live.

The wolf stopped, looked at the lowering sky, and lifted his broad nose. He sniffed the wet air. No scent was there. The rich greens of the forest were gradually turning black. The trees piped the last bit of sunlight downward from the sky. The ground grew dark and braced itself against the coming night. On this evening the cautious beast could see the mountains that formed a distant wall. The mountains gave the horizon a beckoning voice. To live, he knew he must one day respond to that call.

His was a land he walked alone; all of his kind had been killed by hunters. All people, as far as he knew, were hunters. All were killers. He had seen the skins of others of his kind, nailed to posts, drying in the wind. The forest was silent because it was empty of life. The forest once spoke with the voice of bears and the noonday scream of the condors. But now the groves were voiceless. The conversations of the wilderness were mute. The silence was all that screamed now. The condors were gone. Even the trees of the forest seemed to grieve their loss of place as they prepared to die. Cities grew by flinging concrete at the wilderness. Nothing could stop their encroachment. Wherever the city advanced, creation lost its voice. The spotted owls still offered the mellow tones of their throaty wails. But the great animals were mostly gone. Nothing howled or roared in the forest.

The wolf bent his great head down and licked his giant forepaw. He looked at his reflection in a nearby puddle of water. He was but a beast, unable to give thought to what he saw. Still, he was a study in power and freedom. His powerful haunches and his broad paws and his chest drove his strong forelegs through the dying realm that once had been his kingdom. He had survived because he was a wise king. He had remained a living king because he never forgot that death was always possible. He had only lived by never taking any second of life for granted. He ran. He lived.

He walked one more full circle in the center of the silent forest. The temple of the huge construction machines now circled him like a Stonehenge set in steel. At length he stopped. He rested then stood erect. It seemed there was little reason to slink or crouch in the friendly, deepening dusk made misty by the recent rain.

He paused once more, looked cautiously toward the sunset, and moved away from it toward the darkening forest. He suddenly raised his head again. His snout probed the air. His fur bristled on the back of his neck. He was suddenly paralyzed by the sensation that he was being watched. He stopped near a shrub, crouched, and listened. Yes! Yes! It was there! It breathed hate, and it was there. He knew the threat. He had been watched so often, he could feel the weight of leering eyes and gun sights.

The calm was shattered by rifle fire. In an instant the wolf felt a searing pain in his left shoulder as he heard the explosion in the brush. White-hot pain tore his wet fur and shot his own red life onto the wet earth. With a powerful thrusting leap, he bolted into the brush.

"Jee-Haw! Holy Joseph!" cried a distant voice, just before the second explosion that snapped a small tree at the wolf's left. "Missed completely that time," cried the voice behind the high-powered rifle that boomed a third explosion.

The shots ended, but the wolf ran. The only noise the wolf heard now was the sound of his own form crashing through the wet brush. Now his fur was matted with blood, but his leg did not seem to be broken. He knew he must stop the running as soon as it was safe. He seemed to know that his own rapid loss of blood would soon destroy him. When at last he felt he had left the hunter far behind, he instinctively tended to his bleeding shoulder. He ran to a plot of ground that was void of grass. He folded his front paw underneath him and jammed his bloody wound into the wet earth.

The dark mud clotted his silver pelt. He lay silently, his fur stained with rain, blood, and the cool, congealing mud. In spite of the cool mud, his shoulder was on fire. The night came slowly, the darkness gathering about him and caressing his pain. Mercifully, by midnight, the bleeding had stopped. The hunger that had driven him to risk his ill-fated visit to the walker's camp was now forgotten. The pain caused him to whimper.

The moon set and the sun rose before he tried to move again. By midmorning he was strong enough to make his way toward the river that was the northern boundary of his vanishing world. The rain of the past few nights would make the hurried river swollen to overflowing. He knew he would soon hear the yellow machines roaring somewhere in the distance. He felt he must somehow get across the white rapids but had no idea how. The river was all but uncrossable when it was not at flood stage. Now it would be nearly impassable. He must find a way.

In the bright light of morning, he came at last to the river. He paced nervously among the trees on the bank. Suddenly he came to a small flat boat, wet on the inside but still floating on the unsteady and violent current. On the bank, moving upward from the boat, were deep ruts left by a small machine of some sort. The ruts themselves smelled only faintly of people, perhaps the hunters. No one had been near the boat that morning. It was moored by a rotting rope tied to a small tree. The wolf crashed against the tree with full force, but it wouldn't budge. He began to gnaw at the thin rope. The rotting fibers frayed quickly, and the rope was broken.

He was not prepared for the strength of the current, for no sooner was the rope severed than the small boat moved rapidly away from the bank. With a leap, the creature soared from the bank and tumbled into the boat, nearly capsizing it. The rotted craft rocked dangerously in the current before it settled upright and floated out into the river. The wolf lay in the wet floor of the craft with his muzzle on the edge of the boat, peering at the forest on the far side. In the next half hour the boat careened around a stone and moved toward the center of the river. It turned around and around as it drifted through miles of trees, not approaching either bank. While it floated, the huge animal slept, dozing in the afternoon sun of his drowsy and uncertain odyssey.

Suddenly the wound began to throb and bleed again. The animal's leap to the small boat had no doubt torn it open. The river seemed to be narrowing and moving increasingly faster. The huge animal swayed unsteadily as the boat rounded a bend in the river. There the hurried water slowed. The beast was moving now in the shallow water near the north bank of the river.

The bobbing boat at last drifted so near the bank it struck a rock. The force of the white water threw the craft and its wounded passenger almost vertically into the air. The wolf pitched headlong into the river. He could not swim against the heavy current. The ordeal of the past few days had left him too weak to struggle against the foaming water.

The river moved so swiftly around him he could not see any blood, but he was once again bleeding. Trying to swim toward the shore as he tumbled in the rapids, he crashed against several more rocks. At last his heroic struggle to live began to fail him. Weakened by the continuous loss of blood, he found himself succumbing to the cold water that hurried the blackness waving across his vision. The animal lost consciousness. A cold and turbulent darkness glazed his once keen eyes. A strange, thick roaring gathered in his ears. His wound colored the water. The river thundered on.

CHAPTER 6

Rhonda Shapiro welcomed the afternoon sun by putting on a pair of shorts and a nylon windbreaker. She was stunningly beautiful, though any woman long-ignored by her husband rarely believes herself beautiful. Her chin was a bit square, but it seemed to prop up her strong face with character. Her green eyes were clear. Her cheekbones were strong. Like that of an old German movie star, her voice was so alto-low it was melodic.

But she didn't feel herself to be either melodic or attractive. Her mind these last few months had rarely been clear. It was always moving in the dull mist somewhere between trauma and Tylenol.

Now five days after the murder of Victoria Billingsley, Rhonda had decided the tragedy would not keep her inside her home and leave her cowering in fear. She talked of it—it was all so near at hand. Her neighbors had taken to locking their doors at noon and hiding in fear behind their suburban security systems. But Rhonda was far from squeamish over the killing. In spite of the horror, she would not abandon the sunlight.

How slowly her sluggish days passed. Her long marriage to Paul seemed so much longer than it had been. Once, Paul had been Mr. Excitement, before he began reading his own press clippings. His fame in the world of psychiatry had at first moved him from Mr. Excitement to Dr. Excitement and then, at last, to Dr. Aloof. He became the role model for all compassionate drones. Paul had married Rhonda, promising her that she would always be number one in his life. But ever so gradually his work had become his primary mistress. At first Rhonda found herself hoping that his work was his only mistress, but of late she had lost faith even in that issue. Paul rarely got home in time to ask her how her day had gone. She had long since quit caring how his had gone. Paul never remembered her with flowers. In fact, he never remembered her at all. The one decent thing he had done for her was to provide her with a riverfront house on Snoqualmie River Road.

She loved the house, and she loved the river. The roaring water talked to her, quietly in fall when the water was low, silently in the winter when ice slowed its conversation. But it always roared its tumbling dialogue in the spring when the snow was melting and the anxious water bubbled in laughter as it passed her house. She had worn a slim path along the bank from walking the edge of the river. She would play Windham Hill music; their tuneless songs on her iPod always matching the spring music of the river. She liked songs that went nowhere. They were a reasonable accompaniment to her dull days.

She looked at the kitchen clock on the expensive oven she never used. It was time for her afternoon stroll along the hurried current. The river never ignored her as her husband did. She mixed herself a martini. Taking two olives, she ate one of them and threw the other in the glass. She walked out the patio door and down the cedar steps to the river path, stopping a couple of times to enjoy the warm afternoon. The sunlight felt good after days of constant rain. She sipped her drink and moved along the river path. She hesitated in a shady section of her walk and studied a crack in one of her sandal straps, noticing a couple of slugs on the ground around her feet. She wandered on. At last she came to the trunk of the old fir tree that had fallen nearly parallel to the river. It had been struck by lightning long before Rhonda had discovered it. Its dark heart was old and charred, probably as black as it must have been that long-ago day it was struck by lightning.

The black-hearted log had become an oasis in the arid days of her life. It, like her, seemed dead at the core. The burned-out heart of the log was an ebony oracle, reminding her of what she knew so well. Sooner or later her marriage would have to end.

Her mind went back to the place she and Paul had met: the psychiatric care unit of a Seattle hospital. It all seemed so right back then. To be sure, her mother had warned her not to marry a non-Christian. Rhonda remembered the little Methodist church her family had attended when she was a child. She had never cared for church. It was the sermons mostly. They were long and usually denounced as sin all the things she most enjoyed.

Now she wondered at her mother's words. Here on the cusp of middle age, she felt that Christians were not her kind. "I wonder what in the name of heaven my kind is," she mumbled to herself. She swirled the olive in the martini that had become too tepid to enjoy.

Her eyes watched the hypnotic water rushing by. It seemed to her a symbol of time itself. Life was passing her by while she waited and watched. But for what? For that unsuspecting windfall or some Apocalypse or a second chance—some last-minute hope that she might get pregnant late in life? In reality she'd quit dreaming of a second prince. She counted on no illusion of a late-life call from another Mr. Wonderful waiting in the wings when she and Paul finally split up. She wondered what Paul would want as his part of the divorce settlement. She would want the grand piano that neither of them could play. She also would never be able to part with her grandmother's sterling and, above all, the house. She could live here forever, the old woman of the river. She smiled.

She ate the olive, extended her arm, and poured the last of the warm martini in the river. It made a series of bubbles on the deep green shadows. Her eyes followed the white trace of froth until it thinned and swirled against the bank.

It was in studying the martini froth that she caught sight of a mop of soaked fur snagged in a bramble. She could see it was some kind of dead animal, and she walked from her log to scrutinize it further. "It must be a beaver trapped in the current," she mused. It happened all the time when the melting snows tore away the dams upstream. It took only a minute for her to change her mind. The animal was too large for a beaver. "A dog!" she exclaimed. "It must have died trying to free itself from the river." She almost envied anything dead. Still, she hated for anything to contaminate the water in her private section of the beautiful river. The dog was so large, however, she was not sure she could pull it out. She grabbed at the heavy muzzle, trying to pull the animal's soggy form onto the bank. Her hands closed tightly around the dog's snout, giving her the strangest sensation that the lower jaw of the animal was trying, ever so weakly, to close upon her hand. She paid little attention to that unthinkable sensation. With all the effort she could exert, she managed to pull the dead brute upward onto the shore. She dragged it up six or eight feet away from the edge of the water and surveyed its impressive size. She noticed a well-washed, gaping hole in the dog's front shoulder. *He must weigh more than a hundred pounds,* she thought.

The sun fell full on the animal's wet and matted fur. She knew he would be dry before long and therefore somewhat easier to lug into a rather shallow grave that she was now convinced she must dig. She returned to the house and fetched a spade from the toolshed behind it. In fifteen minutes she was back at the site. She approached the dog and began digging a grave a few feet off the path. The ground, emulsified by all the rain, was so soft that it took her only a quarter of an hour to create a shallow grave. The hole was only a foot or so deep but deep enough. She returned to the dog.

His fur was now mostly dry and incredibly soft on his underbelly. Rhonda was convinced he could not have been dead long. She stroked the fur and said aloud, "What a crying shame, poor thing!" She reached down and grabbed his muzzle to drag him to the grave. The animal's lower jaw snapped weakly shut against her hand.

"You are alive!" she cried.

CHAPTER 7

Levi Twist had irregularly dated Dr. Shapiro's assistant in the past, but he had decided to actively pursue her following his last visit to Shapiro's office, which had marked the end of his professional relationship with the psychiatrist.

Levi seemed to have a natural modesty, but in truth he very much prized his compromised morality. He found he enjoyed the bawdy humor of nightclub acts. He stalked the world for suitable entertainment, always avoiding X-rated movies and for the most part R movies as well. He liked old Disney movies that gave him a feeling of being normal. Still, he also had a dark side that frequented pornography shops.

Following the death of his wife, he had lived alone. He never talked much about himself, and he never brought his dates to his place. His pad was his pad. *Pad* was not an adequate word to define his large Snoqualmie River Road mansion. Still, it was the short three-letter way he referred to his home. His castle, like himself, was always well-groomed and neat and was the lonely bunker where he schemed and planned his way to conquer his world.

This Fortune 500 hero was an orphan. As a baby he had been left early one August morning on the steps of St. Catherine's orphanage in Portland. An old abbess had found him on the back step of the rectory. He was a darling child whom the nuns prayed would one day enter the priesthood. It was safe to say that the nuns at St. Catherine's had spoiled him by overdoing their affection for him when he was quite young. By the middle of his teens, he was arrogant and rude, and the sadder-but-wiser nuns were wistful over their failures to produce a candidate for the priesthood. In fact, he was so rebellious during his teen years that the sisters of St. Catherine's began to pray he would never enter the priesthood.

Levi Twist was such a renegade that the nuns of St. Catherine's lost all hope that he would ever be a good Catholic. In his sixteenth year, Levi announced that he was not a Catholic at all. "I am quite taken with Mohammed," he said rather arrogantly. The disappointed nuns were certain that his talk of becoming a Muslim would cause the entire Islamic world to shudder. Still, he stated his faith, as the nuns cringed. "I will never turn back. The Qur'an means more to me than life itself." He loved watching the devout sisters caught up in their despair over his love for the Muslim holy book.

This was, of course, untrue, but the nuns were destroyed by Levi's abdication of the true church. Their feelings of suffering and failure delighted the smirking teenager. There were two pictures of the pope at the orphanage. One was of the seated pontiff and the other of the standing pontiff.

Three of the nuns saw him take a black marker and draw a mustache on the seated portrait of the pope that hung in the vestibule of the orphanage. What he drew on the standing pope earned him six weeks of detention. When he was eighteen he was formally evicted from the convent for spitting in the communion wine. The nuns of St. Catherine's had had enough. They asked Levi Twist to leave the orphanage and join the army.

As is true in so many cases, the army completely changed Levi Twist. He was barely eighteen in 1968 when he finally reached Vietnam. The war seemed to teach him a compassion the nuns had never managed. He won the Medal of Honor for valor. He single-handedly saved a company of men by holding an entire cadre of Vietcong at bay for several hours while his company was evacuated by helicopter.

After the war was over, he found military life boring and left the service, taking a job at Pacific Woods. Tenure and promotion and good looks were his trio of friends, and these three companions at last landed him at the top. There was no doubt about it. He was a self-made man. The untimely loss of his wife had clouded his view of himself and his ability to make life work on his own. But he gradually reentered the world of social life.

It seemed his destiny to meet Della Singleton, his psychiatrist's assistant. Della was a fringe benefit of his many counseling sessions with Dr. Shapiro. He loved her, but he had developed that late-life fear of all commitments and was especially gun-shy about marriage. Although he was twenty years older than she was, he was furious in his ardor.

Gun-shy was an inappropriate metaphor for Levi Twist. During his years of military service, he had developed a love of firearms. He had become a champion marksman, and after the war he developed a passion for hunting. Big game was his bag, as he loved to pun. Even with his initially meager salary at Pacific Woods, he had managed to save enough to afford small-time safaris for big-game hunting. The cost-and-licensing difficulties of foreign hunts had forced him to hunt mostly on North America. Besides, his early apartments were too small to exhibit the taxidermied trophies he collected.

In some ways his wife had never understood him, and since her early death, his various appetites and hobbies no longer fell under mortal authorization. He was free to run both himself and Pacific Woods any way he chose, with no wifely interference. A second marriage had never appealed to Levi Twist, but women in general were another matter. The psychiatrist's secretary had wakened Levi to all kinds of new dreams for himself. Della Singleton was the one woman he felt he might one day ask that crucial question to. He had slept with Della, but only on a few occasions. Levi had no moral compunctions about it, but Della believed that all sexuality belonged within marriage. She therefore felt a little guilty about their permissiveness. Their nights together always led them both to talk earnestly of marriage, but Levi never allowed the conversations to continue long. He did make further promises not to "do it" again.

But every weekend seemed to find him on the verge of need. He needed Della. He was hungry, ravenous. And after all, it was Friday night. So taking Della to dinner and a movie was just the hors d'oeuvres to fit the indulgences he imagined.

Levi so much anticipated his date with Della that he smiled as he slipped his heavy legs into his slacks. He was humming an old Mel Tormé tune his mind hadn't named. He pulled on a gray polo shirt and reached for his loafers. "You beast!" he said aloud, shyly grinning into his mirror.

He passed through the library of his huge home then the door and out through the laundry room. He opened the garage door, walked to his red Corvette, and got in. The sports car had a black interior and black glass. In many ways the car was too sporty to fit his corporate mystique, but he liked it anyway. He loved the feel of the Corvette as it responded to his senses. He never merely drove off. He usually roared out of the driveway and then rocketed away from his castle.

The hollow tailpipes gurgled thunder as Levi roared down the street. He liked roaring, whether in the boardroom at Pacific Woods or in his Corvette.

"Hi, Della!" he called as he pulled up in front of her condo fifteen minutes later. Della was waiting for him on the porch. The April evening was comfortable, and she had decided to wait outside for Levi. She ran down from the porch as he ran to meet her. Halfway down the walk they met, embraced, and kissed. "Grrr!" he growled as his eyes fell on her trim body.

"Grrr!" she growled back. It was unclear which of them was the most eager predator.

He hurried to open the car door for her, buffing her cheek with a mock fist and smiling in approval at her appearance. "Grrr! You smell great!" Della slid into her bucket seat. He reached across the black leather console and patted her knee. She smiled at his practiced forwardness.

Della was falling in love, and she knew it.

There was a part of Della that felt guilty loving Levi. She had never been good at concealing her moods. Her love for Levi really showed. When he called she was always ready—no matter what inconvenience the time or circumstances of his coming might present. She knew what she wanted out of life. She wanted Levi—not his wealth or corporate social structure. She wanted Levi Twist for the more normal things that his protection and security might represent. What Levi wanted out of life was Della, and yet he could never bring himself to ask the question both of them wanted him to ask. On those occasions when their feelings had gotten away from them, Della always thought about the advice that her old Baptist grandmother had given her: "Della Singleton, you save yourself for just one man." It was too late for Della to do that. She had now given herself to Levi so many times she couldn't claim to be saving herself. She wished she could undo those times, but she couldn't. As she saw it, her grandmother's warning to her was not irrelevant, just not totally usable.

After they had enjoyed dinner and a movie, Levi took her home, following her into her condominium for a late-night snack. They sat by a set of French windows, looking out through the plate glass at the streetlights beyond. Della seemed suddenly troubled. Levi, of course, noticed.

"Where's our relationship going, Lee? You're fifty-ish now, and I'm thirty-one—where's it going?"

"It doesn't have to go anywhere tonight, does it, Dell? It's not like a trip we book with a travel agent. It's not going anywhere; it's just OK." Levi reached across to Della and took her hand. He knew they needed to resolve the issue, but he didn't want to work on it right then.

"Why can't it go somewhere?" Della said, refusing to abandon the issue.

"Della, if this is a proposal, I should be doing it, and I'm not. I like my life just the way it is. I love you, but at the moment I'm free and you're free—no messy joint income tax forms to file. Isn't that good enough for now?"

"Lee, it's good enough for now but . . ."

"Aw, c'mon, Della. Tomorrow night we'll have an early date, and then we'll come home and talk about it, OK?" Levi was agitated.

"Levi, I didn't want to have to tell you like this, but there's something else you've got to know."

"What is it, Dell?" Levi grew suddenly serious as he saw the look on her face.

"I'm pregnant." Della looked down. She was on the verge of tears.

Levi reached out instinctively toward her. "Della baby, don't cry. Are you sure? Are you?"

"Yes, Levi, I'm sure. I saw a gynecologist yesterday." Della fought back the tears.

"Well, you'll just get an abortion."

Della thought of her Baptist grandmother and broke into uncontrollable tears. "Lee, I want this baby—our baby!"

"Della, I know you would make a splendid mother—but I'm not ready for this yet." It was an odd statement that caused them both to wonder why a fifty-three-year-old millionaire wasn't ready—and if he ever would be ready. Levi, looking sheepish, went on. "Abortion is the smart thing. We both need time to think about this. Someday marriage will be right for us. But we mustn't let a crisis crowd us into a future we're not ready to face."

Della knew that she could never live with herself if she aborted Levi's child . . . no, if she aborted their child.

Suddenly Levi reached out and took Della's wrist and wrenched it in the vice of his intention. He was strong, and Della felt the pain of his grasp.

"Get an abortion, Dell!" Levi nearly bellowed the phrase.

Della burst into tears.

Only gradually did Levi release his grasp. He stood and left without speaking, slamming the door on his way out of the house.

She sat in silence for a long time. Her apartment was quiet. She had never felt so alone before. Suddenly she didn't feel at home in her own home. She thought of Victoria Billingsley. Exactly why she thought of the woman she had no idea. She did not live too far from the riverfront condo where the horrible murder had occurred. The natural fears had grown common among single women in northeast Seattle. She tried to get her mind off the murder. She returned to thinking about Levi and her unborn child.

His roughhousing left Della in both fear and doubt. Doubt because she wasn't sure how far Levi would go in a real crisis. Fear because . . . well . . . just because.

CHAPTER 8

Henry Demond was the janitor on West Wing 1 of the psychiatric clinic. He was running the vacuum system outside the open door of A-6 when he caught sight of Father Peter sitting on his bed, talking. The priest had spent the first two and a half weeks of April in daily therapy sessions but had shown little progress. Tuesday, April 18 had dawned, and Henry always cleaned the West Wing floors on the third Tuesday of the month.

Ignoring the roar of the vacuum system, Henry approached Father Peter, watching him with interest. The old priest was at the moment catatonic and oblivious to both Henry and the vacuum cleaner left roaring in the hall.

"Excuse me, Father Peter, did you want something?"

Father Peter, lost in his own catatonic world and utterly oblivious to the janitor's query, continued speaking. "Can you stand the return of the fires of Olympia?"

"What fires?" Henry knew Father Peter was not seeing him but a nightmare of some sort.

"This is the truth that shouts against the lie," said the vacant-eyed priest. "The fire that burns is a purging fire. Only the first flames sear. What happens next? My friends, there will be a rain of fire above the Space Needle. This burst of flame will occur just before the exodus begins. There's always a pillar of fire before an exodus! When you see the fire, turn your back on the flame and face the unburned mountain where dwells the snows that quench all flame—the mountains where dwell the wolf and owl."

"Hey, you," called a student nurse to Henry. "Get this stuff out of the hallway."

Henry was so absorbed by the words of the catatonic priest that he missed the nurse's call, which seemed so much less than the roaring vacuum.

"Hey, you," the nurse was hollering as she approached Henry. The enthralled custodian heard nothing until she thumped him on the shoulder with the inhaling end of the vacuum hose. His coveralls adhered to the nozzle of the hose. She pulled it out and his uniform followed, popping off the end of the sweeper hose and then slumping flat against his chest. Henry's gaze turned from the priest's silent lips to those of the nurse. "Mr. Demond, you can't leave your machines running unattended in the hallway. This is a hospital."

"I'm sorry, nurse. I . . . I . . ." Henry dragged the vacuum back into the hallway and stomped the foot switch. The loud whirring stopped.

"What were you doing in Father Peter's room?" the nurse asked.

Henry was embarrassed. "I thought he needed something. I saw his lips move and—"

"His lips are always moving. Forget it."

"Nurse, has there ever been a fire on the Space Needle?"

"Whatever are you talking about?" the nurse said.

"Father Peter just . . . never mind." Henry picked up the hose of the vacuum and moved down the hall. "Father Peter is a real loony tune," he said as he walked away.

When the vacuum was put away, Henry sneaked up the back stairs and went back into Father Peter's room.

The old priest was still speaking: "The planet of life is dying. This blue garden in the black galaxy is in danger unless those who live there can begin to care about it and act to save it. We are going to teach everyone that the planet itself is special to God and its resources are unrenewable. We must make the human race understand that they are stewards of a perishing planet. They have to see that they must act to save their world.

"So come, O beast, and eat our children. Teach us, O Kinta, thou wolf of the new apocalypse that kindness by devouring our children in the night. Destroy life to teach us how precious it really is. Blaze a pathway of light from the tiny cathedral. Set Sister Joanna on her exodus of redemption. Save all your dying Eden with this ebony madonna of hope."

A nurse tapped Henry Demond on the shoulder. She wagged her finger at him in a no-no gesture that clearly told him he must leave the catatonic priest alone. He obeyed dutifully, but the odd prophecy of fire on the Space Needle would not leave his mind. He somehow had the feeling he had stumbled upon a madman's prophecy. To know the future obsessed the custodian with the thrill of power. And after all his erratic ramblings he had spoken of Sister Joanna and the Pathway of Light Cathedral. That was Henry's church, and Joanna was Henry's pastor.

CHAPTER 9

The following morning Dr. Paul Shapiro left while Rhonda was still asleep. He left for the clinic fifteen minutes later than he usually did and was going to be late for his first appointment. He drove hurriedly down the I-5 then exited onto the congested route toward his office, checking his Rolex chronometer every minute or so. His mind filtered through the events of the past week and settled to consider the odd arrival of Father Peter, the doctor's unwanted patient. He could not simply dismiss him; it was against the law. But every day the old man stayed in his care, the bills continued to mount.

Threading his way to Queen Anne Hill through the heavy traffic of the central city brought even more time to examine his thoughts, and Rhonda came to mind. She had refused to sleep with him, and her refusal had prompted their worst argument yet. Their marriage seemed irretrievably doomed. He usually recommended marriage counseling for others in his same situation. Paul, however, was more eager to throw in the towel than to seek help. He was convinced that the work necessary to save their relationship was greater than the enjoyment he would derive from it, even if the marriage came suddenly and miraculously to a better state of health.

He squinted through the windshield as he drove through the car-lined side street. The morning sun struck a window of a small shop and threw a terrible glare into his eyes, temporarily blinding him. At that precise moment he felt a thump under the front of his car. He felt the whole side of his BMW rise sharply. He knew instantly that he had run over something.

A woman at the side of the street cried out, "Oh no! Stop!"

He immediately brought the car to a stop, shuddering to think what he might have done. He could see in his rearview mirror a small form lying in the road. A husky black woman was bending over a child crying, "Oh no! No!"

Paul leapt from the car and ran back to the woman kneeling over the broken form at her knees. She appeared to be trying to pick the little girl up.

"Please, I'm a doctor. Don't pick her up."

The woman looked at him with both contempt and a brokenness of soul. "If you're a doctor, do something!"

Paul bent over the little girl and felt her wrist. "She's still alive," he said as he took out his handkerchief and blotted a trickle of blood that was running out of her mouth. "Are you her mother?"

The question was needless. Tears were coursing down the woman's face.

"Can you call 9-1-1?" Paul asked, handing her his cell phone.

The woman rose to comply. She was thickly proportioned but regal. Her torn spirit revealed a kind of inner light spilling out of the fissure in her soul.

"Never mind. I'll do it," Paul said. "You just watch her, and don't try to pick her up," he repeated. Paul Shapiro was a take-charge person, and he began to possess the chaos and order it with his organized demands. "You there," he yelled to a bystander who had rushed to help, "go to the corner and try to slow the traffic coming over the hill."

At that precise moment, a policeman in his cruiser happened over the hill and braked to a stop, blocking the street and turning on his flashers. Within seconds he had radioed for help. Then the officer sprang from the squad car and cried as he ran up, "Is she alive?"

"So far," Paul replied, "but she's badly hurt. She will need all the help she can get, if she pulls through this one. Officer, I hit her!" It was the first time that Paul had thought to comment on his fault in the matter.

The officer turned to the grieving woman, "You're Mrs. . . . ?" The officer stopped and waited for her to fill in the blank.

"I'm not Mrs. anything," said the hurting woman. Through her anxiety she stiffened her spine and assumed a regal reply. "I'm the Rev. Joanna Nickerson. This is my little Janie. I was walking her to school when she tore free and darted off between those two cars there—I think she was going to race me across the street. I just don't know what got into her little mind, Officer." She broke into tears.

"I'm so sorry . . . so *very* sorry," Paul said, touching her heaving shoulders.

"I understand," said the mother. "She was so small. The morning sun was so bright I know you couldn't see her. Feel her pulse again, would you, Doctor?"

Paul complied. "It's still there, Reverend." Paul felt odd on his knees in the middle of the street, calling this stout, grieving madonna "Reverend." "Should one of us go call Mr. Nickerson?"

"Ain't no Mr. Nickerson. He died in a bar fight down on the wharf three years ago, right after I was called to preach. Oh my poor little Janie . . ." Tears cut across her round face. She stooped and felt the little girl's brow. "She's all I got now. We're just gonna have to ask the Lord to keep her alive."

It was all the preface she gave before she clamped her eyes shut and launched into a prayer of earnestness that tore at the crowd now gathering between the psychiatrist's vehicle and the squad car. "Lord, you know how much Janie means to me. Lord, I can't live without her. Lord, you know better'n anybody, I ain't never had much reason to live except you and her. Lord, let her live. Don't cut my reason for being in this world down to nothing."

Reverend Nickerson stopped at this point and raised her large black arms into the air. She began to sway as she remained with her knees firm on the concrete where her little Janie lay before her. "Lord, you gotta come now. Lord, you gotta come. Come now." It was a chant that she repeated over and over as the tears continued rolling down her cheeks. Paul was indicted by the sad litany as he felt the tiny wrist again.

In a moment the distant whooping of an ambulance siren could be heard. Soon it was at the site. The white-coated paramedics carefully rolled the little form onto a small sheet and lifted it prone onto a stretcher and then into the ambulance. Joanna Nickerson now left her knees and continued to chant, "Lord, you gotta come now. Come now. Come now, Lord, you gotta come!"

Paul helped her to her feet. Both of them ducked into the back of the ambulance just before it screamed away toward the city hospital.

The psychiatrist felt the uneasy rocking of the ambulance and watched the electro-cardiac monitor keeping track of Janie Nickerson's pulse. A paramedic hovered over the little girl, causing Paul to crane his neck in an effort to keep the life monitor in his field of vision. He was disturbed that she lay so silently with no signs of life at all. The monitor, however, still read things in her favor. "At least her pulse is strong, Reverend Joanna," he said.

"Come on now, Lord. Come on, you gotta come," was all the black woman could say. Even in the dim light of the ambulance, a thousand glittering beads of sweat had broken out all over her ebony skin.

Paul rubbed the little girl's arm. He could tell the right one was broken, but the left one was still intact. Some of her ribs were crushed, and a spot or two of blood on Janie's little dress told him emphatically that her bones had punctured her skin in two or three places on her side. Dr. Paul Shapiro was not in the habit of praying, but he was so moved by the plight of the desperate woman and her dying child that he felt like praying himself. It was an odd sensation, and he allowed it to pass.

"Come on now, Lord. Come, sweet Jesus!" Joanna was now changing her litany slightly.

"Momma." It was a single word but so welcome it stopped the prayers of the preacher.

"Now you just lay real still, honey." The Reverend Nickerson patted the little girl's arm.

"Momma, I'm scared."

"'Course you are, honey, but you lay real still. Don't need to talk either, you hear Mommy?" Janie closed her eyes then opened them again and looked around the ambulance. Her eyes fell on Paul. "Momma, who's that?" When Janie tried to point, her broken arm flopped aimlessly to one side. Janie appeared dumbfounded. "Momma, what's wrong with my arm?"

"Now honey, you just lay real still, you hear? This man's Dr. Shaporti." Paul Shapiro smiled. "He's gonna make you well, honey!"

Paul knew that sooner or later she would find out that he was a psychiatrist and not really into emergency medicine—probably by the time the ambulance reached the hospital.

"Momma, I'm sorry I got hit by a car. You won't spank me for running in the street, will you, Momma?"

"Lands no! Now Janie, you be quiet, 'cause Dr. Shaporti don't want you to move at all. You just lay real still, honey."

"OK, Momma."

For the next two minutes no one said a thing. The ambulance driver and his assistant said little. A third member of the rescue team was trying to keep the oxygen mask on Janie, who kept moving her head. Paul motioned him away and told Janie not to move her head for any reason. When they reached the hospital, they wheeled Janie off to an examining room. Paul stayed with Joanna.

"I must tell you, Reverend Nickerson, I'm a psychiatrist."

"Lord have mercy, a shrink!" she gasped.

Paul looked down.

"Dr. Shaporti."

"Shapiro," Paul corrected.

"Yes, well . . . I think if more people would just trust the Lord, there would be less need of you 'sigh-kiatrists.'" She had an interesting way of saying the word.

"I suppose you're right," Paul agreed, "but then if everybody'd be good, we wouldn't have much need for preachers."

Joanna grew quiet.

"Mrs. Nickerson," said a tall, thin man who approached. "I'm Dr. Jamison. We must operate on your daughter. Will you sign the release for surgery?"

"Of course . . . only, what do you think? Will she be all right?"

"We can't say for sure. She's bleeding internally, and we have to get it stopped, even before we set all the broken bones."

"Oh, Dr. Shaporti," she moaned. She signed the papers. Dr. Jamison thanked her and turned on his heel and left the room. Joanna fell to her knees and began to chant again, "Come on now, Lord. Lord, you touch little Janie. Come on, sweet Jesus."

Paul stood and walked down the hall, took his cell phone from his pocket, and dialed his home number.

It was the first time in a long time that Paul Shapiro had called home during working hours. Although he usually ignored Rhonda, he suddenly had a furious need to talk to her. He wanted so to tell her about the accident. After the fifth ring, the receiver clicked.

"Hello," said Rhonda.

"Rhonda, this is Paul," said the psychiatrist, feeling somewhat relieved to hear her voice.

"Paul," she said abruptly, "can you call back later? A man from the phone company is here. I can't talk now. Call back later please."

Paul felt abused. He needed to talk, and she was giving him the brush-off.

"Rhonda, can't you be there for me? I need to tell you something. Why can't you give me just five minutes of your 'very important' homebound agenda?"

He knew the answer to those questions. There was too much in their past that didn't welcome words. Paul wanted to talk—he even needed to talk—but Rhonda had decided against it. She almost hung up on him. Neither of them said anything for a moment as Paul walked back toward the emergency lounge. Even before he got there, he could still hear the Reverend Joanna's "C'mon, Lord. Come, sweet Jesus."

"Paul, the phone man says he knew Victoria."

"Victoria?"

"You know, the woman down the road who was murdered, whose face was eaten off."

"Well, why is he in our house talking about that?'

"Gotta go, Paul." She hung up.

Paul could tell Rhonda was scared. He was scared too. All his life he had dreaded the notion that he might run over a little child. He was plenty scared.

CHAPTER 10

Rhonda Shapiro had told Paul the truth: a man from the phone company was there. The Shapiros had been having some buzzing problems on most of the upstairs phones. Rhonda was determined to get it fixed. She was surprised at the large extent of the trouble the phone man seemed to be going through, just to inquire about what she supposed would be a simple repair problem. She wished the repairman would just hurry and get through with his work and leave her alone. But on he worked. He checked all the small connect boxes and even replaced a red wire in one of them.

"The phone in the upstairs bedroom is old. It's got a bad buzz. It should be replaced, Mrs. Shapiro," said the repairman. "I've got a few new ones in the van if you'd like to pick out one; my selection isn't the greatest. You'd probably rather just pick up one at the Phone Center next time you're downtown. I'd like to make the commission, but, honestly, you'd be better off if you do your own shopping."

"Thank you, I'll take care of it." Rhonda was in no mood to pick out a phone from the repairman. But there was something special in his shy manner that made her feel good about the human race. She was wearing a white blouse that Paul had bought for her years ago. Paul had liked it in the earlier, richer days of their relationship because it was so enticingly low cut. She suddenly felt that perhaps the repairman was stealing glances at the blouse for the same reason.

Rhonda turned away from him and then turned suddenly back toward him. Now he was gathering his tools and putting them in a little gray chest. He was about to leave when suddenly she felt some remorse that she had been so accusing in her mind. She then decided to play the hostess, if only to break her feelings of guilt in having misjudged his glances. He was on his way back to the van when she offered him a bit of hospitality for his kindness. "Cup of coffee?" she asked after he had loaded the last of his equipment back into the van.

He closed the double rear doors of the van and smiled at her. "Yes, I guess so." He accepted her gesture hesitantly. She disappeared into the house and in a couple of minutes reappeared with two steaming cups of coffee.

"Cream?" asked Rhonda, reading his monogrammed name off his blue uniform.

"Black will be fine," the repairman answered.

When he had taken a couple of sips of the coffee, Rhonda asked him how long he had worked for the phone company.

"Since I got out of the service . . . after 'Nam." The telephone man paused, shifted nervously, and abruptly changed the subject. "Ma'am, I know you must have read about Victoria Billingsley. She was killed only a couple of miles back toward town on this same road. I'm convinced that everyone who lives along this road needs to be careful. You know, Mrs. Shapiro, the press is saying the Billingsley woman was murdered by a dog. But from the description in the papers, I don't think any dog I've ever seen could decimate a body like that."

Rhonda winced.

"It would have to be some bigger animal, in my opinion," said the repairman.

Rhonda fidgeted. The phone man was serious. He really did seem to feel that Rhonda was in danger. She was so moved by his concern for her safety that she was about to confess the story of the dog that she had pulled out of the river. Then she froze, deciding not to bring the matter up. She stood and leaned against a section of the ornamental iron fence that surrounded the Shapiro home. For a moment or so the telephone man also leaned on the railing and looked out over the distant river. He suddenly left the fence, drank the last sip of coffee, and handed her the empty cup. He thanked her for her hospitality. As he turned to go, he smiled at her and said, "Well, Mrs. Shapiro, you can't be too careful. If I were you, I'd stay inside, especially at night and above all when you're alone out here."

"I'll remember your advice. Thanks."

Rhonda watched his truck drive away. She could not, in point of fact, imagine what her own husband was going through at the moment. She remembered that he had called but decided not to return the call.

She walked back into the house and into the kitchen, returning to the sink. She noticed a calendar on the wall. It was Wednesday, April 19.

She was glad the phones were fixed, but to rest for awhile she turned off the ringers and even powered off her cell phone. Once again Paul tried to call her. This time he was only invited to leave a message. Oblivious to his need, Rhonda relaxed into a short nap that lasted until 1:30 in the afternoon.

Then she woke in terror.

A man dressed in black slacks and a black turtleneck was standing over her. At first she thought she was having a nightmare. But as he reached for her, she knew it was all too real to be a dream. She knew that she was about to be victimized if not murdered. She thought of the dog murderer and looked at the horrible size of her crouching assailant. He was wearing a rubber Halloween mask over his face. The mask looked like Richard Nixon. She tried to scream, but the scream was too breathless with fear to find any volume. She rolled from the couch and onto the floor. The extra distance that her assailant now had to reach down left him precariously unbalanced, and as Rhonda rolled into his feet, he lurched into the cushions of the couch, tripping over her.

She was thoroughly awake now, on her feet and running toward the back door of the kitchen. She felt his proximity, prompting her to reach for the coffee pot that was still hot and mostly full from the morning coffee she had served the phone man. She threw the scalding liquid on the chest and stomach of the masked intruder. He spat out a curse and doubled over in pain. Again she knew that she had stopped him only momentarily. But while he took a moment to deal with his own pain, Rhonda ran out the back of the house and down the pinecone-covered footpath toward the toolshed.

Ordinarily the great trees that hid their home seemed like those of paradise, filling her with peace and security. But now the loneliness of their residence all but paralyzed her with fear. She ran for all she was worth. But her assailant had now recovered his intention and moved even more rapidly and forcefully toward her. When she was at the door of the toolshed, he caught her once again. His hands were the biggest that she had ever seen. With them he grabbed her and pulled her tightly against him. She now gave up all thoughts of wriggling free and escaping. His very strength and size told her she could never outrun him.

He crushed her small body against his huge hulk. He was breathing heavily, and his breath came through the hideous dark slit in the rubber lips of the ugly mask. Instinctively Rhonda wedged her left elbow between herself and her threatening oppressor. In vain she tried to push him away with her right hand. Her left hand fumbled behind her for the twisted latch that locked the small door of the shed. He flattened his forearm against her face, pinning her head to the wall of the shed. Then he was pushing her toward the ground. Mercifully her left hand fell at last upon the latch and clawed at it, managing to twist it open just as the huge man shoved her to the ground.

The shed door exploded open. Like a 200-pound cannonball, the animal she had rescued from the river bolted into the sun.

"What?!" the intruder cried as the brute shot past him and then wheeled and turned.

"Get him, dog!" Rhonda screamed.

The furry brute snarled at the attacker. His ears lay flat against his head, and the hair on his neck rose in irregular ridges of fur. The assailant seemed unable to adjust so quickly from his rapacious advances to cope with the animal's crouching, frightful appearance. During his temporary stupefaction, Rhonda struggled free. Before he could turn to pursue her again, the animal's crouch exploded into a lunge. Two hundred pounds of brute force struck the man in the chest. The huge predator's muzzle tore into her assailant's upper chest. Blood ran dark through the turtleneck. In a vain attempt to defend himself, the man threw his arm between himself and the dog and tried to push him back. Now his arm also was torn by the savage fangs. There was more blood.

Pushing himself against the shed, the man in the mask got to his feet. His right arm grabbed the back of the dog's neck and pulled his snarling muzzle up and away. Powerful as the man was, he knew he would not be able to hold the beast for long. It was then that Rhonda noticed a phenomenon, stranger than she would ever have been able to imagine. The man's powerful arms held the beast for a moment or so. It was as though he knew the beast. Then Rhonda heard him say very clearly to her in a deep-throated accusation, "You ugly slut! This is no dog!" Then he looked at the animal and said, "So it is *you*, Kinta . . . I thought I finished you off in the Lee West Construction Camp."

The blood gushing through his turtleneck quelled further speech. With his huge right hand he reached out one final time for the throat of the brute, intending to tear it out. Rhonda instinctively reached for an old tire tool leaning against the shed. She swung the iron tool, crashing into the rubber mask that covered the man's head. He staggered forward and released his hold on the animal. Rhonda ran into the woods, and the animal ran after her. Her dazed assailant stumbled forward for a moment, shaking his head to clear it. He stood looking down at his torn and blood-soaked clothes. He knew he needed medical attention. He yelled at Rhonda as she disappeared into the trees. "If you tell anyone of this, I'll come back and kill you. As for you, Kinta, your life is also over!"

His very threat caused Rhonda to shudder. She watched from the safety of the forest as the man stumbled through the trees toward the sheltered road. He climbed into a car and sped away. Rhonda could not even see the color of the car let alone read the number off the license plate. The animal's ears lay back as though he wanted to run after the escaping car and attack again.

"No, Kinta . . . stay, boy," Rhonda said. It suddenly struck her that she actually called the dog by a name—the name her assailant had used. It somehow seemed to fit, and she stroked his huge head and said again, "Kinta!"

Rhonda was relieved to hear the diminishing roar of the disappearing car. Soon the woods were as quiet as they had been before the whole incident occurred. Only after a long time did she and the dog move back toward the house. The intensity of her fear gradually subsided. Terror was new to her. Rhonda had been afraid very few times in her life. She retraced her steps across the back deck and into the house, not even stopping to pick up the spilled coffee pot that now lay on top of the stained carpet before the patio door.

She turned on the phones but had no intention of calling the police. She believed with an acute terror that the attacker would do as he said and kill her if she reported him. Instead, she went directly to the cabinet where Paul once kept a small handgun. It was no longer there. She locked the front door and turned the burglar alarm on. It was a feature she had protested but Paul had added anyway to their remote retreat. Suddenly she felt a chill. What if her horrible assailant had returned to the house through the front door. Painstakingly she began to check every point of entry in the house. The huge animal moved ahead of her, sniffing his way down every dark hallway. Finally the dog walked over to the bearskin rug in the great room and lay down upon it. Rhonda knew it was his signal to her that everything was all right. She had never felt such a sense of peace as she did in surveying the brute as he rested with his muzzle on the broad head of the bear.

"Good boy! You are a good dog. No, you're a *great* dog. *Kinta* he called you. How did such a nice dog—" Rhonda stopped midsentence. "He also said you were no dog. What did he mean by that? Are you, Kinta? Are you a dog?"

Rhonda had the frustrating feeling that he could almost answer. "You're not a dog, are you?" Kinta lifted his head and whimpered.

Rhonda smiled—her first since the crisis at the toolshed. "You're a . . . !" She was suddenly struck by fear again. She ran to the library off the master bedroom and came back with a big picture book, *Wildlife of North America*. She consulted the index and then turned the pages furiously. She stopped and looked at the picture in the book and then at the animal. "Kinta," she said, "you're no dog."

Kinta looked at her quietly, as though her discovery was welcome to both of them.

CHAPTER 11

The sudden ringing shattered the silence and made Rhonda jump. The landline phone rang a second time before she set aside her jitters and moved methodically toward it. She put her hand firmly on it—it rang again. She felt the vibration of the bell through the receiver. She looked at Kinta and took courage. Why was she so hesitant to answer? In the middle of the fourth ring, she lifted it suddenly off the hook. "Shapiros!" she almost shouted at the receiver.

"Rhonda? Are you all right? You sound like you're on edge." It was Mimi Jenkins, her nearest neighbor.

"Oh, Mimi, yes, fine," said Rhonda.

"I can certainly understand your being a little shaken."

"You can?" Now Rhonda was insecure. How could Mimi know?

"Yeah, I heard about Paul on the radio."

"Paul? Radio?" Rhonda was completely confused.

"You know—the little Nickerson girl."

"Whatever are you talking about—Nickerson girl?"

"You know, the accident."

"What accident? Mimi, what on earth is going on?"

"This morning . . . I thought for sure you knew. This morning Paul ran over a little girl on Queen Anne Hill."

"Oh, Mimi!" cried Rhonda.

"I'm surprised Paul didn't call you."

"He did call me while the phone man was here, and I abruptly told him to call back later, only later . . . oh no . . . Mimi, Mimi! I've had the phones off for most of the day."

"Rhonda, are you sure you're all right? Rhonda, you're not all right. Something's wrong, and I'm coming over. I'll be right there."

"Yes, I'm fine! Don't come over! Mimi, please, I must be alone." Rhonda bit her lip to cut off a sob.

"Well, OK, but call me if things get too heavy. Understand? Promise me, Rhonda Shapiro!"

"I promise. Thanks for your call. Good-bye."

"Are you sure you're OK?"

"Yes. Good-bye, Mimi."

"Good-bye, Rhonda."

Rhonda hung up the receiver and immediately dialed the hospital.

"Hello. Dr. Shapiro's office," said a familiar voice.

"Della?"

"Yes. Rhonda?"

"Yes. Is Paul there?"

"He's with a patient, Rhonda. Do you want to hold, or shall I have him call back?"

"No, he might not. I'll hold, Della. Please tell him I'm calling and see if he can talk to me right now. I need to talk to him. Do you understand?"

Della was surprised by Rhonda's insistence although she knew more about the Shapiros' marital problems than Rhonda suspected.

Rhonda's mind drifted back to the horror of her encounter with the masked assailant. In her reverie she forgot she was holding the phone, and her chin began to quiver in the reliving of the experience. The phone was silent for more than four minutes when the sudden volume of Paul's voice in the receiver called Rhonda back to reality.

"Hello, Rhonda," Paul was noticeably cool.

"Darling, can you forgive me? Please, it's important to hear you say it. I had no idea about the accident. Paul, I had the phones off this afternoon—please, do you forgive me?"

The phone was silent. Paul was overwhelmed at the near-desperation in her voice. It was so unlike Rhonda to beg his forgiveness, and she hadn't called him "Darling" in years. Paul was all but speechless. The silence welded the dead receiver to Rhonda's hand. Because of Paul's long silence, Rhonda had the odd sensation that the phones weren't working again.

"Paul! Are you there?!" Rhonda shouted into the unresponsive receiver.

"Yes . . . yes . . . I'm here. Are you all right?"

"Do you forgive me?"

"Of course, and I love you for asking!"

"If you forgive me, then I'm all right. How is the little Dickerson girl?"

"It's Nickerson. She's in stable condition. Rhonda, I feel so ashamed, hitting the child. The sun was in my eyes. I couldn't help it!" Now Paul sounded desperate to Rhonda.

"It's OK, Paul. Please don't blame yourself like this."

"I don't know if I'll ever be able to sleep again," Paul continued. Then he realized Rhonda was crying.

"What's wrong, Ronnie?" he probed.

"Paul," she wept, "Paul, promise me that you'll come straight home from work. What did you do with the gun—the handgun?"

"What are you talking about?"

"Please tell me," Rhonda begged.

"I will not. Rhonda, what is going on?"

"Promise me you'll come straight home. Where are the extra keys to the Cherokee?"

"They're in the valet case on our dresser, but don't try to drive it. What on earth is going on?"

"Will you come straight home after work?"

"Yes, Rhonda, I will."

"Paul, I have a dog—a big dog—he's in the house with me. I'm frightened."

Paul had thought so often of Victoria Billingsley. Now the idea that Rhonda was in the house with a big dog terrified him.

"Where did you get a dog?" he sounded almost critical. Realizing he might be a little irrational, he instantly softened his tone. "That's fine, Rhonda. Get a pack of dogs if you want to, only don't do anything foolish." Paul worried Rhonda might be suffering from the beginnings of some paranoia.

"Do you forgive me, Paul?"

"I said I did."

"Will you come straight home after work?"

"I only have a couple more appointments. Dr. Nefton can take them. I'm starting for home now!"

"Oh, thank you . . . thank you."

"Good-bye, Ronnie."

"Bye, Pauly."

Paul hung up, uneasy. Her desperate thank-yous made him feel suddenly needed in her life. Paul knew that something had happened to Rhonda. Something real or imaginary was terrifying her to the extent that she at last needed him. Whatever she faced, he knew that she no longer felt competent in being alone. She had not needed Paul for years. She hadn't called him "Pauly" for a decade.

He strode toward his assistant's desk. "Good-bye, Della. I'm leaving. Call the center and tell Dr. Nefton to take my last two appointments." He turned on his heel and walked out of the office. Della was as befuddled by Rhonda's call as she was by Paul's sudden leaving. But she envied Rhonda. She had someone—she had Paul. And even though they were the most unhappy couple she knew, in a crisis, Rhonda had someone to depend on.

It took Rhonda awhile to let go of the conversation she had with Paul. She sat holding on to the phone for a moment, reluctant to hang up and afraid it might ring again. When she finally lowered the phone from her ear, she thought she heard the distinct sound of a receiver clicking the audio buzz of her own receiver into silence. Could someone have been listening in? Now she was being paranoid. It was time to get hold of herself.

Her eyes fell on the silver brown fur of the wolf. Should she have him inside the house with her? She thought of Victoria Billingsley.

CHAPTER 12

Paul Shapiro got out of his car and walked to the front door of his house. He was surprised to find it locked. Rhonda loved walking freely in and out of the house on days like today. Puzzled, he pressed his own doorbell. He was startled when a huge hulk of fur and fangs lunged at the glass side panel beside the door. The snarling animal soon sensed the futility of trying to get at him through the glass and retired to his haunches. Still showing his fangs, the beast kept his ears laid back.

"Kinta!" shouted Rhonda from inside. The brute turned from the glass at her words and slouched away, only staring at the door as Rhonda relaxed the dead bolt and chain. As Paul stepped into the house, she nearly bowled him over in an embrace.

"Oh, Paul. Thank God, you're home!" She clung to Paul for a moment and then released him. He saw tears mingled with terror in her eyes. He was about to speak when she pulled at his sleeve to draw him across the room to the couch. Suddenly she stopped their progress, turning back to the front door to secure it. She sighed with a kind of healing relief as she looked gratefully at her husband. Paul could not remember how long it had been since she had looked at him like that. She smiled at him and crossed the floor, taking his hand and sitting down with him.

Paul's eyes moved from her to the great animal whose neck fur was still ruffled with suspicion. The beast's eyes made him feel an overwhelming sense of terror in his own home. Paul's terror subsided only as Rhonda reached out and drew her husband close. A kind of odd reverence gathered about them. They were sensing something each had lost somewhere in the fog of their selfish years. It was oddly instantaneous, like something had fallen upon them out of their younger lives.

They were together, and they wanted to be as such.

Paul had injured a child; Rhonda had been attacked.

The mystery of their sudden togetherness postponed their speaking for a long time. Each seemed afraid that even the shortest phrase would destroy the new mystique. Something had revived their horrible marriage to life again. Paul was the first to break the spell. When words finally came to him, they came all at once.

"Rhonda, wherever did you get that dog?" Paul's eyes were wide in astonishment.

"Pauly, his name is Kinta, and I didn't get him just today. I've had him in the toolshed for a couple of weeks now."

"My goodness, Ronnie, why? What is going on?"

"Pauly, first tell me about Janie Nickerson." The mood that had just prefaced their conversation was so sacred it had stolen Paul's frazzled mind. It was the first time all day Paul had actually *not* thought about Janie Nickerson.

"Well, she ran out from between two cars on Queen Anne Hill. I ran over her twice."

"Twice?" Rhonda nearly shouted the question.

"I mean with both the front wheels and the back wheels. Oh, Rhonda, I'm so ashamed!" Paul's confession released tears from his eyes and a storm of need that caused him to reach out to his wife. He held onto her with a kind of passionate requirement he had long forgotten.

"But why should you be ashamed?" protested Rhonda. It was the first time all day she had *not* thought about the attack of her horrible assailant.

"Ronnie, if you could have seen her, silent on the pavement with blood running out of her mouth." Paul stopped his narration. He seemed so far away, so broken, so unable to stop or go on. His description brought tears to her eyes.

"Will she live, Pauly?"

"Yes . . . no . . . I don't know. She was quite lucid before her surgery. Children are always so bright. It's hard to tell what condition they are really in. It's hard to tell if she will live or not."

"Paul, I am ashamed that I turned off the phones at a time when you really wanted to talk."

Paul and Rhonda felt a cleansing sanctity that neither could explain. Why, all of a sudden, was a marriage that had been important to neither of them suddenly so essential to both of them?

"Rhonda, I don't know what's happened to you, but today when you called me 'Pauly,' I felt that our marriage might find a way again. For the first time in two years I actually caught myself hoping it would. Ronnie, you're a beautiful woman."

He stopped. She threw her arms around him. She kissed him as she had not kissed him in years. Paul could tell she meant it. When the kiss was complete, Paul opened his eyes. Kinta was resting sleepily and unconcerned on the bearskin rug.

The sight of the huge animal reminded Paul that the euphoria he felt was an uneasy cluster of tangled events.

"But what about the dog?" Paul asked, trying to make the unreasonable things in life explain themselves.

"Darling, it's not a dog." Rhonda clipped her sentence short. She suddenly got up, walked to the other end of the couch, and picked up the book on American wildlife. She plopped the large volume in Paul's lap and pointed to the picture. Paul read aloud the label on the picture: "American Timber Wolf?!" Paul looked at the wolf and suddenly felt an urge to leave. He moved his body toward the back of the couch as though his three-inch retreat would give him some added distance and safety. Kinta slept on.

"Is he dangerous?" asked Paul.

"That depends on who you are," Rhonda said.

"I'm your husband!" he shouted. "Is he dangerous or not?" Paul instantly felt ashamed for his flash of temper. He fidgeted on the couch then settled back into the cushions.

"No," Rhonda replied. "That is, I don't know. He tried to kill a man this afternoon."

"What on earth! What man?"

"Paul, the man deserved it, so I hit him with a tire tool."

"He doesn't look like it hurt him." Paul was confused.

"Not Kinta, my assailant!"

"What assailant? What are you talking about? Who did you hit with a tire tool?" Paul smiled at the idea then laughed out loud, sure that it was some kind of joke. "OK, Ronnie, out with it. Who did you hit with a tire tool?" His mirth faded, however, when he saw his wife on the verge of tears.

"Pauly, I had to. The man was trying to kill Kinta." Rhonda started over. "I took a couple of aspirin and lay down to take a nap about 11:30 this morning. Around 1:30 I was awakened by a tall man dressed all in black, wearing a rubber Halloween mask. He looked like Nixon, Richard Nixon. He grabbed at me and started trying to kill me or rape me or whatever. I threw myself off the couch and pushed him off balance. He stumbled, and I wriggled free, and then he came at me again. This time I threw the coffee pot at him. It burned him severely, and then he became really enraged. I ran outside and managed to get to the shed where I have been keeping Kinta. The attacker caught me there, but I managed to let Kinta out, and Kinta flashed past me and attacked him. The man's throat was gushing blood, and there were claw marks all over his chest when he finally got control of Kinta. He was a huge man, and it looked like he was going to break the dog's . . . er, the wolf's neck, and so I smashed him with that old tire iron."

"What . . . how . . . ?" Paul stammered. "Who was he? I'll rip him apart."

"When he staggered to his knees," Rhonda went on, "he dropped Kinta, who backed away with me. Then we ran into the trees and hid out until we heard him start the engine of his car. He had parked along the river road. I heard his car drive away, and awhile later I went to the house with Kinta."

"Did you call the police?"

"No, Paul, I didn't."

"Why not? Darling, a man like that needs to be arrested. There's something you're holding back. What is it, Ronnie?"

Rhonda leaned closer to him. "Pauly, you've got to show me how to drive the four-wheel drive. I've got to learn. Promise me that you won't tell anyone about this. Nobody has to know, do they?"

"Of course they have to know. I'm calling the police right now."

"No, please, Pauly. There's more. He said if I told anyone, he'd come back and kill me. Please, promise me!"

"Ronnie, I can't promise you that. The man needs to be locked up. The police can handle him."

"Paul, no. That's not all. He knows Kinta."

"Who, your assailant? How do you know that he knows Kinta?" Paul felt funny calling the animal by its first name.

"Well, I know because when the man saw Kinta, it was very clear both of them had met before. If you could have seen how Kinta acted toward him. It was like they were old enemies. In fact, that's how I know the animal's name. The man called him Kinta. I hadn't given him a name at all until that moment."

"Ronnie, Kinta greeted me like I was an enemy a moment ago, and this is my house! We've got to get rid of this dog . . . or wolf. What else are you keeping out in the toolshed?"

"Nothing, Pauly, and Kinta did not greet you like he greeted that man. Kinta did not greet you like an enemy, Pauly."

"Well, he has a splendid way of showing friendship. Where did you get Kinta? Ronnie, there's still a lot you haven't told me. Now give me all of it."

"A couple of weeks ago, I found him in the river, just past the fallen tree on the footpath. He was nearly dead. I thought he was dead at first, and I was digging a hole to bury him. I found out he was alive. It was clear from the gaping wound in his shoulder that he'd been shot. I put him in the toolshed to care for him and—"

"Rhonda, do you know how weird all this sounds?" Across the room Kinta rose. Paul stopped.

"Here, boy!" Rhonda called.

"God protect us, he's actually going to come!" Paul moved back into the couch as far as he possibly could. The animal advanced—a study in power, brute power.

"Here, boy," said Rhonda again. "This is Pauly."

The intelligent head swiveled until the muzzle was dangerously near Paul's knee.

"Extend your hand, palm down, to be sure," said Rhonda.

Paul reluctantly and cautiously followed her suggestion. Kinta sniffed then opened his jaw and extended his tongue. It fell on Paul's hand, scratching across it like fine sandpaper. Paul felt his skin crawl all the way to his elbow.

"He likes you!" Rhonda laughed. She took the massive head in her hands and shook it just like a child with a teddy bear. Paul's eyes widened at Rhonda's courage.

"Nice doggie," Paul ventured as he reached out his hand and patted the fur between the sharp ears. "I can't believe I'm doing this."

Rhonda dropped the huge head and stood abruptly.

Paul immediately backed into the cushions of the couch again.

"Why don't you two kiss and make up, and I'll fix a little dinner," she said.

"If you go to the kitchen, I go to the kitchen. Tell him to back off so I can get up."

"C'mon, Kinta. We'll all go to the kitchen," said Rhonda.

They did, Paul following cautiously behind the woman and the wolf.

"We can't keep him, you know," said Paul, nodding toward Kinta as Rhonda chopped a head of lettuce.

"Of course we can, Pauly."

"Rhonda, what's happened?"

"What do you mean, Pauly? I stared existence in the face today; maybe somehow God doctored my sick view of marriage. Pauly, how do I know what happened? I was nearly raped and—"

"But Rhonda, only yesterday you wanted a divorce, and now it . . . it's like we were at first. I feel like I have just fallen upon the Earth for the first time. I need you. This is the way we were meant to be. Now at last we can live."

"Well, yes, but . . ." Rhonda reached for a hot pad and opened the oven, checking on the two filet steaks roasting there. "Paul, I have the oddest feeling that today is some kind of pivotal point in our lives. That our world, maybe all the world as we know it, has changed. It will belong to us, but . . ." she hesitated. "But, Pauly, I have this feeling that while life for us is coming together—a marriage closer and better than it's ever been—we are going to go through a time of great stress, of . . . I don't know."

"What are you talking about, 'a time of great stress'?"

"It's that man in the mask. There's something more in his relationship with Kinta than either of us can under- stand. The man mentioned that he had tried to shoot Kinta in the Lee West Construction Camp. I checked today—Lee West has no construction going on this side of the river. And Lee West has been shut down because of the renewal of the spotted owl controversy. I called a state naturalist and asked him if there were any wolves in the state south of the river, and he said no. But Kinta was there. He had to have been there before he somehow crossed to this side of the stream."

"So even if he was the last wolf south of the river, what does it all prove?"

"It proves that Kinta must have lived south of the river at one time when this man took the shot at him, yet no one saw it or would ever have imagined it possible. Don't you see? The man said he'd kill Kinta. I've got to stop him. Now that this horrible man knows he's still alive, I've got to smuggle Kinta to some place of safety."

"Rhonda, why not just report him to the police and let them handle it?"

"Paul, you know that since Victoria Billingsley was killed, every large animal in this part of greater Seattle is suspect. Especially Kinta. He's a wolf; there's no way the police would take his side. The minute we report him, the authorities will think for sure that he did it. That's why I can't report him. The police would take him away."

Now Paul Shapiro, in fear, felt the hair bristle on the back of his neck. "Rhonda, how do you know Kinta *didn't* kill Victoria Billingsley?"

"Because, Paul, I just know he wouldn't do that!"

"Do you remember the day you pulled him out of the river?"

"It was Wednesday I think. It must have been on the fifth of April— No, it was Thursday, I remember now, because I had canceled a dental appointment I had for the day. It was Thursday, April 6."

"Well, Rhonda, Victoria Billingsley was killed on the first. How do you know it wasn't Kinta—before he was shot?"

"Pauly, he just wouldn't do that!"

"But, Rhonda, don't you see if Kinta, or whatever his name is, could tear this man's shoulder, couldn't he have torn the body of Victoria Billingsley as well?"

"But he didn't—he just wouldn't. And if we report him, the police will come and take him away!" Rhonda was fighting back tears now. Paul decided to press her more gently toward his logic.

Rhonda broke down. "Pauly, please don't report Kinta. They'll kill him and he's innocent and I am indebted to him for my own life."

Paul drew Rhonda close in an embrace. "OK, Ronnie, let's drop it, and we'll think about it for a day or two."

Paul sat in a kitchen chair while she finished preparing dinner. Kinta sat by Paul's chair. The psychiatrist absent-mindedly ran his fingers through the wolf's fur. He had been so absorbed in Rhonda's talk he had not even realized what he was doing. When he did, he withdrew his hand in fear. Kinta's head never moved, but his large green eyes rose toward the top of his head in warm entreaty; he whimpered an intense plea that was almost a command. Paul reached down again and continued stroking the animal. Rhonda smiled and reached to smooth the fur on Kinta's neck.

"Easy there, Rhonda. He's not a house pet, you know," warned Paul.

When dinner was ready, Rhonda dimmed the lights, making the single candle on the small table appear suddenly brighter. She sat, and Paul reached across the table and touched her hand. "I can't believe how much I love you, Ronnie," he said.

She smiled. "Paul, do you know how to pray?"

"Funny you should ask. I actually felt like praying today when the Reverend Joanna was praying for Janie." Paul cut a piece of his filet and stuck it in his mouth.

The Shapiros talked quietly of all they had missed in recent years. The day was strange. The night somehow also would be strange. Maybe they were destined, at last, to have a child.

Paul wanted to put Kinta back in the toolshed for the night, but Rhonda bristled.

"OK, I'll sleep with a wolf in the house, but it's weird." Kinta's presence, like an angel's, seemed to bless his long-dead marriage. For all the wrong things that had happened that day, life for the Shapiros was right for the first time in years. Rhonda felt that God had come to them personally to make them truly one in marriage.

They made love by the fireplace in the living room. Afterward, Paul marveled that after so many empty years of marriage healing might be on the way. How could it happen? How could they both know it so instantly? How could so many wonderful and horrible things have happened in a single day?

They held each other. Paul suddenly felt Rhonda's body become tense.

"What is it?" he asked.

"Tomorrow it begins," she whispered.

"What? What begins?"

"Paul, I don't know, but if I leave, I'm going to our old mountain cabin. You're the only one who will know where I am. I'll drive the Cherokee and take Kinta and the gun."

"Honey, you know nothing about guns."

"Pauly, you must tell me where it is."

"OK, OK. I'll lay it out for you in the morning. But don't leave the house tomorrow. Stay inside and keep the doors locked. We'll keep in touch by phone. But I don't want you to go up to our cabin yet, OK?"

"Maybe I'll wait a few days, but honestly, I'm afraid, Pauly."

They both crawled into bed as exhausted by their conversation as they were by the events of the day. Neither of them uttered a word when Kinta stood, stretched, and walked to Rhonda's side of the bed then lay down again. Her hand fell from the edge of the bed and felt his warm fur. There was a kind of security in his nearness. She soon slept.

Paul listened as her breathing became rhythmic. He thought of her trembling prophecy and of the wondrous turn in their relationship. How odd that he half believed her.

"Shapiro, you old fool . . . that's what happens to old psychiatrists," he said aloud. "They start believing their delusions. You're going to end your brilliant career locked up with all those patients you used to treat." When he closed his eyes, he could still see Janie Nickerson lying unconscious on the concrete.

Soon all three of them, the Shapiros and their wolf, were asleep.

They were awakened at 7:30 the next morning by the ringing of the phone. Paul rose suddenly and looked at the clock. "I've overslept. Thank goodness the phone rang." He stumbled across the room and nearly tripped over Kinta. He was startled all over again. In the soundness of his sleep he had forgotten all about Kinta. The huge animal paid him no attention. His mind eased, and he picked up the receiver.

"Yes . . . hello," he said, rather confused. "Yes, this is Dr. Shapiro . . . no, we don't have any unregistered animals," Paul lied. "Who filed the report? . . . No, you can't come over and look around; we won't be home. No . . . look, buster . . ." Paul slammed down the phone.

Rhonda, who'd also been awakened by the phone, remarked, "Paul, it's begun now. The man who attacked me has reported Kinta. Now the police will come, and they'll take Kinta. I can't let that happen. The wolf is innocent—he saved my life. He can't be a killer. He saved me; now it's my turn to save him." She hurried to Paul, and he held her. "I won't let it happen, Paul. Do you understand?"

"I . . . I think so," he said softly. Kinta looked their way and stood. Silhouetted against the glass wall of the master bedroom, the wolf loomed silver, large, and strong.

Paul paused. Rhonda looked as though she were thinking over all the recent events.

"Don't you see, Ronnie, darling, if Kinta could tear the chest of a man, he could certainly—"

Rhonda looked stunned, that Paul would even think the animal might harm her.

"I don't mean to frighten you, Ronnie, but I just couldn't bear to come home and find you like they discovered Victoria Billingsley."

Paul wanted to pray again.

CHAPTER 13

While Paul Shapiro was doing his best to get acquainted with Kinta, Joanna Nickerson began the evening service. The singing was usually vibrant for the midweek prayer meeting, but Reverend Joanna played the piano quite cheerlessly. Her little Janie was so much on her mind she broke into tears several times during the service.

"Now brothers and sisters of the Pathway of Light Cathedral, we have to pray for my little Janie. She's laying quiet at the hospital just waitin' for our Lord to heal her. Now let's pray."

Joanna sobbed while most of the members prayed. They circled Joanna and placed their hands on her as they began praying for Janie Nickerson. The cacophony of their voices swelled into merging "Precious Jee-suses" and "Yes, Lords." Tears flowed and hands flagged the air above. Some looked into the ceiling fans, and some stared at the dark flooring beneath their shifting feet. They swayed, prayed, and worshipped, praising and singing over and over with a rich sincerity. They began as one to sing one of the congregation's favorite choruses: "Father we love you / Lord God triumphant. / Come in your glory / And touch our empty lives with grace. / Then will we praise you, lift your name. / Then will we honor you / With lips made clean by flame."

The rolling chorus was repeated a full eight times. Sister Joanna then served up a rippling arpeggio and started singing it all over yet once again. When the music had gone on as long as she desired, she stopped the singing by rippling only on the treble octaves as she asked, "Who among us, in the name of our Lord, has a word of joy?" Joanna's brokenness signaled a brighter mood than she felt.

None seemed willing to speak, and Joanna Nickerson tried once again. "Who among us, in the name of the Lord, has a word of prophecy?"

"I do," said Henry Demond, as he stood.

"Yes, Brother Henry." Joanna was surprised then hesitant. "Brother Henry, are you sure?" In the two years she had known him, Henry had sat quietly through the boisterous worship at Pathway of Light. He rarely came to the "joy services" on Wednesday nights. Henry dutifully waited for Joanna's permission to come forward. Joanna, regaining her composure, nodded her permission. "Then you come on up here, Brother Henry. Stand by the piano and give us the word."

Henry came forward. He had never given a word of prophecy before and felt awkward about the task. But as soon as he reached the front, he pivoted and immediately bellowed, "Brothers and sisters, there's gonna be a fire on the Space Needle—then when the flame has burned an exodus to the wilderness, it will face the snows of the mountain. Come all ye who are lethargic in the face of majesty. Between the fire and snow will come the dawn of Eden born again."

Everybody was listening. Henry felt important having the gift of prophecy. He was smiling and immensely proud of how mysterious he sounded to all the members who looked at him in awe. He pushed his prophecy now that he had their attention. "So brothers and sisters, God's gonna judge the Needle—and the Needle will burn while the angels of terror arraign the planet for judgment!" Henry stopped. He really knew nothing of what he was talking about. But it sounded sincere, and everybody was listening. It felt good to prophesy even when he had no idea what he was talking about.

"Whew! Henry! Is that all? Precious Jesus, I hope so!"

"No, I am not finished," Henry grew quieter and more mystical. "When the fire has fallen, it shall be thee, dear Pastor Joanna, and thy wolf that shall lead the exodus of God's people into the mountains to cry out for the salvation of his world. As Moses' mountain was Sinai, thine shall be Rainier."

"My wolf! Henry, you sit down. Sister Joanna don't got no wolf, and she's not about to lead an exodus anywhere. You sit down, you hear me?"

"I will, thou exalted and ebony madonna of hope!"

"That does it! Don't you call me no ebony madonna of hope! I ain't nothing but Sister Nickerson. That's all I am and all I ever wanted to be. You sit down. That's just about enough of your prophecy."

"Okeydokey!" said Henry, sounding a little less prophetic. He returned to the back of the little church and sat down.

Joanna, befuddled by the abrupt and startling prophecy, asked, "Is God gonna burn the Needle clear up, Brother Henry? Will it come on Judgment Day, Brother Henry, or sometime sooner?"

"Just about anytime now," said Henry.

"'Just about anytime.'" Joanna's words were less a question than a restatement.

Joanna tried to preach, but all she could see in her mind was her poor little Janie. Her heart was not in the worship service. And Henry's odd prophecy was a major distraction to her mind. His overwhelming confidence distressed her. The other members of the church also were stunned and missed most of Joanna's sermon. But there was a greater hindrance to her speaking. All the time she was preaching, Henry Demond just sat smiling on the back pew like he knew something that even Sister Joanna was unable to guess.

———

It had been a long day for Joanna, and she was glad when all the brothers and sisters of the Pathway of Light Cathedral were gone. It was a short distance to her Queen Anne Hill flat. She used the walk back to her apartment to sift through the muddled events of the day. During all the confusion she thought of Dr. Shapiro faithfully waiting for the outcome. She loved her little Janie, but in no way could bring herself to dislike Dr. Shapiro because of the accident. She felt that was just the way life was sometimes. Only Jesus could sort through the injured souls and heal all the broken things.

She fell asleep on the couch. It was a shallow slumber that allowed her tired mind to wade through manufactured images of things wild and unconnected. Reverend Nickerson dreamed of Seattle and heaven, of Janie and Henry Demond. In her dream she roamed through the green mists of some pristine Eden. She saw children in green forests frolicking and playing with huge tigers. Her little Janie, completely healed, was there and quite healthy, running and playing with the others. All the serpents of the sea were sleeping and coiled among the flowering trees of this dream world. Even in her sleep, Joanna smiled, knowing that the day would come when there would be peace throughout the whole world. As she wandered around the wondrous forest of her dreams, she saw a great lion lying down with a lamb. No, it wasn't a lion. It was a wolf. But wasn't a lion supposed to lie down with the lamb? She felt confused. Just as she began to grow angry at the inappropriate wolf lying down with the lamb, one of her favorite prophets invaded her dream. Isaiah happened to come along. Joanna was not the type to be silent even in her dreams. She began to argue with Isaiah over the discrepancy in the image.

"It's supposed to be a lion, isn't it?" she asked Isaiah.

"Well, that's the way I originally wrote it," answered Isaiah, looking a little sheepish. "But listen here, Sister Nickerson, I could just as easily have written that it was a great wolf; it wouldn't matter."

"But you said it was gonna be a lion in the Good Book. If you're gonna write it in as a lion, it ought to stay a lion."

Joanna just couldn't let Isaiah get by with something less than he had written in the Bible only because she was dreaming.

"Joanna, I tell you, it just doesn't matter. It could just as well be a wolf as a lion. You're being too pushy, Joanna," said the offended Isaiah. "Look here, I'm one of the major prophets. Who do you think I am, Henry Demond?"

"OK, Ike," Joanna said with a little more respect. "It can be a wolf as far as I'm concerned." Somehow she wished she hadn't called him "Ike."

"Thanks, Joanna, for seeing it my way."

Joanna felt better. She liked the major prophets best when they took a little time off from throwing their thunderbolts at hypocrites and began to act more ordinary, more human.

In the swirling mists of her dream, she walked away then turned to wave good-bye to Isaiah, but saw both Isaiah and Henry Demond walking off together toward her beautiful little Janie, who was playing with the huge wolf. The dream stopped, and Joanna moved to a deeper level of sleep, untroubled by a cheeky prophet.

CHAPTER 14

On the afternoon following his unusual prophecy, Henry Demond was again privy to the voices within the catatonic and tortured soul of the priest.

"The rainforests are dying. The oceans are dying. The deserts are growing. Whole species of beautiful living creatures each year perish from the planet. And come all you, the unconcerned. It is time for us to correct this error. We all must teach the ignorant that the value of life lies in its significance to God. There glows and flows the living harmony—the balanced coexistence of all living things. All life is interdependent. Only when people have a real regard for all living things will they finally esteem themselves. All things—human and subhuman—must live or die together."

The priest's conversation trailed off. At length the old priest's lips moved again. "Thursday, April 20 is the day of Holy Flame! Today, my friends, comes the fire."

Henry Demond felt strangely exhilarated by the old cleric's words.

"Are you back in my room, you nosy janitor!" shouted the priest, coming all too quickly out of his stupor. Henry saw him reach for his stainless steel water bottle and dashed from the room.

It seemed to the janitor that Father Peter knew nothing of the odd voice that issued from within him during his catatonic trances. Henry Demond, on the other hand, knew everything. Henry was determined to stay as near to Father Peter as he possibly could. He found the old priest's mental meanderings too intriguing to ignore. Besides, it was his best hope of feeling spiritually significant at church. All that came to him through the priest's dementia was causing quite a stir at the Pathway of Light Cathedral. The poor psychotic priest was creating Henry's new reputation for prophecy.

A few blocks away two men linked together by clumsy security rigging worked on top of the Space Needle. At 2:30 that afternoon, welders working with acetylene and old hosing accidentally tore a hose, and flame at first spurted out of the ripped hose. Then the flame gathered in a gushing eruption. A ball of fire exploded over Seattle, and flames shot out from the roof level of the Space Needle. At that very moment a reporter for the *Seattle Times* was walking near the base of the Needle. "Whoa!" he cried to no one in particular. "Did you see that? It looked like an explosion on top of the Space Needle."

The flames faded, quickly convincing his senses that nothing had been there at all. However, a tourist to his right had been running a video camera.

"Excuse me, sir, I'm Harry Fick from the *Seattle Times*. Did you see anything through the view finder?" The question was needless. The man's face was blanched with fear. The fleeting vision of the fire had to be on his tape.

Joanna got home early that night. Inside her small, immaculate apartment, she pulled a chair up to the TV, got a glass of milk, and waited for the evening news. She continued to think about Henry Demond's word of prophecy. It was a queer word. Indeed, it was a most surprising word for a man who never once had spoken aloud during his years at the Pathway of Light Cathedral. She switched on the set to see a newscaster directing the audience's attention to a shot of an unexplained phenomenon at the Space Needle that very day. *Somebody else must have tried to commit suicide,* thought Joanna.

She heard a reporter saying, "At three o'clock this afternoon, a large fireball appeared directly above the Space Needle. Those in the Needle at the time were completely oblivious to the fire and light. However, hundreds of visiting tourists all over the city observed the fireball, and a tourist from Las Vegas happened to be videotaping the skyline at the moment of the occurrence. Reporter Harry Fick was able to obtain this footage."

The camera work was obviously amateurish, but the footage was spectacular. Joanna watched in astonishment. The fireball was half as large as the saucer-shaped restaurant and observation tower atop the Space Needle. The whole scene etched itself in Sister Joanna's brain.

"It must be some kind of sign!" Joanna said aloud in the empty apartment. "Lord, I know you're coming again, and that's OK with me. But when you made a prophet out of Brother Henry, you just about outdid yourself. But if Henry

Demond has the gift of prophecy, help him prophesy something a little less fiery next time!"

Joanna had the oddest feeling that Henry must somehow be in league with God's gracious Spirit. Henry's fireball was on the news! Henry really must have the gift. But it was just too much for her to ponder that what Henry prophesied was being reported on TV. It was all too confusing, and she gave up thinking about Henry's fireball and began praying for her little Janie once again.

Then she stopped praying. She suddenly remembered the rest of his prophecy. She was an ebony madonna in charge of an exodus to the mountains.

CHAPTER 15

After spending a leisurely morning with Rhonda, Paul arrived at the clinic near lunchtime. "Happy Birthday, Della," he said as he walked through the reception area. "And how about lunch? I mean, because your birthday's tomorrow and you get the day off, what if I take you to lunch today and we celebrate early? TGIT. Thank God, it's Thursday!"

"Sounds great!" she smiled. "I'll get my purse."

Soon they were in Paul's BMW, cruising along a back street. Paul drove her to one of their favorite fish-and-chips places.

In the past it had been easy for Paul to enjoy the lightness of their being together because he had felt trapped in his dull marriage. But following that severe and wonderful day when Paul had run over a little girl and also recovered the lost joys of his life, he really was a new man. He felt secure enough to take Della to lunch, confident that their friendship would remain platonic. After a wonderful, if fearful, night at home, Paul thought mostly of Rhonda even as he listened to Della. The two of them talked for the longest time, picking unenthusiastically at overfried fish and under-fried chips. They decided to settle the greasy aftertaste with a cup of cappuccino.

Della, suddenly eager to unburden herself to the psy-chiatrist, announced, "Paul, I'm pregnant." The statement's suddenness, not its truth, startled Paul, as it came abruptly from one totally unused to making such significant disclo-sures about herself.

As a psychiatrist, Paul Shapiro was used to abrupt con-fessions, and with Della as with any other client, his face showed little or no aftershock. "Levi Twist is the lucky cluck, I suppose?" Paul smiled and waited for her to tell him only what she wanted to and nothing more. Paul secretly wished it were someone else, for he held no high opinion of his for-mer client.

"Yes, of course, but he's skittish on marriage. He says an illegitimate child would ruin his corporate legitimacy. So I guess the number one question is whether or not I'm going to keep the baby."

"Do you want a baby? What would you do with one?" Paul realized the first question invited a reply; the second sounded as if he was either accusing or advising her. She apparently brushed aside any sense of accusation.

"Yes! I do want it! It's just that I'd rather the baby have a father."

"So."

Now she *had* said more than she intended. She checked herself, having no intention of going further. It was her problem, and she would have to work it out. She found herself suddenly delivered by the server who interrupted her confession with "More cappuccino?" The two words were enough to get her off the hook.

"Please." She handed him the small cup. "And be sure it's good and hot this time."

Della looked calm as she sipped her cappuccino, but the tears that formed in the corners of her eyes told Paul that she was a woman living so close to the brink that she could go over at anytime. He felt such a strong yearning that he reached out and touched her hand. There was no romantic contact in his touch, and Della understood that. But there was a world of spiritual compassion; she understood that too.

"Della," Paul's voice was suddenly so quiet Della had to lean toward him to be sure she didn't miss the counsel that was issuing from the gentle center of his soul. "I've been around long enough to know that you're dealing with a lot more than you're being open about."

Della blotted the corners of her eyes with the napkin that had been serving as a coaster for her cappuccino. "Paul, would you mind taking me home?"

He only nodded and patted her hand. Somehow she felt that just being with her boss would bring a sense of reprieve from the fear that she and Levi would never marry. But Paul was far more willing to listen than she was to talk.

While she stopped at the women's room, Paul paid the tab, walked back to the table, and left a tip. Della emerged from the powder room, composed and with her makeup carefully reapplied to her eyes and lips. They left the restaurant and climbed into his BMW. Paul knew her abruptness in leaving lunch was a form of self-protection.

They drove to Della's condominium complex in silence. Paul, noticing a hot-red Corvette in front of Della's place, exclaimed, "Wow! Nice wheels!"

Della was suddenly all sunshine at the sight of the car. *Maybe he's come to propose,* she thought. *Maybe life isn't so bad after all.* "Paul," she said, "stop here! Let me out!"

Paul pulled his BMW to the curb, slightly past Levi's car. Della pecked him on the cheek, saying, "Thanks so much for lunch." She opened the door and stood outside Paul's car.

Paul did not immediately pull away. He studied the scene playing out in his rearview mirror. Levi Twist had gotten out of the Corvette, looking like the corporate fashion plate he was. He was somehow too titan, too proud to be only a CEO. Della walked toward the red car and Levi reached for her, drawing her to him. He swallowed her in his thick arms and kissed her. She pushed against him at first and then yielded and snuggled into his muscular limbs. He handed her a bouquet he'd rested atop his car. Della joyfully accepted the bouquet and kissed him yet again. Perhaps it would be a happy birthday for Della. Maybe their unborn child would have a father after all. They walked toward the door of her condominium as Della fumbled in her purse for her keys. She opened the door, and soon both of them were inside.

Paul put his car in gear and drove away. He called the receptionist at the clinic, telling her that he was taking the rest of the day off. He swung the car onto I-5 and started home. *Home* was not the uncertain word it once had been, for something new had been born there. He was anxious to see if all he'd seen in Rhonda continued to live.

As he drove home, he felt alternating joy and bewilderment about his life. Except for the uncertain status of Janie Nickerson and the haunting feeling that Della was involved in a potentially unfulfilling relationship, life seemed glorious. Rhonda's new need of him had awakened him to the euphoric feeling that life really was worth living. He continued to think of Rhonda until he finally pulled into his garage.

Rhonda was sitting on the front stoop of the house. She was dressed in a chambray shirt and a pair of jeans that made her look like a lithe fashion model. It surprised Paul that he thought of her that way. She was sitting with her arm around Kinta, who lifted his head and swung it in the direction of Paul as he walked up to Rhonda. Then Kinta seemed to lose interest in the psychiatrist, laid his head back on Rhonda's knee, and fell into a doze in the afternoon sun.

"Hi, hon!" said Paul.

"Hi, Pauly," Rhonda grinned.

She stood. They embraced.

"Ronnie, it feels good to be alive!" Paul beamed.

They kissed on the doorstep and entered the house. The rebirth of their marriage still astounded Paul.

It had a mystical effect on Rhonda too. She was amazed, stupefied really, that Paul had come home from work early twice in two consecutive days. All at once, Rhonda's face brightened. Paul could tell that she was about to erupt with something she couldn't contain.

"Pauly, there's wonderful news! The hospital called and said Janie Nickerson is going to be fine."

Paul was ecstatic. "Well, half of my troubles are over! Tell me that the man who attacked you has been permanently jailed, and all of my problems will be over."

Of course, Rhonda could not say that. She hoped and prayed for it, but time would tell.

Paul found a book that Rhonda had obviously checked out from the library just that morning: *The Vanishing Timber Wolf*. While Rhonda was preparing a small rib roast, Paul began to read the book. When dinner was finally underway, she returned to the room to find Paul reading the book.

"I see you're reading the wolf book," she said. "Have you come to the place where it says there are less than ten wolves in the entire state of Washington?"

"Rhonda, you know that Kinta can't stay," he said, answering her question with a confrontation.

"Pauly, listen to me. I know that Kinta will not be ours forever, but I feel an odd responsibility for him at the moment. I still can't get over the feeling that he's in danger." She paused. "Paul, did you know that wolves mate for life? Do you think that this fact could be a kind of sign for our marriage? I mean, let's face it—Kinta seems to have touched everything broken in our marriage with an eerie healing."

"Whoa there! Are you saying that our marriage has been restored by a wolf? That's a bit much—a lot of credit based on an odd happenstance."

Rhonda tossed her head to show she disagreed. Then she reached out and took the book from his hand. She turned to a page near the middle of the book and said, "Listen to a few lines from Rudyard Kipling's poem 'The Law of the Jungle':

'Now this is the Law of the Jungle; / It's as old and as true as the sky. / The wolf that shall keep it may prosper / And the wolf that shall break it must die. / As the creeper that girdles the tree trunk, / The truth runneth forward and back: / For the strength of the pack is the wolf, / And the strength of the wolf is the pack.' It's beautiful, isn't it?"

Paul had to admit that it was. "But even if they mate for life and are fiercely loyal, they are still wild animals. The Humane Society suspects us already. Once the nature lovers find out that we've got Kinta, they'll be merciless until we release him. We must take him into the wilds and set him free. It will be best. Remember that bear they caught in the suburbs a couple of years ago? They took him up into the highland by an old Jeep trail and let him go. That's what they'll do with Kinta, and that's the way Kinta would want it if he could have his way."

"But what about the man in the mask? He said he had tried once before to kill Kinta, and he'll try again until he does it. Kinta saved my life; somehow I feel it's my turn to save his if I possibly can. . . . Besides, they won't release him into the wild. He's more likely to be on the FBI's most wanted list as the killer of Victoria Billingsley."

Paul felt uneasy about Rhonda's fiercely protective view of the creature she had rescued. "OK, but let's talk about it tomorrow," Paul acquiesced. "What do you say we take a little walk down the river path while the roast cooks?"

They changed into hiking clothes and strode onto the path. Kinta, not to be ignored, followed them. They talked of their delight in Janie Nickerson's improvement. Paul told Rhonda about his lunch with Della. At length their conversation moved on to the possibility that Rhonda might really have conceived a child, and if she had, what changes would have to be made in both their lifestyles.

Paul paused to lean against the giant hulk of the old log where Rhonda said she had spent so much of her time. Rhonda leaned back against Paul, looking nowhere, but Paul stared into the dark spaces between the smaller tangled trees of a nearby thicket. He watched Kinta nosing around the base of some of the larger shrubs in the thicket. Kinta stopped and raised his head and whimpered an almost puppy-like sound that seemed in sharp contradiction to his regal demeanor. At his whimper, Rhonda walked over to inspect the thicket as well. She had the odd sensation of a fetid odor in the air, like meat that was spoiled or nearly so. "Pauly! Pauly!" she shouted abruptly. "Quick!"

In a few strides Paul was at her side.

The Shapiros were staring down at a fly-clotted piece of meat wired to the tongue of a large-animal trap. Paul took a nearby rock and threw it at the lever, and the steel teeth clamped instantly together, launching the spring-loaded mechanism several inches off the ground. Kinta, wide-eyed, drew back. Momentarily scattered, the green flies buzzed back to the meat now resting underneath the closed steel jaws.

The Shapiros looked at each other. They knew who the trap was for, and they knew Rhonda's assailant had likely put it there.

"We'd better get back to the house," Paul said.

Kinta followed at their heels. They both felt watched. Their pace doubled. They didn't look back.

CHAPTER 16

Father Peter had no idea it was either Saturday morning or April 22. His mind, like his stare, was vacant. In a dream-like stupor, Father Peter saw a beautiful woman entering his room. He stared upward into the face of the woman, who was crying, "Hark, hark, hark!"

"I'm harking," said the old priest. "Who . . . who are you?"

"Thou knowest well who I am," she replied. Peter did know, of course. It was the Virgin of Stockholm. He had never had the courage to tell her that in his schizophrenic dreams he often confused her with the Great Whore of the Apocalypse. Both of them inhabited his wild dreams, but when he thought it all through, Father Peter knew which was which. The Great Whore of the Apocalypse wore false eyelashes and loads of costume jewelry. The Virgin of Stockholm was blonde and wore only a light blue shift. Also, the Virgin of Stockholm used only Elizabethan English. The Whore talked more like a Brooklyn waitress.

"Rise! Greet the day! Hie thee to the forested mountains, lest thy time come upon thee and thou forgoest thine hour of visitation," said the Virgin. "The realms meet at coming midnight. Get up, oh thou that sleepest!"

The priest smiled and drew back

"Hasten, thou sluggard. Fly! Fly! Fly!" The Virgin came to the side of his bed where Father Peter was trying to put on his shoes. His eyes were still bleary, and he couldn't make his shoelaces obey his fingers. "Poor priest," she said, "Let me!" And so she bent down and began to tie his shoelaces.

"No, please," begged the priest. "I am not worthy that you should tie my laces."

"Yea, verily thou hast spoken the truth and thou art not worthy. Neither art thou deserving. Nevertheless, 'Use every man after his desert, and who shall 'scape whipping?'"

"Haggai?" asked the priest while she continued to tie his shoes.

"Hamlet," she answered.

His shoes tied, she beckoned for him to stand, and they walked off into the morning. Even though Peter talked to her as they walked along, passersby who saw them observed only an old priest walking along by himself, mumbling and making his way toward the Space Needle with a sack of old clothes under his arm. He slouched his way along with his shoes gaping because the laces were untied.

———

After Paul Shapiro called the hospital and checked on Janie Nickerson's continuing recovery, he picked up the Saturday morning paper and read a ghastly front-page headline of a crime now many hours old. The dog killer had struck again on Friday night. Staring up at Paul from the front page was a picture of two young women who had shared a fashionable condominium not far from the expensive duplex where Victoria Billingsley had died. *They were probably lovers,* thought Paul.

The article detailed the death of the two young female executives using the same words from the description of Victoria Billingsley's death: horrible, savage, eerie.

Paul's mind raced ahead to the issue of Kinta. He felt more shock than horror as he continued reading. "'Their faces and throats were horribly torn as if attacked by a huge animal of some sort. The scene of the crime was chilling,' said Officer Gary Jarvis of SPD's Homicide Division." The article went on to express the dismay of the victims' carpool companion who had gone looking for them when they missed their morning ride. He discovered their bodies and immediately reported the double murder. Again the attacker had come and gone, undiscovered by any witness.

Paul was about to show the article to Rhonda when the phone rang and he heard her say, "No, it is not convenient for you to pick up our dog today!" Her voice trailed off, and she hung up the phone. "Paul," she was nearly in tears, "it was the Humane Society. They know. They're coming today for Kinta. They say we cannot keep him. I asked who filed the complaint, but they said they couldn't release that information. What are we going to do?"

Paul embraced her. His right hand, still holding the paper, encircled her waist. "Rhonda, did you sleep well last night?"

"Like a log. Somehow, in spite of all we've been through, I slept the entire eight hours without ever waking. Maybe it's because Kinta was here beside me. Maybe I was just so worn out emotionally. But I did sleep soundly. How about you?"

"Yeah, me too," he said. "Do you think there's any chance that Kinta could have left our bedroom during those hours and then returned to us before we woke?"

"I don't see how. All of the doors and windows were locked. He was here when we went to bed and here when we woke up. I think he had to be here all night."

"Take a look at this." He handed her the paper.

She colored. "Paul, Kinta was here all night. This ought to at least put your mind at ease concerning any possibility that Kinta could be implicated."

"I guess you're right. . . . I know you're right. Kinta could not be involved, and yet you know as soon as the police and the Humane Society get together, Kinta will be the number-one suspect in all of northeast Seattle. We both know he's innocent, but we'll never make a very good case, I'm afraid."

"That's why I'm leaving today, Paul. I'm taking Kinta with me. It's the only way we can keep him out of this."

Paul knew she was right. There was no other way.

In the next thirty minutes he helped her pack the Cherokee. When at last it was loaded with clothes, extra blankets, and all the food they could pack, Rhonda asked Paul to go to the toolshed and get the rest of the dog food. He huffed and puffed to get the fifty-pound bag to the Jeep, resting it on the bumper a minute before throwing it in the back.

"Rhonda, how long have you been feeding Kinta out of this bag?"

"Since I pulled him from the river nearly three weeks ago," Rhonda said, heaving a box of canned goods in the car.

"Well, he sure hasn't eaten much of it!" Paul's voice held a measure of alarm and a lot more volume than it needed. He was upset by something.

"I know, Pauly. I don't think he likes this dry dog food—probably too much dried vegetable in the mix and not enough meat. I think big dogs . . . er, wolves . . . need something to eat with more of a meat base."

"Well, Rhonda, *what* has he been eating?"

Rhonda rounded on him. "Paul, if this is some kind of slur on Kinta's character, I won't have it. We've already discounted every reasonable possibility that he could be involved in these killings, so stop it."

"But how could he have regained his strength and look so great just from eating a few handfuls of dry dog food over such a short time?"

Rhonda walked around the Cherokee and embraced Paul. "I don't know," she said. "Maybe he did jump out the back of the shed and catch a rabbit or two. But he's no killer."

They kissed, deciding to drop the quarrel at the moment of their parting. They kissed once more and looked at each other, attempting to smile.

"Ronnie," Paul blurted, "do you think that sometimes the little people of this world get involved in unseen issues that are too large for them to comprehend? I can't help feeling as though our little lives have become the stepping-stones of giant forces."

Rhonda listened but didn't answer, instead directing the conversation toward her more immediate concerns. "Paul, thanks for letting me take the gun. I doubt if my cell phone will work in the mountains, but I'll call you at work from some phone in a few days. I'm leaving."

"I love you," he said. "Do what you have to do, but please be careful and, above all, let's keep in touch." With terrible uneasiness, he watched Rhonda and Kinta climb into the Cherokee. She had obviously been practicing how to drive the stick shift. Still, the car jerked its way out of the drive as Rhonda tried to gently let out on the clutch. Paul watched the Jeep roar down the tree-lined driveway, turn onto Snoqualmie River Road, and get swallowed up by the forest.

He walked back into the house and got a glass of water. He couldn't quite finish all the water and dashed the last of it into the sink, noticing that the small kitchen window over the sink was open. It was so small and so inaccessible above the deck that they had not had it latch-monitored in the security system. The window had been open all night. As he closed it, a horrible possibility occurred to him. *No human intruder could enter or leave by the small opening, but a wolf could.*

He looked outside and saw that one of the cedar posts of the deck stairs had been knocked loose as though something large had hit it at high speed. A small rain gauge on top of the post had been broken by the same impact. Maybe Rhonda's assailant had broken it. Maybe . . . but it was directly in line with the small window that had been open all night, and if Kinta had leapt through that window, it might easily have been he who dislodged the rain gauge.

If Kinta were the killer, he was now alone with Rhonda, who had so much faith in Kinta that she allowed him to sleep on her bed. Indeed, she slept most soundly when she was nearest to him. Terror seized Paul. He tried to pray it away. "God . . . Ronnie!" It was the shortest and most intense prayer he had ever prayed. It was all nouns and names, and yet he felt somehow that God understood short prayers whose bad grammar polished their need.

CHAPTER 17

On the same Saturday morning Rhonda Shapiro had left for the cabin, the attorney for Pacific Woods woke to the chatter of squirrels on the crisp morning air. Eric Compton, still feeling good about his corporate coup, took a sip from his cup then poured the last of his bitter coffee on the weak campfire. The coals smoked and spit, hissing steam back at him. He stuck the cup in the top of his backpack and slipped his arms through the shoulder straps.

Eric's tall frame, square chin, and thick eyebrows and mustache gave him the appearance of a noble woodsman. He walked about fifteen minutes up the trail before resting against a tall tree to observe and celebrate the morning. How he loved the high country. He was so mesmerized by nature that he gave little thought to the career that lately had worn him down with the corporate agenda. Friday nights found him eager to spend the weekend among the glorious trees. The trees he loved; his job he tolerated. He hated his job not for its tedium but for its conflict with his love for nature.

Eric rationalized that while these trees would soon disappear on giant logging trucks, their cutting would mean a new surge of economic life—both in Seattle and at Pacific Woods. He knew his business coup would spell new jobs and a better way of life for all those at Pacific Woods who were suffering from the recent layoffs. But in the six years since he'd left Harvard and been working for Pacific Woods, he'd realized he worked for a company whose very name meant controversy in Seattle. Still, his rising personal expenses—his Mercedes SL and his luxurious sea-cliff apartment—left him more eager to embrace the successes of Pacific Woods as his nature-loving spirit slowly ebbed away. A good lawyer, Eric knew how to face down those unreasonable environmentalists who had been responsible for the Pacific Woods layoffs, earning the respect and rewards of his company. He had also managed to weld the logging interests of Pacific Woods and the building interests of the Lee West Construction Corporation into a giant legal amalgam. That corporate coup had opened 83,000 acres of the south bank of the Snoqualmie River for logging and 4,000 acres of suburban forest ranches.

The action had made him the darling of the firm overnight. In fact, while he and Levi Twist lived on immensely different social planes, Levi fully admired the executive clout Eric Compton could wield, and it was impossible not to notice how good Eric always made Pacific Woods look at press conferences. When any battle between ecologists and

Pacific Woods was over, Eric always stood smiling before his corporate victory.

At the moment he was holding in his hands the destiny of 50,000 more acres—a large tract of nearly all first-cut forests. George Callahan owned most of the grove and generously lent his name to it all. Eric had managed to buy the rights from all of the landowners except one stubborn holdout—a second-generation immigrant named Isletta Borg. Her court case against the Pacific Woods takeover had been financed by an army of legalist tree huggers. It was Isletta's parcel of ground that had prompted Eric's weekend hike. He was anxious to see what the tree huggers called his coming sawmill empire.

Even so, his hike through the forest was not totally prompted by his legal ties with Pacific Woods. To be truthful, the trees fed his spirit. He wished that he didn't love them quite so much as he did. Ironically, it was only after his first major corporate victory, the Southbank project, that Eric discovered his love of backpacking. He loved the sweet smell of a forest after a rain. He exulted to find a white thicket of mushrooms overarched by ferns. He enjoyed spotting hummingbird nests and trying to tell a common hawk from a soaring golden eagle. His love of nature lured him most powerfully when he walked through the shadowed light of the sentinel firs that made every grove a kind of temple.

Eric felt a supernatural splendor in his relationship with the wilderness. He had hiked both the Olympic coast trails and the Shasta wilderness of northern California. As he hiked this trail, his mind turned toward simple things. He picked up a huge stick and dangled it here and there on the ground like a cane he didn't need. He was walking a new path.

After thirty minutes, this pursuit at last led him to a level meadow about 200 yards long. He heard women's voices in song somewhere near the front of the grove—probably a weekend gathering of feminist naturalists singing their Gaian hymns. Finally he came close enough to observe the gathering by peering through the thick bushes.

The women had finished their song. One offered a kind of prayer: "O Gaia, Mother of the world and all of us, your children, teach us to harmonize the inner vibrations of our lives with the resonant universal hum of all life. We bless your motherhood and adore your child, the goddess daughter, who lives around us in the rocks and trees and beasts and birds. Daughter of god and mother of all gods, swim the living waters of the oceans. Walk the forest, the living testament to the glory of your motherhood. Make us brave enough to teach the world the true nature of Gaia and her love for Earth, her poor ravished child."

"Amen!" the other women intoned. They joined hands and lifted their arms above their heads, calling upward to their feminist matron, "Glory be to the mother and the daughter and to Sophia, the nourishing trinity of all living things!"

Gradually their rapture ceased, and they began to break into smaller groups. The path Eric was on led straight through the center of the clearing where the nature service was just breaking up. Should he go around the group or right through them? True, the trail was as much his as theirs. He walked toward the group. He tried to whistle a tune nonchalantly as he passed through them but became self-conscious once in their midst and stopped short.

Most of his observers smiled at his sudden appearance at their gathering. Eric doffed his cap and said as cheerfully as he could, "Good morning, girls!" He immediately recalled that *girls* was a bad choice of words.

"How big do *boys* grow where you come from?" shouted one of the women. He decided not to reply and walked on through their midst. Unfortunately, the cap he had so ceremoniously doffed was a Pacific Woods cap. Another of the women seeing the cap shouted, "Tree killer!" Eric quickened his pace. He was almost through the clearing when one of them shouted. "Daughters of Gaia, it's Eric Compton, the lawyer!" With that, three or four of the largest of them began walking toward him. Eric saw blood in their eyes and was about to break into a run when the female leader called out forcefully, "Please, Daughters of Gaia. Remember our holy goddess invokes all who would follow her to be charitable to all who come into our midst, even tree-killing male attorneys."

Eric could tell that the tension was easing. "Praise be to Gaia, the kind one!" he offered, much too loudly. It sounded a lot like blasphemy, even to Eric. He was about to dash away when he was unexpectedly rescued.

"Would you like a cup of coffee?" asked the female leader.

"Uh, yeah, yeah sure," Eric replied, wondering how safe it would be to reject the woman's hospitality.

He slipped off his backpack, selected a comfortable stump, and sat down just as the tall woman handed him a cup of coffee and a few other women nearby walked away whispering.

"I'm Isletta Borg," the woman offered as she selected a second stump, sat down, and extended her hand. Eric couldn't believe it—the very woman who had kiboshed the Callahan deal by refusing to sell her 10,000 acres of trees to the company. He tried not to flinch, pretending that he didn't know who she was.

"Eric Compton," he said, extending his own hand.

"Yes, we know who you are," said Isletta. A regal woman, she had enough of a Scandinavian accent that Eric guessed she was a recent transplant to the United States.

"Isletta Borg of Denmark?" he ventured.

"Sweden, actually!"

"This Gaia thing—is it New Age?"

She bristled. "It's not a 'thing,' Mr. Compton. Gaia is considered the mother goddess of us all, treasuring the Earth and all living things."

Isletta gestured with willowy arms, her deep blue eyes flashing. Her husky Marlene Dietrich voice was musically intriguing.

"Yes, well I'm not a Gaian myself," Eric responded. "I don't send money to Billy Graham or anything like that, but I am a Christian." Eric was forthright, and he followed his words by taking a forthright sip of coffee.

"You can tell that these women take their faith in Gaia seriously. Most of them don't have much use for you, Eric." Isletta shook out some grounds from the bottom of her cup. "Tell me, are you out this morning looking over Pacific Woods' next conquest?" She gestured upward into the trees.

"Surely you saw the posted procurement. These are our trees, Ms. Borg. They belong to Pacific Woods."

"Trees don't belong to people or companies or sawmills or future subdivisions. These trees belong to Gaia."

"Well, unless Gaia gets down here to defend them, she's going to own a lot of plywood and chipboard."

Isletta looked skeptical. "Do you know what the largest thing that ever lived on Earth is?" she asked.

"Roseanne Barr?" he said, hoping to inject some humor into the conversation.

She stopped, looked at him, and grinned before she went on. "Gong! Wrong! The largest thing that has ever lived on this planet is one of the Sequoia redwoods not too far from Fresno. There's enough lumber in that one tree to build 400 homes."

She paused, momentarily uncertain.

Eric cleared his throat. "How many?"

"Well, 200 homes."

Eric again protested her statistic by cocking an eyebrow.

"OK, OK, 164 homes, but that's as low as I go." She smiled in acquiescence.

Eric's own smile turned into a laugh. Tension dissipated.

"Are you a priestess of Gaia or something like that?" he grinned.

"Not really. We don't have priestesses. I'm only a lowly neophyte, but they let me lead the worship because I used to be in community theater. Ever hear of the Sacramento Mask and Wig Club?"

Eric looked vacant.

"Oh, never mind. To be really honest, I also think this Gaia stuff is a lot of hooey, but I go along with it because these women are the most adamant about their cause, which is to stop all you enviro-rapists."

"Looks like they hate men as much as they love trees."

"How about another cup of coffee?" Isletta redirected the conversation.

"Tell me, Isletta, is this coffee from one of those plantations where poor Juan Valdez is drubbed into the fields to pick coffee beans by some bloodsucking Colombian cartel? If it is, so help me, I'll have a cola with my Danish from now on."

Eric looked so serious that for a moment Isletta stammered, "I . . . um." Then she caught his joke. She smiled. "I told you, I'm Swedish."

Eric smiled back at her. "I'd still like to buy you a cola sometime. And I'd like to point out that there's a lot of injustice out there. Most of us get pretty selective in our causes." He rose. "No more coffee this morning. I want to make the high rapids before I start back to the city. But I wouldn't mind your phone number."

Isletta glanced at the women looking on. Some thought she was too friendly to the infamous attorney. "I'll call you," she said as she stood up. He pulled on his backpack.

"Don't wait too long," he counseled then turned and walked up the trail.

CHAPTER 18

"What do you think of these killings?" Della asked Levi. Her question was innocent enough, but it seemed to stir Levi.

"Notice all the victims were women. Probably all lesbian executive types."

"Aw, come on, Lee," said Della. "That's pretty crass. Surely you don't approve of anybody being killed this way. It's horrible."

"Now Dell, a lot of these executive women are sick with corporate power. Sick."

"Hey! Simmer down!" She kissed him on the cheek. "Honey, it's going to be a wonderful evening, and I don't want you so riled up that you lose all rational ability to celebrate with me."

Levi's intensity softened at her rebuke. After a moment he smiled at her. They walked from her apartment to Levi's Corvette. He opened her door for her, and their date began. They went to a movie then stopped by Fannie's Fondue Follies and split an order of chocolate and fruit fondue. The hostess seated them at a perfect little corner table. The candlelight was just right for Levi's plan. When the main course was over, he drew a little box out of his pocket. Della's eyes flashed with anticipation. It was a beautiful ring. It encircled a scroll of paper that had a date written on it: Saturday, June 17, 2006.

"Della," Levi looked down shyly, "I want you to be my wife, and I want to apologize for being so cruel the other day. No child of mine will ever have to grow up without a father. I'm an orphan myself, for goodness sake! I know the pain of that. I guess our unborn child has just brought it all clearly home to me. I've done a lot of thinking about all my years in the orphanage with the nuns. I just don't want that to happen to a child of mine. And you know, Dell, I am really suffering a lot of guilt for saying that you should have an abortion. I was out of my mind. God forgive me . . . how could I ever have suggested that? I mean, our little baby is *our* little baby, and I could never live with myself if I let some quack obstetrician cut it apart with a curette." Levi was suddenly more intense than he needed to be.

Della was glad for his conclusions, but she did once more see ravenous intensity stealing over Levi. Still, she was glad that he was agreeable about keeping the baby.

They kissed.

Della looked again at her ring and then they kissed again, this time more exuberantly. When their embrace was over, she crushed the paper with the wedding date in it into a ball and threw it into the air, shrieking "June 17 . . . MRS. LEVI TWIST!" They kissed yet again.

Then Della thumped him playfully on the chest.

"Ow!" he said, drawing back. "My stitches!"

"Stitches?"

"Yeah," he said, "some fatty tumors removed this past week. I've got quite a set of football laces on my chest. I can't even go to the gym and pump iron for at least two more weeks."

Levi looked momentarily embarrassed. He settled back into his chair and straightened himself as if to signal that he had gotten control of his wildly romantic overtures.

"Dell, darling, can you ever forgive me for suggesting the abortion?" He reached over and patted her stomach. "This son is ours. Do you know, Della, if you had actually gotten the abortion, I believe God would have held me responsible for the murder of our unborn child. Thank you for not obeying me. I love you so much right now, and I love our little one too. Tomorrow I'm going to deposit 500 shares of Pacific Woods into his little savings account. It's soaring on Wall Street since Compton's coup. Our little child will be rich when he arrives by way of the golden stork!"

"When *he* gets here?" Della cocked an eyebrow.

"OK, OK, when it gets here."

Della wasn't sure she liked *it* any better than *he,* but she gratefully received another warm embrace. Yet he was somehow, once again, not himself. "Levi, you haven't been watching cable television and gone and got yourself born again, have you? I don't think I've ever seen you so wound up."

Levi laughed. "Know what I think it is? I think just the thought of being a father has for the very first time knocked a little sense into my head."

Della smiled. "You know, Lee, this is the very best day of my life. I have never been happier. I am getting older; I thought I'd never be a mother or a wife—and to find out in a single month that I am going to be both is some kind of wonderful!"

Levi looked grateful too. "Dell, I came back from 'Nam as a kind of pristine Freedom Fighter. I wanted no more war. Then after my wife died, I withdrew from much of my world. I wanted to be left alone. Then I met you. I gotta be honest, Dell; in a way, you have been my savior. I guess I'm pretty old-fashioned too. It must have been those old nuns at the convent, but I really believe that all sexuality ought to occur within marriage. I want to apologize for any advantage I might have taken of you. I must confess I really want you, but I know that I have no real right to you before God until our vows are promised in the church. I know this may sound a little twisted, but in a way I'm glad we had sex and you're pregnant, 'cause I think this was life's way of saying, 'C'mon, you lunk, and get with it. Marry Dell. She's your right woman!'"

He seemed suddenly talked out. Della was glad. He was being a bit too evangelistic about things. In a little while they left the restaurant. The red Corvette full of two happy passengers moved swiftly through the traffic. Della knew that Levi wasn't the most poetic soul in the world, but he was a sterling man who got overexuberant about things sometimes. Still, honesty was his second nature.

As they moved along the rain-washed street, they passed a group of anti-abortioners gathered in protest around a small clinic. Della looked at them as Levi drove past. Levi stomped the brakes and pulled the car suddenly to the curb. As her mouth dropped open, his car door swung open and Levi exploded from the Corvette and hurried toward the protesters. Della got out of her side of the car more slowly. She watched in horror as Levi ran up to the door of the clinic, obviously violating the distance that the law permitted between the protesters and the clinics. Even the protesters were amazed at his aggression. He startled the group by running his big fist through the glass storm door in front of the clinic's main door.

Della left the Corvette and ran to Levi. She was instantly on him, trying to pull him away from the door. Unfortunately, she was not able. His hand had been cut by some small shards of the broken glass. Bloody as it was, he still raised it above the crowd and shouted at the dark clinic, "Baby killers!" The breaking of the glass set off a loud alarm. The jangling siren caused Della to break into tears. The other protestors, hearing the alarm, fled into the darkness. Levi noticed Della's small frame shuddering in sobs. He snapped out of his hysteria and anger, grabbed her, and ran with her back to his car. They sped off into the night.

Almost at once, as though perfectly synchronized with Levi's tantrum, the night skies opened and the rain began to gush down. When the police arrived to answer the alarm, they found only rain-washed shards of glass in front of a deserted clinic.

The incident wrapped Della's spirit in a leaden mood she could not shake. Nor could she fight the tears that came so readily to her eyes. On the same night that Levi had made her the happiest woman in the world, he had behaved so violently, so erratically, that she no longer felt safe being with him. He walked her to her door. She didn't ask him in, and the rain was falling too hard for Levi to stand at the door very long. She pulled an umbrella from her purse and opened it, giving him enough protection to offer a few moments of conversation.

"Della," he began, "I don't know what made me do that. I know these baby killers are wrong and that abortion is wrong, but I mustn't deal with these matters in such lawless ways. It's been a hard day, Della. I'm sorry. Can you forgive me?"

"Yes, of course, Lee," she blubbered. "I love you. But honey, I want you to stay in control of yourself."

"I am in charge, Della. I've just been overstressed. I've been edgy ever since your boss refused to renew my prescription."

"Lee, I want you to come back to the clinic. I'll talk to Paul—I know he'll see you again if I ask. Would you consent to an appointment?"

"Oh, come on, Dell, I'm not crazy or anything. Besides, he was pretty firm when he told me not to return. I'm just stressed out, that's all."

"Would you, Lee, please?" She was unwavering.

"Yeah, well sure, Dell. But first give me a chance, and if you feel like I'm losing it, I promise, I'll go, OK?"

"OK," she agreed.

Lee leaned forward and kissed her. "Look, Dell, I love you, and I'll love you until the day I die." He kissed her again. "And I love that little fellow there too." He patted her stomach. "Here's to June 17."

"I love you, Lee," said Della and then repeated, "June 17."

She went into the condominium and watched out the front window until she saw the taillights of the Corvette disappear down the rain-soaked street.

"Lee, I love you so much," she said to the empty room. "Please don't get sick on me."

She could still see her fiancé striding up the sidewalk and ramming his massive fist through the clinic door. "Oh, my darling, I'm so afraid for you . . . for us." She looked down at her stomach and said sadly, "And for *him*."

—————

Three hours later, Renée Thomkins entered her apartment. She noticed that the window on the left side of the door was broken. All the glass was gone except for a single shard that stuck up like a stalagmite from the bottom of the sash.

She thought for a moment that it might have been done by the boy next door, who was always playing ball in the front yard. She was sure it had been broken long enough to let the rain soil the carpet. She put the key in the door, determined to quickly fetch the sponge mop and soak up as much of the intruding rain as possible. She knew she would have to tack some plastic over the opening till she could get it repaired.

In the darkness, she closed the door behind her and locked it. She was about to turn on the lights, when in the darkness she heard a low gurgle issuing from a corner of the room. The outside streetlights illuminated nothing in the darkness but a pair of feral eyes and white teeth. There was an animal . . . a snarling evil.

The hair rose on Renée's neck as the evil darkness gathered some unmeasured bulk and flew at her, sending her sprawling against the wall. Her head struck the corner of a heavy antique coffee table as she collapsed. She was instantly unconscious in the darkness. That was good. The next few moments were not ones to remember. Only the coming daylight would reveal how merciful the darkness really was.

CHAPTER 19

Cary Jarvis was called to the site of Renée's assault and found himself obsessed with yet another murder. Three killings in two nights. In completing the crime report he scratched Saturday, April 22 on it. Renée was the fourth victim, killed exactly three weeks after the first one occurred. Jarvis sat brooding over all he didn't know. He had promised himself he would not be obsessed, but obsession had been his lot with any investigation he had ever known. Crimes always began as puzzles and ended as compulsions. He could scarcely sleep while any unresolved clues dogged his thoughts.

Four people had been mutilated in these murders. He struggled to put together anything that might link them all to a single killer. But what kind of killer was it? Was it really a dog? Certainly it was more than a random animal roaming the streets. The killer was flawlessly picking its victims on the basis of their gender. Not only were they all women but women with corporate clout. This was as self-proclaiming to all of Seattle as to Jarvis. He was now convinced that Seattle's vicious night stalker was the accomplice of an evil mastermind of some sort. The dog that killed was, at least, being driven or led by some psycho to the various scenes of crime.

Jarvis knew that while each crime scene had broken windows, the animal was not, in his opinion, breaking those windows by leaping through them. Animals do not prowl around, leaping through glass. Further, every window of entry was the one in the house not hooked up to the security system. No animal is smart enough to always pick the one window without an alarm attached to it. The animal was definitely being guided to his victims.

Still, this was not the general conclusion in Seattle. Most people believed that all of the vicious murders were perpetrated by a huge dog. Gary Jarvis was not altogether convinced that it was a dog; it might have been some other kind of animal being illegally kept to provide its owner with such sick pastimes. The unsolved and unconnected pieces of his investigation kept him confused for most of the day.

Besides Gary Jarvis, another man couldn't sleep that same night. When Eric Compton returned to his apartment late on Sunday evening, he was tired. He warmed a can of beef stew, washed it down with buttermilk, and stared at the calendar. It was April 23, exactly two weeks after his first probe into the possible Callahan purchase. When the stew and buttermilk were gone, he washed his dishes and left them on a wooden drying rack. He walked out onto the high deck of his Puget Sound apartment and stared at the sea for a long time. He always enjoyed looking at the water. It kept him from taking himself so seriously. When his sea-staring was done, he took a shower and collapsed in bed. There he tossed and turned most of the night.

What greeted him as he opened the *Seattle Times* on Monday morning was a picture of Renée Thomkins. He was stunned by the story that stared up at him. Renée—his friend Renée—had become the fourth victim of the strange and savage killer simply known all over the city as *the dog*. The paper was filled with the gruesome story of the latest *dog killing*. Eric remembered that Renée had told him of her knowledge of Victoria Billingsley, and together the two of them had also discussed the two other women who had been victims as well. Eric thought about the other three murders. Everyone seemed reluctant to admit that the killer dog was being led to the vicious killings by the real killer.

With Renée's murder the pattern was confirmed. Those who were being killed were corporate women. With Renée's death, the news spread through Seattle and began to create a sense of panic within Seattle's community of women executives.

Why Renée? Eric wondered.

On Wednesday, April 26, Gary Jarvis went to Renée's funeral, just as he had gone to the funerals of earlier victims. He hung around the edge of the mourners, who were few and female, mostly executives. At every funeral he looked around for anyone who might have been involved in the murders. These murders invited the kind of funerals that lured murderers to show up just to *enjoy* the fruits of their crimes.

Jarvis was now convinced that someone had trained the attack animal. But now he had the task of identifying why executive females were the target and what, if anything, was the common denominator that related all four of them to the animal trainer.

The funeral minister used the typical Resurrection and "dust to dust" passages of the Bible along with some bits from Job and Psalm 23. After the committal service, the crowd gradually disbursed.

Eric Compton stayed after the others were gone, leaning against a tree and reflecting on his long friendship with Renée. Several others from the company had attended the funeral to honor Renée's memory, but they left long before Eric.

Gary was also lingering. Gary couldn't help but wonder if Pacific Woods' young superstar attorney might be involved somehow.

"Excuse me, sir, I'm Gary Jarvis, SPD." Gary felt that it was an abrupt introduction of himself. He could see that Eric was hurt over the passing of his friend.

"Eric Compton, Pacific Woods," Eric responded matter-of-factly.

"I know who you are," said Gary. "You've been in the news so much lately, I guess everyone must know who you are." Gary paused. "There are a lot of environmentalists who don't much care for you."

"But a lot of working people who do," Eric defended himself.

"Did you work with the deceased?" Gary already knew the answer.

"Yeah, she was our corporate accountant. We worked side by side at Pacific Woods. We spent a lot of time together."

"Only at work?"

"Only at work, Mr. Jarvis." Eric was irked at the detective's forwardness.

"Now simmer down, Mr. Compton."

"I'm sorry," said Eric with diminishing hostility. "If I can be of help in cracking this serial violence, I would very much like to do so."

Gary proceeded with questions about the duration of Eric's friendship with Renée and his knowledge of her private life. Nothing of interest emerged until Eric suddenly remembered, "Renée knew Victoria Billingsley!"

"How did she know her?"

"They hung out at the same lounge, a place off the 405 in Bellevue called . . ." Eric's mind went blank. "What was the name of the place? It's a lounge off the 405. It specializes in haute culture—lots of Seattle's executive women meet there after work." Eric couldn't remember what Renée had told him.

"Well, I'll nose around that Bellevue exit off the 405. If there's more than one lounge, I'll give you a call and read them off to you."

"I'm sure I could identify it," said Eric.

"Could you give me your home phone number in case I do need to get back to you?"

Eric seemed glad to be of help to the detective. They parted company just as the cemetery crew arrived to close the grave.

———

Gary had no trouble finding the My Kind lounge. A few elementary questions to the evening bartender revealed that not only had Victoria Billingsley and Renée frequented the lounge, but the other two "dog victims" had also been customers there. From time to time all four victims had come there after work. Now the only question that remained was who was the one person all four victims knew. The bartender hadn't a clue. No one ever came into My Kind who would be remembered as a vicious-looking-apt-to-be-a-serial-killer type.

Jarvis got to interview another bartender, a female, but she had no clues to offer. Nothing made sense to Jarvis. He ordered a soda, munched disinterestedly from a bowl of pretzels on the bar, and left so distracted that he tipped the bartender twice.

CHAPTER 20

Friday, April 28 was a very special day. The Reverend Joanna Nickerson stepped out of the cab and held the door for her little Janie, who followed her onto the sidewalk. She paid the fare, and the cab whisked away from the curb. Joanna switched Janie's hospital suitcase from her right hand to her left then used her right hand to pull Janie up to her.

"Janie, honey, praise the Lord, you're home! No, Janie, *we're* home!"

"Oh, Momma. I'm going to be real careful from now on. I'm sorry I ran out in front of Dr. Shapiro's car."

"Well, don't you think about it anymore, child. We are home! Jesus done made you well!"

"Momma, does Jesus make everybody well?"

"Well, what a question, honey! 'Course he does!"

"Well, Momma, what about all those people that are still up in the hospital? He didn't make all them well, did he?"

"Well, honey, sooner or later, he will. Either here or in heaven, everybody who's ever been sick is gonna get better.

In the here and now, sometimes folks gotta die, but sooner or later they all get better!"

"'Here, there, or in the air,' everybody gets better, don't they?"

Joanna smiled. She had used the cliché so often that now her little Janie was using it too.

"They sure do, child. Now, Momma's done got you a present—a big surprise for your homecoming."

The child's eyes brightened. Even though she was too large to carry, Janie was scooped up in Joanna's ample arms and carried up to their front door, where Joanna almost dropped her. A man in used blue coveralls was standing right in front of the door. Joanna was momentarily shaken, certain there was no one there the moment before they arrived.

"Hello," the stranger said kindly.

"Good . . . good morning," stammered Joanna, trying to regain the composure his sudden presence had startled out of her. "Who are you?"

"My name is Father Peter. I'm a client of the man who ran over your little Janie."

"You know Dr. Shapiro?"

"Yes, but that's not important. I'd like to talk to you about a group of trees out east of Seattle called the Callahan Grove."

"Is this some kind of survey? 'Cause me and Janie just got home from the hospital, and if you don't mind, I'd like to spend a little time with her."

"I know she's meant a lot to you since your husband went away." Father Peter tenderly patted Janie on the cheek. Ordinarily a stranger touching her daughter would have filled

Joanna with fear, but Father Peter's doing so didn't bother her at all. "My, hasn't she grown since she was born over at Grosvenor Hospital seven years ago . . . next month."

"Who the devil are you?" Joanna blushed. She knew immediately that *devil* was the wrong word to use.

"I told you, Joanna, my name is Peter—"

"You just said Father Peter."

"Well, whatever, it doesn't matter, but I've got to talk to you."

"About trees?"

"Yes, exactly. You do believe in trees? You don't believe that they should be destroyed, do you?"

"Well no, no I don't. Not needlessly. I think trees are made by God, and like everything else God made, they should be treated with reverence and respect. Still, I'm no tree hugger. And I gotta be honest with you, Father—when it comes down to siding with trees or people, I'd pick people every time, 'cause Jesus died to save people and not redwoods."

"Well, we're not out to save redwoods; it's more like primal forests of any type—Douglas firs for instance."

"Well, I still believe Jesus would pick souls over Douglas firs."

"But you'd vote to save as much of either one as you could, wouldn't you?"

"Well, honestly, Father Peter, I've never thought that any of God's good world should be uselessly destroyed. I mean, it's not just trees we ought to be concerned about. There are a heap of little feathery things alive in these forests, and each of them play their little part in making the world a wonderful place to live. But, Father, I'm just a preacher at the—"

"Pathway of Light Cathedral. I know, but you know all those dreams you've been having about Isaiah? Where do you think those dreams come from, Reverend Nickerson?"

Joanna's mouth fell open. "Won't you come in?" she asked, opening her door. He nodded, following Joanna and Janie inside. Joanna set down her little Janie, who flew back into her bedroom to be sure her toy chest was intact. Joanna heard a happy shriek; Janie had discovered her surprise. Janie ran back into the room even more excitedly than she left.

"Oh, Momma. A new canopy bed . . . just like in Snow White." She threw herself into Joanna's arms with such force she nearly tipped her mother off the couch. "Momma, can Father Peter see it too?"

"Well now, honey, I don't think Father Peter would care about it too much."

"It's pink, isn't it?" asked the priest. He took little Janie's hand and walked her back to her bedroom. Joanna was twice amazed—that he knew the canopy was pink and that she felt no fear in seeing this strange man walk her daughter back to the child's bedroom.

When they returned to the living room, Joanna was putting on a pot of coffee. The old priest held Janie and sat her down to read *Snow White* to her. Janie knew the story so well that occasionally her lips moved right with his.

Soon Joanna carried Father Peter his cup of coffee and sat down across from him, sipping from her own cup. "Now take your book back to your own room, Janie. You can read it yourself. Father Peter and I have to talk."

"Why can't I have Father Peter read it to me?"

"Now, Janie, don't make a fuss." Joanna cocked her eyebrow and stuck out her chin. Janie knew there was no use arguing and went back to her room.

The priest took a sip of the coffee. "Ow! What is this stuff?"

"Maxwell House, chicory blend. Now, Father Peter, how can you know practically everything about me and ask me what a cup of coffee is?"

"Well, I'm not from Seattle."

"Father Peter, who are you anyway? And what's with all this tree stuff? If you're not from anywhere around here, where are you from that they never serve coffee?"

Ignoring her question, Father Peter answered, "I, for one, am getting tired of the way that people are treating this world. They scrape the earth, burn the earth, pour oil on the waters, and dump their rusted car bodies into every green creek there is."

"Well, you're certainly right about that. Humankind has messed up just about everything. I reckon that it's 'cause there's so many of us. Did you know that when the second angel sounds his trumpet, a third of all the creatures on Earth are gonna die?"

"Yes, I knew that."

"You do? So where does it say that in the Good Book?"

"Revelation 8:9."

"Well, I'll tell you this, Father Peter, many of the men in my congregation work at those lumbermills. And when the trees aren't being cut, our members don't work. And when they don't work, they don't eat and they can't pay their rent.

So don't talk to me about saving trees when my congregation is hurting because of some tree-hugging crusaders."

"Well," he began, "trees are meant to be used for shel-
ter and warmth. But you can't just cut 'em down and leave
Earth a planet of rotting stumps. Still, I'm troubled by these
New Age philosophies that get so anxious to save the trees
that they forget that all of Earth was meant for the use of
humankind."

"Father Peter, you think we ought to be cuttin' or plantin'
trees?"

"Yes to both. Cutting and planting is the way God wants
his world used—that's how you use the world without using
it up."

"Joanna," he went on, "do you think you could get the
members of the Pathway of Light to do a weekend campout
in the mountains?"

"Maybe, but it would have to be for something pretty
important."

"For the trees of the Callahan Grove. If you could help
save the big trees, would you?"

"I don't know. I'm in the business of saving souls, Father
Peter, not trees. By the way, you been saved yet?"

"No. It's not necessary where I come from."

"Nonsense, child; it's necessary wherever you come
from. Say, you're not one of them New Agers we got all over
this town, are you?"

"No, I'm not a New Ager. But I am concerned about
Earth, aren't you? And I'll tell you, Sister Joanna, we gotta
stop all this destruction of the beautiful world that our heav-
enly Father made. Did you know that every year twenty-

three more significant species perish from the world and are never seen again? Ever hear of the passenger pigeon?"

"Nope."

"Know why you've never heard of them?"

"'Cause I don't hang around much with pigeons, passenger or otherwise."

"Well, you've never heard of them 'cause there's not a one of them left on the earth. People hunted them out of existence. It's been the same tale for hundreds of other species that have made their homes in the big trees for centuries. Now the big trees are up against the wall. But the answer isn't to worship them or refuse to cut them. The answer is—"

"What kind of priest are you—out there loving trees like you were Johnny Appleseed? Why don't you get you a church like other priests?"

The priest was silent. Joanna went on. "Well, if the men at the Pathway of Light Cathedral could go back to work, I'd be most grateful to help with any plan you got."

"Well, Joanna, a lot of the men of your congregation work for Pacific Woods, am I right?"

"Yes."

"Challenge those men in your congregation to incite a whole city to get ready for a big march. It'll attract more attention than the march on Washington."

"I don't know if all Seattle will follow me, but the people in my church would do anything if they thought Jesus was askin' them to." She looked in her coffee cup. Empty. She got up to refill it in the kitchen, pausing to take Father Peter's cup as well, but he begged off, "No, please, not for me."

She walked to the kitchen, but when she returned, he was gone. She hadn't heard him leave. She went to the door, opened it, and looked up and down the street. He was nowhere to be seen.

"Janie, Janie!" she called.

Janie came flying into the room. "Where's Father Peter?" she asked.

Joanna hugged her close. "Oh, thank the good Lord, you saw him. I was just calling you back to me to be sure that you saw him too. He really was here, and I am not going loony like your poor Uncle Claude."

"He didn't like coffee, did he, Momma?"

"No, honey, he didn't."

Twenty minutes later, when Joanna tried to put Janie down for her nap, Janie began to protest. But Joanna insisted. "It's for your own good. The doctor says you need to take your naps every day until you're completely strong again."

When Janie had drifted off to sleep, Joanna decided to have a little nap herself. She lay down on the couch and quickly dozed off. She dreamed her doorbell was ringing. In the dream, she went to the door and was surprised to see that someone had painted it green and thumbtacked a fir bough to it. While she stood there studying the bough, the doorbell rang once more. She opened the door and wasn't at all surprised to see Isaiah standing in front of her. A spotted owl sat on the prophet's shoulder, blinking its big yellow eyes at her.

"Come in, Ike," she said.

Isaiah seemed a bit cool. He came in without speaking and took a chair. The owl seemed indifferent.

"What's the matter, Ike?" asked Joanna.

"I think you need to hear what Spotty has to say. Go ahead, Spotty."

"Well," said the small owl to Joanna, "I think you seemed a little dismissive about the plight of our kind upon Earth. How can you call yourself a woman of God and not care what happens to the likes of me and my poor family? Once these Callahan Grove trees are all gone, we'll be all gone too. My little owlets were all hatched up in those big trees, and I'd sure appreciate it if you would do all you can to help Father Peter make sure my owlets and my grand-owlets and my great-grand-owlets get their chance at life too. Now what was the name of your little owlet?"

"My daughter is not an owlet. She's a human being, and her name is Janie. And what's more, it sounds to me like you're falling for all of this New Age stuff. You spotted owls have caused the world a heap of trouble. You've blocked progress, shut down industries, caused people in the lumbermills to lose their jobs. So I'd appreciate it if you'd just shut your beak and move down to Oregon until all the jobless people in Seattle have gone back to work. In fact, Ike, you can just leave my house and take your loud-mouthed owl with you."

Isaiah stood up angrily with his owl and slammed the door on the way out.

In the real world, Janie ran in from her own room, slamming her door at the same time as Isaiah in the dream. Joanna awoke, wondering about Isaiah and his owl.

Janie ran up to her mother and jumped in her lap. "Momma, I want you to read about Bambi and Thumper and the Owl. Momma, can animals talk just like us?"

"Land sakes, Janie, no." Joanna stopped and thought for just a moment, remembering. "Uh, I don't think so, honey. Momma doesn't want to talk anymore about this right now."

CHAPTER 21

"Gary Jarvis, Homicide," said the detective, standing framed in the clinic doorway. Paul Shapiro noticed Gary's imposing six-foot, broad-shouldered, dark-haired presence, complete with lantern jaw.

"I'm Paul Shapiro. Won't you come in?"

Gary entered Paul's office, and they both took a seat. There was a prolonged silence. Paul fiddled with the pens on his desk, noticing that his calendar read Thursday, May 4.

"I tried to call your home, but there was no answer," Gary began.

"Yes, my wife will be out of town for awhile."

"We had a caller who informed us that your wife is illegally keeping a large, vicious animal at your home."

"Large, yes. Vicious, no. But she's not here in Seattle anymore. She took the animal away with her into the mountains for a brief stay."

"Dr. Shapiro, can you think of any reason we might need to question her? Is there any light she might shed on the

case? Surely both you and your wife know that the dog killings have occurred not very far from your home."

"Yes, of course we know. But believe me, Kinta had nothing to do with these murders. It's not possible. Besides, Kinta
is not a dog—he's a wolf that my wife rescued from the flood
waters of the Snoqualmie only a few weeks ago."

"Kinta?" It was the first time Gary had heard Seattle's
possible killer given a name. "Why not, Dr. Shapiro? Why
couldn't the killer be the family pet?"

"Well, first of all," Paul launched into his habitual numbering and organizing of his responses, "from all that I'm
reading in the papers, the SPD believes that the animal now
has a trainer and is selectively killing only corporate women
executives. Second, Kinta wasn't even at our home in Seattle
during the last murder of Miss . . ."

"Thomkins?"

"Yes, Miss Thomkins. Rhonda and Kinta had already
been gone for more than half a day when that murder
occurred."

"Is she so far away that she might not have driven back
with the animal and then, after he had done his dirty work,
returned with him again to the mountains?"

"Mr. Jarvis, if you are suggesting what I think you're
suggesting, forget it. I won't have you accusing my wife or
implicating her in any way in these bizarre crimes. I must
confess that when the Victoria Billingsley murder occurred,
Kinta had not yet come into our keeping. I do know for sure
that on the Friday night the two women were murdered,
Kinta was asleep by our bed all night."

"Dr. Shapiro, after the Thomkins funeral I had a look around your place. I noticed a square hole in the back wall of the shed where a window had once been. It was clear from my hasty inspection of the shed that you had been keeping Kinta in that shed. The empty window casing would have allowed plenty of room for the dog or wolf to have jumped through it."

Paul had used the same logic against Rhonda when she had defended Kinta against the same possibility. Suddenly he found himself hoping that Gary had not noticed the broken rain gauge and bent deck post.

"I've got one other question for you, Dr. Shapiro."

"What's that?"

"You've got a bent post on your rear deck across from your small kitchen window. Any idea how the post got knocked out of line? It also seems to be the only window on the back of your home that isn't armed with your security system. It appears to me that something might have come through the window and struck the post with such force that it knocked it out of line."

Paul became more defensive. "You are putting two and two together and getting five. Ronnie and Kinta had nothing to do with these murders."

"Still, I think we're going to have to question your wife, Dr. Shapiro."

"Mr. Jarvis, I don't think questioning Rhonda would be of much help to you. I'm sure she could offer nothing more than I have already told you. Try to understand this, officer. Rhonda has been under a great deal of stress lately. I'm not even sure that she could stand up to much questioning now. She's just not emotionally up to it."

"Dr. Shapiro, what I think you are suggesting is an obstruction of justice. You're aware that we could subpoena her if necessary?"

Paul bristled a little but said nothing. His silence seemed to cause the detective a little uneasiness, and he shifted in his chair.

"Mr. Jarvis," Paul began slowly, "I feel like I need to share something criminal that we never reported. It seems unrelated, and yet I think it might explain the bent deck post."

"Go on," urged the detective.

"Several mornings after the Billingsley murder, two things happened in our lives that desperately complicated our relationship. I ran over a seven-year-old girl on Queen Anne Hill near my clinic. The little girl, Janie Nickerson, miraculously survived and was just released from the hospital." Paul felt he had to quickly tell the story of Janie and her recovery just to experience again that sense of release in knowing that she was nearly well.

"Well, I know you must be immensely relieved."

"Oh, believe me, I am. I am."

"But how is this related to Victoria Billingsley?" Gary pursued.

"It's not related to the killings, but needless to say, it did add to the strain that both Rhonda and I have felt. The same day I struck this child with my car, a masked man entered our home and assaulted my wife. He was dressed in black and wearing a Halloween mask that looked like Richard Nixon."

"You personally saw this man?" asked Jarvis.

"No, I was at the hospital with the Nickersons. But my wife told me about it, and I have no reason to doubt her."

"Did you report this to the police?"

"No. I felt that we should have reported it, but Rhonda said her assailant threatened to kill her and Kinta if she informed the authorities. Further, she believed that having the police come out would only implicate the wolf in crimes that he did not commit. At any rate, the man first assaulted her on the deck, and I believe that this is when the post was bent. She got free and ran toward the old shed, where he caught her and the most serious part of the assault began. It was then that the man attacked her, apparently with the intention of rape. But, thanks be to God, Kinta attacked him, and in the process she hit him with a tire tool."

"The wolf?"

Paul smiled, remembering that he had felt the same sort of confusion. "No, not the wolf, the intruder—because he had Kinta by the throat and was trying to kill him. In fact, the animal had attacked the man and had thrown him to the ground, tearing into his upper chest with his massive jaws. But the man was very powerful, Rhonda said, and had managed to get the kind of grip on Kinta that would have allowed him to kill the animal, even though he had been severely wounded. Because Kinta had acted so instinctively to save her, she responded with the old tire tool that she had picked up from the shed."

"So your wife runs with wolves and tire-tools her assailants?"

Paul smiled. "No, no. Rhonda is a very feminine and sweet and demure type."

"Who keeps a wolf and a tire tool to ward off rapists?" Gary wasn't grinning.

Shapiro also grew serious. "Anyway, after the tire tool thing, the assailant fled. Maybe you could check the hospitals and clinics and see if, on Wednesday, April 19, anyone reported into emergency medicine for a lot of stitches to the chest and—"

"Tire-tool repair? OK, Dr. Shapiro, I'll do that, but I wouldn't bet on it. Whatever happens, we are going to have to question your wife on the whole business."

"I'll have her come in for questioning, or if you're up for a two-hour drive, I'll take you to where she is. There are no phones up there, and it's not marked on any maps."

"Not necessary. But if you draw me a map, I can find the place. I'll go up there tomorrow."

Paul agreed and in a few minutes had drawn the inspector a map. They exchanged farewells.

Paul was relieved when Gary was gone. He hated to spring this on Rhonda because she had no phone at the cabin and there was really no way to let her know the inspector would be paying her a call. Oh, and Kinta. Paul could not help but think of Kinta. He desperately hoped that Kinta would behave himself when the inspector came to call.

While he turned all of these thoughts over in his mind, the phone rang. He could hear Della saying in the next room, "Yes, Dr. Shapiro is in. May I say who's calling?" Then the buzzer on his desk phone sounded abruptly, and he reached forward and picked up the receiver.

"Hello?" said a familiar voice.

"Oh, Ronnie, thank God it's you! Where are you calling from?"

"My cell phone won't work way out here. I'm calling from a pay phone at the bottom of the mountain." Rhonda's voice sounded weak and distant, nearly buried by an obnoxious audio hum. "Darling," she went on, "anything further on the death of Renée Thomkins?"

"None so far as I know. I've just finished talking to a Gary Jarvis, a homicide detective. Ronnie, I want to come up on the weekend and see you." Paul decided not to share the inspector's suspicions about her.

"OK, that sounds great," Rhonda said, not suspecting that she was now a suspect in the serial killings. "Any further signs of the masked intruder?"

"No."

"Any calls from the animal rights people?"

"Not that either."

"Paul, I've been practicing with the pistol. I'm pretty good. I can hit a tree if I'm not too far back."

Paul laughed, which felt great. His wife's flight to protect Kinta had left him so uptight he hadn't done much laughing. "Ronnie, please don't shoot your foot off. Remember, Wyatt Earp was only successful in Dodge City because he never fired his six-gun until it was out of the holster."

"Well, I'm no Calamity Rhonda, but I wanted to practice just enough that I wouldn't be afraid of it in case I ever needed it. I still have the feeling that the man in the mask will be back." She changed her tone. "But I am looking forward to seeing you when you're up here tomorrow night. Can you come tomorrow night?"

"No, honey, I've got to speak to that colloquium at the university. Forgive me?"

"OK, but first thing Saturday morning. Be careful—it took me two hours to get up here, and I've got the Jeep. There's a washout about a mile off the asphalt. Hug the inside of the road. If it doesn't rain a lot between now and then, you should be able to make it in the BMW. Pauly, I do miss you. I can't tell you how Kinta enjoys the forests. I never use his leash. He wanders away in the night and sometimes the early morning, but he's always back way before noon. He won't come in the cabin much, though. It's like he was born to be outside. Well, Pauly, I need to get back. When you come up, bring some extra blankets and groceries."

"Ronnie, Janie Nickerson went home from the hospital on the weekend. Her ribs are still taped, but other than that she's her normal, busy little self."

"That's wonderful. I'm so glad. Well, I'm looking forward to seeing you. Oh, I almost forgot. There's a strange group of women at the bottom of the Callahan Grove. They're camping there. I passed them on a hike. They sit in a circle and sing nature hymns. They seem a little weird, but I might try to meet them. It might be one of the environmentalist cults who are going to protest the Callahan sale. Well, I really do have to go. Good-bye, Paul."

"Good-bye, Ronnie. No, wait! Police Inspector Jarvis is coming up to talk to you tomorrow afternoon or evening."

"At the cabin? Here?"

"Yes. I drew a little map of the place and how to get there. Rhonda, we have to cooperate with the police on this matter. A lot of people have died, and they and we have to clear Kinta on this matter. Just tell them what you know."

"Very well, but—"

"One other thing: I told them about your assailant."

"Why? You know they'll just take it out on Kinta. Why did you tell them?"

"Rhonda, we have to be open about this. We don't want to hide things from the police. Just tell them everything."

A long silence ensued. "All right," she finally acquiesced.

"Rhonda, I love you. I can hardly wait to see you."

"I love you, too, Paul. Good-bye."

"Good-bye, Rhonda."

⸻

Paul hung up and fixed himself a cup of coffee. He saw three clients before noon, the last of whom was Emma Silone. Emma believed her husband was trying to poison her. She had begun to suffer from these delusions shortly after her stroke. The resulting paranoia about eating anything that her husband had come near had left her anorexic. She also had developed some bulimia in the attempt to deal with what she believed was poisoned food. Over the months since her stroke, her devoted husband had never grown weary of her paranoia and seemed possessed of a need to help her get well. Harvey Silone was an anchor of healing love to his spouse. But in her extreme mental state, Mrs. Silone saw Harvey's loving concern as even more of an attempt to do her in. She was convinced that Harvey was trying to slip strychnine into her Big Macs, which he lovingly brought her from time to time because she had so loved McDonald's before her stroke.

Paul prescribed some more tranquilizers for her, knowing she wouldn't take them once she got them home, fearing that her husband or his mistress would lace the pills with poison. In fact, before her session was over, Paul felt certain she needed to be hospitalized immediately. "Mrs. Silone," he began.

"Emma," she corrected.

"Emma, would you possibly consider coming to spend some time in our hospital? You're obviously a woman under a lot of stress. You're so thin. Why don't you admit yourself to our wing of the hospital before you have a total breakdown?"

Emma Silone sat still, listening. "Do you think it's necessary?"

"Yes, the rest will do you good, and you won't have to worry that Harvey is putting strychnine in your Big Macs. You'll be able to sleep ever so soundly. How about tomorrow morning? Can you check in at nine?"

"Of course, but, Doctor, pray that Harvey won't do away with me in the night. If I'm not there in the morning, I'll be in the morgue . . ." She stopped and broke into tears. "Every night I pray that I will live till morning."

After Emma left, Paul got up to catch some lunch when the phone rang. It was Gary Jarvis.

"Dr. Shapiro, one of the laboratory people found some animal feces on the lawn outside the broken window of Renée Thomkins' condominium. Laboratory analysis shows that it is the droppings of a wolf. From the size of the droppings, it appears to be a very large wolf. The analysis of the droppings shows them to contain traces of processed meat and monosodium glutamate, the kind of ingredients that might be found only in prepared dog food. So when we find a wolf that's been eating dog food, we believe we will have our killer. Dr. Shapiro, I'm going to have to go tonight to pay a call on your wife. I'm afraid the evidence and circumstances are too pressing to be put off until tomorrow."

Paul was speechless, but his heart was racing. Could Kinta be the killer? He had seemed so protective of Rhonda. But could he overlook the damning evidence of the police? Kinta had to be the killer, whatever Rhonda thought of him.

He now had terrible fears for Rhonda's life. Early on, Paul had tried to convince himself that maybe there were two wolves: one of them was a killer, and the other was the gentle Kinta. But deep inside he knew that such an idea was preposterous.

Still holding the phone, Paul was seized with overwhelming fear, forgetting the officer on the other end.

"Dr. Shapiro, are you there?" The inspector's voice shook him out of his lethargy and drove the dark visions of his helpless and possibly mauled wife temporarily away.

"Uh . . . yes, yes, Mr. Jarvis, I'm here," Paul stammered.

"Well, about the wolf. I'm going up tonight to call on your wife. Do you understand?"

"Yes, by all means, Inspector. Hurry, please, but be careful. Oh, yes, Rhonda says the road is badly washed in some places. Hug the inside on the curves. And the guard rail is missing in some places. But hurry, please! This is terrifying news."

"Good-bye, Dr. Shapiro."

"Good-bye, Inspector."

Paul cradled the receiver of the phone. He felt sick.

CHAPTER 22

It was after five o'clock in the afternoon when Inspector Jarvis left the precinct headquarters building. The Seattle traffic boxed him in until almost six. He knew that he had started for the Shapiro cabin far too late in the afternoon. The gloomy skies and intense rain brought the darkness much earlier than usual. He thought he could make the drive to the Shapiro cabin in an easy two hours, but the steep ascent and winding roads were severely lengthening his driving time. To worsen matters, the rain, though abating, was making the asphalt driving surface too slick to hurry. He knew, however, he was in a race with the oncoming darkness, and nothing is darker at night than the high woods of the foothills.

He worried that he would arrive at the Shapiros so late he would likely frighten Rhonda. Still, he used the now-three-hour drive up into the highlands to review all that he knew about the four murders. Apart from the fact that they were somehow linked to the My Kind lounge, nothing else seemed significant.

He was now convinced that the victims were killed by a wolf. He also knew this wolf did not operate alone. No animal could randomly select executive females who happened to frequent My Kind. The animal had to be taken there. It seemed unlikely that the killings were in any way linked to the isolated gay bashings that had been occurring in and around the Queen Anne Hill area.

Then something occurred to him—Victoria Billingsley had been killed on April 1. He had a hunch that just might pan out. He turned on the speaker option of the car phone and dialed. Sergeant Brock answered.

"Sergeant Brock, Jarvis here. Would you do a little research on the gay bashings in the Queen Anne Hill area and find out how many have occurred in the last month or so?"

"Sure, boss!" said the melodious voice on the other end.

"Thanks, Brock," said Gary.

He was about to hang up when Brock told him that his ex-wife, Melody, had called.

"Why?" Gary wondered aloud. "I'm sure the alimony payment was on time."

"She just said to tell you that she wanted to talk to you. And there's a letter from her on your desk that just came in."

Gary thanked the sergeant again and hung up. He wondered about his ex-wife's intentions. She never wrote him. What could she want now?

Probably more alimony. The way she drained him, he could never afford to date any women. But then again, he wasn't interested in other women. Though his life with

Melody had been difficult, he had and still did love her . . . and didn't want another to take her place.

He remembered how happy they once had been. But their relationship had gradually begun to sour, always curdling around the same subject. Melody despised being a cop's wife. She had known too many police widows who never seemed to stop crying. Usually they were trying to support two or three kids on inadequate pay. The thing that she hated most about them was that they never seemed free to marry again. They were martyrs to their martyred husbands.

She had insisted that he leave the SPD. But while he loved Melody, he also loved the police force. He tried his best to convince her that he would not get shot in the line of duty and that he would always be there for her, but it was no use. Gary remembered their last court hearing. He had not wept very many times in his life, but he wept that day. It was the last time he ever saw her. After that day in court, his life became a ritual of post-office support. He mailed her the alimony checks and received back the canceled stubs, proving that she had cashed them.

The weather drew him back to the moment. The rain was gradually becoming stronger. He was now winding slowly through the twisted foothills. Most of the time, the rain was outdistancing the wipers' ability to keep the windshield clear. Twice, the rain became so severe that he had to stop the car and wait for five or ten minutes to let it abate. In spite of the torrent, his thoughts continued to move between the wolf killings and the torch he still carried for Melody.

In considering the murders, he felt more and more certain that the Shapiros must be involved. Too much evidence pointed that way. The murder of Renée Thomkins was the one murder that didn't fit as cogently as the others. If Mrs. Shapiro did indeed have Kinta with her, then either she or the psychiatrist had brought the wolf down from the mountain for the Thomkins job. It was not an unreasonable possibility.

The phone rang abruptly, jarring him out of his thoughts. He pushed the Talk button: "Jarvis here!"

"I thought it was, but you don't have to shout about it," said Sergeant Brock.

"Sorry. It's pretty quiet up in these hills, and I must admit the phone startled me a bit. Did you find out anything about the bashings?"

"Yes, but I'm afraid I can't be of much help to you. There hasn't been a recorded bashing since March."

"Hmm." Jarvis mumbled into the phone. "Victoria Billingsley was killed on April 1. That means, Brock, that the former basher and the serial killer could actually be the same person. Maybe he just wearied of bashing gays and got into bashing executive women."

"Yes sir, maybe . . ." agreed Brock and then hung up.

Suddenly, he stopped suspecting Rhonda and considered her husband as a possible suspect. Shapiro's practice was on Queen Anne Hill, and his home was on River Road, so there would have been logical reasons why he could be implicated in both the bashings and the killings. He didn't seem physically strong enough to manhandle the men, but you never knew. Still, his mind raced to something long ago he had read in some police files. One basher who had been apprehended years ago said that he had developed an animosity toward all gays out of a deep seated preadolescent issue of child abuse. His gay uncle had repeatedly sexually abused him when he was nine years old. He had grown up to become interested in psychology, as many child-abuse victims do. He had ultimately become a family counselor on the Olympic Peninsula. However, he had often driven over to Seattle and tried to catch some poor fellow outside a bar to roll him and take his cash. He had been hard to catch because he would accost people he really did not know, throw a bag over their head, and beat them half to death before leaving them for the rescue squads to put back together.

Perhaps history was repeating itself, and the killer was psychiatrist Paul Shapiro. It was not Rhonda Shapiro but her famous husband who he might soon snare in his net. It all fit so perfectly. Shapiro fit the serial killer's psychological profile. His work address matched the area of the earlier bashings. His home address matched the area of the killings. Most incriminating of all, Paul Shapiro had access to a somewhat domesticated wolf that could easily be his accomplice. Everything fit so cogently that Gary was amazed he had not connected all the pieces earlier.

The only real evidence that he needed to fit together was the common link that all of the murder victims had with the psychiatrist. He ought to try searching Paul Shapiro's patient files. There he might find a common thread that would link all of the victims. The car radio buzzed then clicked into life. Brock was back on the line.

"I just noticed, boss," said Brock, "that your wife's letter was mailed from the very area where you're heading right now."

"Really?"

"Yes, sir—the post office in Carnation, Washington. Isn't that the last stop before you turn up into the wilderness areas?"

"Yes." *But what was Melody doing there?* "Brock," Gary heard himself say, "open the letter."

"Are you sure about that, sir?"

"Yes, just do it and tell me what it says," Gary said.

There was a pause and the sound of ripping paper. "OK, there's an uncashed check—looks like for alimony—returned to you in this envelope. And a note. It says she's gone to camp with the Gaians for awhile. . . . Huh. . . . She'd hoped to find some purpose in life with them, but has instead realized that she wants to reconnect with you."

There was a pause. "That's all, sir," finished Brock, a bit embarrassed.

Gary, although also embarrassed, was feeling some elation. She wanted to see him. Realizing Brock was still on the line, he abruptly said, "Thanks, 'bye," and hung up to enjoy the possibilities in his mind. For the first time in weeks, he forgot about the killings.

He remembered the picture of Melody in her wedding dress that still presided over his sparsely furnished apartment. He remembered their wedding, the glory of their honeymoon. He remembered their fondness for Johnny Mathis and the music of the '50s that neither of them had ever lived through but that both of them loved. They both loved "Chances Are." He found himself humming it as the car moved laboriously up to the higher altitude. His mind raced ahead to the possibility that he might find his wife among the Gaians. The check his wife had returned was not just money in the bank; it was somehow a symbol that he was growing rich . . . really rich in the right things. It was odd that Gary Jarvis was tracking the worst serial killer ever to stalk Seattle, and yet something new was being born even in the midst of all the killing evil.

Ever so gradually his mind returned to the task at hand. Then suddenly in the thin beam of his rain-dimmed headlights he saw something standing in the middle of the road. Instantly he began braking. Then he pushed the brake heavily to the floor and braced himself for the impact. An old man was standing in the rain, and in front of him was a wolf.

His car went into a long slide that threatened to become a skid. He slid over the old man and his wolf and then floated to a stop. He didn't hear the vehicle hit the old man, but he knew it must have. The peppery rain on the metal of the car was now so intense he could hear nothing else. He got out of the car and hastily slipped into his rain slicker. Then with his flashlight he walked back down the road to see if he could find a body. His shoes were red clumps of mire—walking was nearly impossible. He poked around in the muddy weeds and sparse scrubs to see if he could locate the injured. He was getting back in his car when he decided to look in front of it. Ten feet beyond the beam of his headlights was a torrent of cold water rushing through the roadway. The pavement was gone. A washout of some thirty feet in width gushed over the road and fell over a nearby cliff two hundred feet down into the inky night.

Gary stared in horror at what might have happened. Had he not braked for the old man and the wolf, his life would have certainly ended in a watery plunge. "Oh, God, thank you, thank you!" he said with his face turned upward into the streaming rain.

But with thanks came the realization that the Shapiro cabin was inaccessible. He backed a long way down the dark, wet road before he found a place wide enough to turn around and proceed even more slowly back to Seattle. What weird visions and things had come to him in the night! What an odd mixture of pain and glory the day had been. Savage killings and ghosts and love notes and uncashed alimony checks and the hope of coming home to his wife again: "These are such things as dreams are made of," he said aloud into the interior of the car.

It was as if Gary Jarvis was being born all over—as a new man living a new life . . . a charmed life protected by an aging angel on a precipice of horror. Why? There was no answer. Only the cold, clean rain; the rain that had almost destroyed him was suddenly a baptism of hope.

CHAPTER 23

On the morning of the same May day Gary Jarvis had confronted the psychiatrist, Isletta Borg and her Gaian friends had prepared themselves to protest both the sale and the cutting of the Callahan Grove. They were prepared for a long stay on the mountain, ready to take any measures necessary to stop the chain saws. On sabbatical leave from her job at the university, Isletta, though not committed to Gaia, was committed to her surrounding campmates of artists, geologists, ecologists, and others who did not want to see the forests die nor any particular species of wildlife disappear from the earth.

She perused the literature the Gaians were reading: Carson's *Silent Spring,* Pirsig's *Zen and the Art of Motorcycle Maintenance,* and Dillard's *Pilgrim at Tinker Creek.* The Gaians were convinced that the disastrous silent spring was already on its way. They were passionate about the woods and the woodland life that chirped, croaked, and whistled all about them.

This particular morning, still soaking in the wild, Isletta had put aside her books and instead looked through a huge telescope to a nest of spotted owls nearly a hundred feet up in a tree above her. While watching the mother owl return to her nest, Isletta saw a flash of gray wolf cavorting in the morning mist and sunshine. Then Rhonda Shapiro came into view, her long chestnut hair flowing free over her faded blue bathrobe. She appeared to be running after the wolf. Then she stopped and crouched. Kinta romped back toward her. She threw a stick and he shot after it, returning it to her. She caught his large head and pulled his broad snout up to her face and caressed his head before the two of them ran up the trail and out of view.

Isletta was intrigued. She hiked out of the Gaian encampment and the Callahan Grove. Around midafternoon she caught sight of the Shapiros' Cherokee parked beside a small cabin. The day had remained alternately foggy and sunny and very cold. A thin tendril of smoke was coming from the chimney of the cabin.

Isletta approached the front door. She paused, working up the courage to knock on a stranger's door. Finally, she reached up and rapped her knuckles on the wood.

Inside, Rhonda was terrified by the knock. She instinctively reached for the pistol. Outside, Kinta, who had been dozing on the back stoop, awoke and raced to the front of the cabin, skidding to a stop on the wet flagstones near Isletta. He gave no indication of springing at her, but his immense size was frightening enough up close. Isletta drew back in fear. Just then, Rhonda opened the door with her pistol in her hand.

"Now, don't you bite me," Isletta weakly instructed the wolf. She turned to Rhonda. "And for goodness sake, don't *you* shoot me."

Rhonda, slowly sizing up the intruder as nonthreatening, started to smile at Isletta's predicament. Then a laugh leaked out. Kinta looked bewildered by the laughter.

"Down, down, Kinta," she said through her laughter. Kinta backed off. Rhonda lowered her pistol. Isletta, realizing she was in no danger, managed a half grin.

Rhonda, still smiling, began. "Don't tell me: you're selling cosmetics."

"No," said Isletta, grinning more fully but still recovering from the wolf-pistol encounter.

"Well," said Rhonda, deciding that a bit of female company would be welcome, "can I offer you something to drink? I assume you're with the Gaian camp. You must be thirsty after a long walk up here."

"Yes, thank you," Isletta replied, following Rhonda into her small house. "How did you know about us?" She was struck by the beautiful rustic furnishings of the home's interior. In the corner of the great room was a single bed covered with a beautiful handcrafted quilt. Opposite the bed area was a kitchen with an electric stove and a table covered with a checkered cloth under a window that looked out on a distant mountain. Rhonda turned on the burner under a copper kettle. Rhonda gestured for Isletta to sit at the table then sat down across from her.

"I saw your campfire the other night. The next morning, I came down again and watched your dawn ritual through the trees."

"Oh. Do you happen to have a phone in this cabin?"

"No, unfortunately. I do have a cell phone in the four-wheeler, but it won't work up here. But whenever I get lonesome, I go down the mountain to a phone, call my husband, and we talk." She paused. "Are you married?"

"No," Isletta replied. "Actually, none of us Gaians are married."

"Oh?" Rhonda pressed.

"Yes. We are banded together by our common desire to stand against all the human predators that want to gobble up these forests. We have decided to camp here and stand against the Callahan proposal." Her speech grew more passionate. "They may cut these trees down, but they'll have to cut us down first. We've enough cables and locks to chain ourselves to many of these huge firs, and we intend to do it before we let the logging industry grind these beautiful trees into pulp wood."

Rhonda, seeing the conversation had taken a turn toward the intense, attempted to lighten the mood, asking Isletta about her background and other interests. The kettle whistled. Rhonda poured Isletta some tea and offered her a three-day-old Twinkie. Isletta agreed to both, and before long they were finding out all about each other. They talked for more than an hour. Rhonda's tale of how she had acquired a wolf fascinated her tall blonde guest.

Isletta understood her passion to save Kinta from the animal pound. "I guess you feel about your wolf like we feel about these trees and the incredible wildlife they contain."

Rhonda, appreciating Isletta's understanding, ventured more. "I'm actually here to escape some . . . grisly occurrences back in Seattle," she began. Isletta leaned toward her, and Rhonda spilled the incident of the intruder, amazed at how comfortable it was to confide in Isletta. She also shared the whole bizarre tale of her friendship with Kinta.

"So you see," Rhonda concluded, "I'm here because I'm afraid. Not just for me but for Kinta as well."

"Rhonda," counseled Isletta, "why don't you come down the hill and meet with our group. Whatever else they may be short on, these women are long on courage. You'll feel safe, and I guarantee that they'll protect you."

"Oh, I dunno. I never could be a Gaian. I decided that as I watched your ritual through the trees. This kind of stuff just isn't for me."

"Can I be candid?" Isletta launched into her admission. "I was born into the state church of Sweden, and I believe in the Holy Trinity, so all this Mother Earth stuff really isn't for me either. But these Gaians do care about saving the world; and I believe, in this matter, God is on their side. God must have loved it to make it so outrageously beautiful."

That seemed reasonable to Rhonda.

"Anyway," Isletta went on, "why don't you come down and eat with us tonight? It would break your monotony and make us a new friend."

Rhonda agreed. "That would be nice."

"Oh," said Isletta, "do bring Kinta with you."

Rhonda paused. "I don't know. As far as I know he's never been out in the world of people. I'm not sure I could control him if he suddenly decided he wanted a couple of Gaians for dinner. Speaking of dinner, should I bring my own?"

"Oh no. We'd love to share our authentic Gaian fare with you. Tonight it's hot dogs and Ho Hos. The ambiance isn't much, but the company is charming."

Rhonda agreed but thought it best if she brought Kinta on a leash. She knew the leash would do little good if the wolf took a liking to the women in the Callahan camp. Still, the rendezvous was set. Rhonda would be down to the grove for forest vespers at 6:30 or so. Kinta would be with her. Isletta rose from her chair as if to leave. Rhonda also stood.

"Isletta, thanks for spending time with me," said Rhonda.

"And it was so nice of you to be hospitable," agreed Isletta. They shook hands at first and then, because the wilderness seems to invite that sort of thing, they hugged warmly and walked to the door.

"Remember, no shooting or biting, OK?" said Isletta.

"I promise," laughed Rhonda.

CHAPTER 24

Eric visited the Pacific Woods corporate offices around 11:00 on the same evening Gary Jarvis had attempted to reach the Shapiro cabin and failed. The offices were closed, and the eerie atmosphere was marked by heavy silence. When he walked into his own office and flipped on the light, he was startled to see Isletta Borg sitting in his chair behind his desk, drumming her thin fingers on a single file folder. She was dressed in a simple shift that seemed to float around her. Eric, having seen her only in camping clothes, smiled warmly at her appearance. She returned the smile.

"So you've come down from the grove," he said. "Welcome to our boring, high-rise world of glass and steel."

"Hello, Eric," she said. "We have to talk."

Eric's friendliness waned. "What gives? What are you doing in my office?"

"In your Callahan file," she tapped the file folder again, "there are four deeds of abstract, licensing you to sell the Callahan Grove."

"Would you tell me what are you doing with my Callahan folder?"

"Eric, I'm not sure I can make all this real to you, but do you know what the largest living thing that has ever lived upon your puny planet is?"

"I believe we've had this discussion—redwoods."

"Good," she briefly smiled. "You've been paying attention. Now, do you know why any of those trees are still standing?"

"I could guess."

"Because concerned people saw what was happening to the natural resources of the world. Did you know that the Sahara is creeping southward at the rate of 1.4 miles every ten years?"

Eric was getting impatient with the nature lesson. "What's your point, Isletta?"

"My point is that the good Lord must be grieved at the way people often disregard the use of his planet. He made the trees of Callahan Grove, Eric, and he likes them. He made the seed-bearing cones that fall into the dark earth and grow green. He speaks and there is life, water, microbes, snails, slugs. You know I think the Gaians are wrong about Gaia, but they are right about life. God made all of life to reproduce itself." Isletta paused and began drumming her fingers on the table and the file folder once again.

"Isletta, don't tell me that you think God himself is a tree hugger?"

"Let us say that he is rather a tree maker. But after he made trees, he made human beings to enjoy and use the trees. Trees were his gift to people who would use and treasure them. They are the keepers of a whole ecological system. The Callahan Grove is where God speaks both to those who abuse nature and those who worship it. Neither course is right. Eric, you and I have a special role to play in this environmental eruption. Eric, the Gaians want you to work for their side . . . our side."

Eric bristled, "No way." It was laughable. Why would he toss his wealth- and status-giving career for a bunch of trees? Still, he had to confess his love of the big trees was causing him to rethink his value system. He could watch Isletta smile as she saw him changing his views of ecology right before her eyes.

Eric had no idea what he would do or how he would do it. It was quite clear, however, that if he did what she was asking he would lose his job. He didn't know how he would pay his debts. He felt that he was at a decision point—a crisis point. For the first time in his short legal career, he was about to act on what was right and not what was merely profitable. He was about to start life over, to play out his life according to conscience. He was in search of the experience of finding a joy beyond working for a living. He was stumbling somehow upon a sense of calling.

"What if I agree to do it?" he ventured, but when he looked up, Isletta was gone. He sat down behind his desk, thinking hard. Something had been born inside of him—it felt new and light and . . . purposeful. He had purpose. This incredible lightness of being brought a courage he had never experienced in court. He decided to act.

He flipped through his Rolodex to a certain entry and then dialed the number.

"Hello, and who would be calling me at such a late hour?"

"Hello, Callahan?"

"Yes, that's right."

"Eric Compton here."

A jovial note entered the voice. "Well, hello indeed, Eric. You can call me anytime, my boy."

Eric steeled his nerves. "Callahan, I'm not your boy anymore. Pacific Woods will buy your trees, but we can't cut you the $3 million now. Isletta Borg still isn't selling, and the state commissioner is firm: we can't buy any trees unless we buy all."

"I thought you said you could slap Borg with a joint-tax retainer and force her in. She will have to sell ultimately, won't she?"

"No, as a matter of fact, she doesn't have to sell at all . . . ever. She's got the same right to keep her trees as you have to sell yours. She's owned that grove for a long time. And what's more, I'm going to see that Isletta Borg isn't forced out. She's interested in reforestation and conservation. And if she doesn't want to sell, she shouldn't be forced to do it."

Callahan swore into the receiver. "I'm gonna eat you for breakfast, son! Don't even think you'll ever work—"

Eric hung up the phone, knowing he was in a world of trouble.

He also knew he was free. He wasn't altogether sure what his freedom would cost him, but he knew it would be expensive.

CHAPTER 25

The Shapiro clinic had been out of balance for several days with everyone abuzz over Della's engagement ring. Naturally everyone was glad, and some a little jealous, that Levi had at last proposed to Della. They were generally very happy days. Della still had to live with a lingering uneasiness over Levi's actions on the last night they were together. It was mostly his erratic behavior that left her so unnerved. She tried to pass it off as one of those weird quirks that would soon pass. She wanted never to think of it again. She wanted her relationship with Levi to be as normal as it had always been. She wanted it to be all that everyone believed it was.

On Friday morning, May 5, Margery Irons, who worked in the dispensary, bought Della a cup of coffee in the lunchroom. Margery had been gone on an extended vacation when Della had become engaged. But now that she was back, she wanted to hear all about it. As they sat across from each other, Margery said matter-of-factly, "OK, Dell, let's see it."

Della dutifully extended her hand.

Margery took her hand and looked at the ring. She narrowed her eyes with the kind of squint that usually precedes a frown. The frown never came. She looked away and then looked back at it again as though she was trying to be sure of something. Then she smiled and gave Della's hand back to her and picked up her coffee. She took a hasty, hefty sip. It was too hot, and she grimaced at the overlarge swallow that must have burned even as she gulped it down. "Wow! This coffee is hot!"

"All right, Margery, get off the coffee. What do you think of the rock?"

"It's big. Really big."

"But you think it's gaudy?"

"Not gaudy." Margery was choosing her words very carefully.

"Ostentatious?" Della probed.

Margery shook her head.

"OK, then, what gives?" Della was insistent.

Margery reached across the table and took Della's left hand, looking again at the ring. She shook her head sadly. "You really want to know?"

Della nodded. "Yes. Spill."

"Dell, it's a cubic zirconium!"

The words knifed into Della. Then she laughed and waited for Margery to laugh, too, indicating the joke. Margery didn't laugh. She did stand up. "I'm sorry, Dell. I won't tell anyone."

Della believed that she had only said it out of jealousy. She was glad Margery was leaving. She knew her face was flushed because of Margery's snide comment. She was in the process of finishing her coffee alone when Margery stuck her head back in the room and said. "Dell, forgive me." Her head was followed by her whole body as she entered the room. She walked to Della and drew her up from her chair and hugged her. Della made no effort to hug back; her body remained unforgivingly stiff.

Margery reached up with a closed fist and gave her a loving and mock cuff on the cheek. She smiled.

Della didn't. "You're wrong. Levi is one of the richest men on the West Coast. Why would he buy a zirconium? You're wrong! Just . . . just go away."

Margery left.

When Della had regained her composure, she went back to her office. She had little heart for her work the rest of the morning and found herself living only for her lunch hour. As soon as she could get away for lunch, she walked straight down to the jewelers a block or so from the clinic.

"Yes, my dear, it's a cubic zirconium. I can get it for you in pink as well," said the appraiser.

Della fought a stinging in the corner of her eyes.

"But the mounting—it's quite old, isn't it? Perhaps an antique!"

"No, it's new. Cheap. Merely a plated reproduction, my dear."

"Thank you," Della stammered. "What do I owe you for this appraisal?"

"If it were the Star of India you were getting appraised, I'd have to charge for it. But not this paste. I make it a practice never to charge anyone when the appraisal costs more than the gem is worth." He was intentionally brusque. "I don't appraise junk—this is what I call an *identification,* not an *appraisal.*" He stopped short when he saw tears swimming in Della's eyes.

Turning abruptly, she left the shop, and once out of his sight let her tears flow freely. She walked hurriedly into the alley and cried. Only after ten or twelve minutes did she feel that she had gained enough control to go back to work. Fortunately for her, Paul Shapiro had agreed to make rounds once a month with medical students at the Washington Psychiatric Institute. Della was relieved that he wouldn't be there the rest of her long afternoon. She turned her love affair with Levi Twist over in her mind a thousand times. Why would Seattle's wealthiest widower give her a fake diamond? He could afford the Hope Diamond if he so desired. Why? Did she really know him?

What about his odd, vicious behavior? Why would he give her a fake gem? And the most important question: What was she going to do about it?

She took the ring off at three o'clock in the afternoon, determined to give it back to him the next time she saw him. She had decided there were too many things unsettled for her to pursue her engagement. The June 17 wedding they had planned was just too soon, and marriage was too great a step to take only so their unnamed child could have a name. There were some things Lee had to settle psychologically before she would feel comfortable. She would suggest once again that he needed professional help and maybe later they could talk about marriage. But in the meantime, she would bring their baby into the world. It was something she had always wanted, to be a mother if never a wife. She broke into tears once again.

She thought again how emotionally agitated Levi had become at the abortion clinic. Other than that, in every part of their relationship, Levi was always gentle, forthright, and utterly honest. She looked down at her naked finger where the phony engagement ring lately had been. *Well, maybe not entirely honest or generous.* The day was long. Her mind was tired.

CHAPTER 26

Della hadn't heard from Levi for three weeks. Finally, on the Saturday before Memorial Day, she decided to leave her apartment to try to find him in his hunting cabin. She had never been there before, but she knew she would have no problem finding it for she would follow her onscreen travel-mate. She smiled with confidence. She suddenly remembered Margery telling her once that she'd seen Levi walking his dog in Bellevue Park. The statement troubled her. Levi didn't have a dog. A lot of different emotions had welled up in Della, but she simply could not get the issue of Levi's nonexistent dog out of her mind. She put the cheap ring in her pocket and got into her car. The traffic was terrible, but she finally got out of the steel slog and emerged from the city.

The weather had cleared, and Della found her little car moving rapidly north in the late afternoon sunshine. By 6:45 the sun was still high in the sky as she found herself exiting onto the Totem Wilderness Road. Within ten minutes, she came in sight of the cabin. Lee's black Bronco was parked off to one side. She knew he was there.

A second thought struck her: Levi was supposed to be there; she wasn't. How in the world was she going to explain her presence at his private hideaway? She knew now that she should quickly stop the car and return when Lee wasn't there if she wanted to check out Margery's dog story. By the time she had come upon this plan, fully realizing that she shouldn't be there, it was too late for her to turn around and go back. She knew Lee would already have seen her. She dusted herself with a generous amount of bravado and drove off the road and up the short driveway. She parked her car beside the Bronco. She sorted silently through a long catalogue of the most plausible lies and managed to select one just as she heard Levi shout out, "Hello, Dell!"

In another instant he was beside her car, pulling her up from the driver's seat into a warm embrace. "It's great to see you! What in the world brings you up to the cabin?"

"Oh, Lee! You didn't call last night. Why? You always call on Friday nights when you don't actually come by. Anyway, when that sky cleared off this afternoon, I knew I just had to see you. I called your house, and when you weren't there, I knew you'd be here." Della was amazed not only at how easily she had lied but at how cheerfully she could do so.

"Where's the rock?" Levi said, looking down at her finger where the ring should have been. Levi did not speak cheerily. Della suddenly felt it was going to be a bad evening.

"I left it at the jewelers for a little sizing."

Lie number two, thought Della.

"Lee, that is quite a diamond," she said, thinking of the phony ring. It was Della's third lie. After that she quit counting. She passed off her lies with generous smiles. She was so inviting that Levi took her in his arms and kissed her.

In the lock of his powerful embrace, Della felt both comforted and very afraid. She kissed Levi as convincingly as she could, but there was now so much between them that she was fairly sure she was not being very convincing at all. As the overamorous Levi kissed Della, she began to feel that he had more in mind than she would agree to. She tried to pull free, but his intense embrace only became more constricting. Suddenly she heard a roar that terrified her. It was coming from inside the Bronco. It sounded as though an animal was attempting to snarl or bark or both. But it also sounded like his snarl was somehow being muffled.

At the frightening sound, Della squirmed with such intention she broke free from Levi's death grip, crying, "Lee, for goodness sake, what was that?"

"It's just Daimon," he said. "He's my black shepherd. C'mon, I'll introduce you."

"I'm not sure I want to meet him, Lee."

"Of course you do," said Levi as he approached the Bronco. He opened the door, carefully bracing his knee against it. The big dog oozed like fluid anger through the barely opened door. As he did so, Levi grabbed his chest halter, slipping a chain clip into the halter as the animal passed his knee. The car door snapped shut as the dog literally sprang into the glorious evening sunlight.

In a single leap, he sprung at Della but was stopped midair as the chain that held him reached its maximum length between Levi's fist and the heavy straps of the confining halter. Della nearly collapsed in fear as the black dog was jerked backward and fell to the ground.

"Hi . . . D . . . Daimon." Della croaked as she instinctively backed away. "Lee, I didn't know you had a dog."

Levi almost seemed to enjoy seeing her tremble in terror. He laughed more wholeheartedly than Della had ever heard him. "Daimon's a cream puff. There's no need to be afraid. Once you get to know him, you are going to love him."

"About how long will that take, Lee? He looks like he is going to be hard to get to know. What's that thing over his nose?" Whatever it was, she knew that it had kept him from barking or snarling at full volume in the horrible and fearsome first noise she had heard issuing from the vehicle.

"It a muzzle. Daimon can be a little nippy, and I don't like to take him out in public without a muzzle."

"Public? What public?"

"I was going to take him down to the Sound tonight. He likes to run in the tide shallows."

"Can I pet him?"

It was her tentativeness that caused Levi to laugh again. "Of course, you can pet him. I'll take his muzzle off."

"No, no, no need to do that. I can pet him with it on."

Levi laughed still again, "OK, Dell, have it your way."

Della knelt down to pet him, and as she reached forth her hand, she could see Daimon's black lips wrinkling backward to expose huge fangs. He snarled, and she drew back her hand, stood up, and retreated toward her car.

"Don't worry, Dell honey, you two are going to become great friends. It's just that great friendships take a little time.

I'll tell you what, Dell, I'll take both Daimon and you out to the Sound some night and you can get acquainted. In the meantime, help me put him away."

As Levi tugged the chain, Daimon turned reluctantly to follow him. Della followed them both as they rounded the corner of the cabin. There, behind the cabin, was a well-worn path that led to a shed and a dog run some fifty feet in length. The run was made of cyclone fencing. There were lots of bones inside the run and a curious instrument hanging on the fence that looked like a leather flog. It was made of thick strands of raw leather with bits of steel tied in it.

Almost as soon as Della saw the flog, she also noticed that Daimon's flesh was almost universally covered with old scars. She grimaced to think that there might be a connection between the flog and the scars. There appeared to be some four or five new wounds on the brute. There were also six or eight smaller scabs healing on Daimon's back. Her mind flew from the obvious truth that if Levi had done this to the animal Levi was capable of doing almost anything. Suddenly Levi noticed Della looking at the flog.

"Yes, in case you're wondering," he smiled, "I've had to use that flog to break his spirit a little."

"His spirit?"

"Dell, a good dog is made better by obedience. And the strongest-spirited animals only learn obedience through fear. I know you're also wondering why I bought Daimon in the first place."

"Yes, I wondered why you would keep such a vicious animal."

"Hey, now! Daimon is not vicious. Let me show you."

Levi took his muzzle off. The dog looked at him and drew back, and then he looked at Della and bared his fangs. The short, bristly hair on the nape of his neck stood straight up. Della could see him crouch as though he were going to spring upon her.

"No, please," she cried.

Instantly, Levi snapped the halter chain hard and then reached to the fence and grabbed the flog. Levi's powerful arms brought the steel-barbed whip down forcefully across the dog's back a couple of times. Bright red appeared in the dog's black hair. As the red broke upon the steel barbs in the flog, the snarl changed into a whimper, and Daimon laid submissively down.

"See. That's how you make a savage beast gentle."

Della instantly left off feeling sorry for herself and began feeling sorry for the huge dog. How often, she wondered, had the black shepherd felt his "spirit being broken."

Levi used the halter chain to jerk Daimon to his feet. He then removed both the halter and chain and kicked the dog brutally in the side. Daimon flew sideways into the cyclone fencing. Levi kicked him once more into the small steel opening in the fence, and then pegged the metal gate closed as the dog growled at Levi with a look of hate in his eyes. It was easy to see that this huge German shepherd loathed his master.

Noticing the bones that lined the dog run, Della asked, "What have you been feeding poor Daimon?" She wished she hadn't used the word *poor*.

"I've been feeding *poor* Daimon cheap cuts of meat," he replied. "It makes his coat shiny."

Della wanted to say that his coat seemed to be made shiny mostly by scar tissue, but she thought better of it.

As they walked back to the cabin, Levi stopped and kissed her. There had been a day when his kisses delighted her, but for the past few weeks, so many changes had stalked their relationship that Della now felt very afraid of Levi, even when he was kissing her. He kissed so hard that she knew exactly what he had in mind.

In the cabin, things were pretty much as Della had imagined they might be. Levi was a neat housekeeper. Della started to hang up the light jacket that she had worn that day. She got as far as opening the closet door when Levi reached to her and said, "Here, honey, let me!" She did, of course. He was trying to hide something, but what? The closet door opened far enough to reveal a pink nightgown that was not hers. Behind that was a dark Halloween costume. In the dim reaches of her mind, she remembered that Lee had told her the previous fall of when all company employees had worn costumes to work.

Levi took her jacket and put it in the closet in front of both the costume and the nightgown. As he did, he said, "Della, honey, spend the night with me. There's no reason you have to go home tonight, is there?"

"Not really," said Della, afraid to answer any other way. Why was she suddenly so afraid of Levi? She had never been this afraid of him throughout their entire relationship.

"Good," Levi said in that boyish, innocent way of his that she had always loved. "I'll rustle us up some grub. Any objection to steak?"

"Sounds wonderful, Lee," Della smiled.

And for the rest of the evening, everything seemed normal. It was like old times. They talked, and Della even laughed a little. They talked of their coming wedding. Levi brought out a bottle of Chardonnay to toast their future.

When it was time for bed, Lee suggested that they go ahead and sleep together since the couch in the front of the cabin was both small and uncomfortable. Della reminded Levi of their covenant to live chaste until June 17. He looked disappointed for a moment or so.

"How's our little one?" He glanced at Della's stomach.

"I'm sure he's fine," Della replied.

"Dell, baby, I need you tonight."

"Levi, you promised that we could save our best times for the big night."

"Have it your way. You always do!" he flung at her, clearly growing angry.

Della was once again afraid. "OK, OK, Levi."

Suddenly Levi smiled and backed off, "Honey, I'm sorry. I don't want to break my promise to you, and I won't. But I can tell you this, Miss Singleton, I can hardly wait until you are Mrs. Twist. I do love you, and to prove how much, I want to stand by my word. I'll sleep on the couch tonight, and you can have the bed."

Again Levi was suddenly himself. Della smiled, and they embraced. It was getting late, and Della remarked that they both had long days ahead of them on the morrow and that they ought to go to sleep. Levi kissed her in agreement. They kissed again and went to bed. Levi tucked her in bed and kissed her goodnight and took his dutiful place on the couch.

Della soon heard his slight snore coming from the couch in the front of the cabin. She knew he was asleep. She found her own sleep postponed for a two-hour replay of all that had happened to her that day. The ring, the dog, the hostility that had suddenly come into their relationship. She trembled over the man she knew that she could never marry. Still, she could not muster the slightest courage to tell him so. And worst of all, she hid from herself the horrible possibility of Levi's involvement in the serial killings of Seattle.

Sunday morning came swiftly. Levi woke Della with the delicious smell of hot coffee. It filled the cabin. So did Lee's singing. He had a robust and wonderful voice, and Della felt suddenly ashamed that she could ever have suspected anyone who could sing like Levi. It was a glorious way to wake up. Better than that, it was a glorious way to make up. As Della showered and dried her hair, she suddenly wanted to apologize to him, but, in truth, she had as yet made no official break with him or let him know that she was undergoing immense suspicions. Thus there was no real need to apologize.

Inwardly, she was glad that she had not broken their engagement. She felt herself cooling down emotionally. She began to feel that she wanted to reason through her doubts, almost convinced that she might yet come to the point that she would feel sorry she had been so hard on Lee.

Once her hair was dry, she slipped into her clothes. Levi had cooked a humongous tomato omelette with wheat toast. They devoured breakfast with gusto. The coffee tasted as wonderful as it smelled. Their morning flew too swiftly. All too soon Levi kissed her good-bye and threw her her jacket.

It was not a long throw, but somehow Della only managed to catch it by the sleeve. It upended in midair and something came tumbling out of the pocket—the engagement ring.

Levi couldn't see what it was, but Della knew and shuddered. She quickly reached for it just as Levi also reached. To her horror, he grasped it first. Della was nearly struck to stone by the look Levi gave her.

First it was the look of a wounded child. Gradually that soft, wounded look turned to a leer of hard judgment. At last, anger turned Levi's eyes to stone, and shortly after that, he doubled up his fist and sent it flying at Della's face at such a velocity that there was no time to dodge.

His fist caught her face, his military ring tearing savagely at her cheek. As she staggered into the doorjamb, her face was baptized in blood, and she spun outward—out of the cabin into the side of the Bronco. She fell face downward into the soft earth. The pain of Levi's brutality somehow hurt more than the actual blow. She raised herself on her left arm and then rose gradually as she steadied herself against the car. Levi was suddenly there again.

"You're a liar, Della! A filthy, vile liar!" he screamed. "You weren't getting the ring sized . . . you're ashamed of it, aren't you?"

Della's tears were coming so fast, she couldn't reply to his screaming. He looked as though he was going to hit her again. She clutched her purse and stumbled around the corner of the Bronco. Now the cut on her face was flowing copiously, and blood was staining her dress. She fumbled in her purse and found the keys, jabbing them at the lock of her own car. She tried repeatedly to make the key and the lock engage. At last they did. She swung the door open and almost collapsed in the car.

Levi grabbed the door, refusing to let her close it. Holding the door open, he shouted through it, "You slut. Nobody takes off her engagement ring unless she's looking for a chance to be unfaithful. What kind of business are you into on the nights we're not together, Dell?"

Della turned the key in the ignition. The motor jumped to life.

Levi grabbed at her as though he wanted to drag her from the car. She floored the accelerator, and the car spun nearly out of control as it leapt away from her angry fiancé. She managed somehow to keep the car on the drive, but the erratic path that the auto had taken in getting away sent Levi sprawling in the light gravel that the spinning tires spewed at him. Miraculously the car straightened itself in the driveway and roared away. Levi stood up just as she reached the end of the driveway. Even as she pulled the flagging car door shut, she heard Levi yell at her, "I'll kill you, you two-timing slut!"

Della's tears washed her eyes so fast that she could barely see the road to drive. She wiped her eyes, wept, and drove. Mercifully she was soon back on I-5 and headed to Seattle. When she drew near the city, she pulled out her cell phone and called Paul Shapiro's home. The phone rang five times, and she was about to hang up when someone picked up.

"Paul Shapiro," said the voice. It seemed a wonderful voice to Della. It was the most welcome voice she had heard in all her life.

"Paul, this is Della." A sob escaped her.

"Della, what on earth is wrong?" asked Paul. He had to wait for a long time while Della tried to get control of herself. "Take your time, Della, take all the time you need." He waited a good bit longer before Della finally managed to stop the tide of emotions that were tearing her apart.

"Paul, I need to go to the emergency room and get help."

"Della, why? What is the matter? . . . Please, tell me. What's the matter?"

"Paul, I need so badly to talk to you. I know tomorrow is a holiday, but . . . could you meet me at the clinic in the morning?"

"Sure, what time?"

"Eight-thirty OK?"

"Yes, but what about Denny's?"

"No, that's the last thing that I want. I won't be able to go out in public. My face is injured."

"Della, please tell me, what in the world happened?"

"Paul, don't forget me. I need you. Paul, Levi has a dog, a big dog. Daimon is his name. Paul, please, I need to see you."

CHAPTER 27

At the moment Paul and Della were arranging their meeting, Eric was having a meeting of his own with Isletta Borg.

"They look fine to me," Eric said, throwing the sheaf of papers on the tree stump that served as their table.

"But what about that clause 'except for the public good'?" Isletta asked. "I've got to anticipate any possible loophole. Is there any way that Callahan can get a writ of public benefit and force me to give Pacific Woods my trees? The newspapers say he can get a writ of public deference and do it. If he does it, Pacific Woods will pay him more for his own trees, so he wants to force me to sell to enhance his position. What if, by something we're overlooking, those bloodsuckers figure a way to mandate the release? You see, Eric, it isn't just my little piece of inheritance that could be lost. It's not even these trees—it's more . . ."

Isletta stopped and gestured to all of the trees. They were magnificent in the late afternoon sun. They stood like sentinels guarding their little patch of meadow. They looked as strong as Isletta wanted her case against Callahan to be. But inwardly she knew that trees only appeared to be strong. They could stand for centuries, besting lightning and contagion, and still live precariously at the mercy of the bulldozers and chain saws.

"Eric, are these trees safe?" She felt as if she only existed at the mercy of the courts. The law was trying to take her land. "Are my few acres of inheritance at the mercy of the giant lumbering forces with their immense political power? Can they—in some way we don't understand—take my land?"

Eric could understand why she was concerned. Still, he knew her case was airtight. He reached across the sheaf of papers and took her hand. "Isletta, not to worry now. Trust me on this: your case is safe. Even if the devil owned the courthouse and Faustus was Callahan's lawyer, nobody could legally take your land away from you." Eric stopped and smiled at her. He pressed the hand he held. The long slim fingers of her hand seemed to take refuge in his firm, square fingers. She smiled back, stingily at first, then broadly.

He drew her up to her feet. He picked up the papers, and they walked down the trail through the trees. It was that same trail where they had first met. So much had happened in the meantime. Under a storm of protest, Eric had managed to legally separate Isletta's grove of trees from the larger Callahan sections. He had been in the papers again, and all those put out of work by legal bric-a-brac, which had paralyzed the lumber industry, were eager to get back to work. Those who were going back to their jobs had made Eric the most celebrated young lawyer in the whole Northwest. On this particular day he felt particularly good. He was walking with a gorgeous blonde in the middle of an enchanted forest. He had eaten a splendid sandwich for lunch, and although he hated the insecurity of his bold new profession, he knew that he was genuinely in love.

The world for him had opened up and yet removed itself. It was not a real life he was living; it was some kind of fairy tale. Even now as he walked through the forest, he felt like some corporate Prince Less-Than-Charming walking with the Forest Queen. If she would only kiss him, it would turn Callahan into a frog and they would all live happily ever after. But Eric's Forest Queen seemed a little uneasy about her kingdom.

"Eric," the Forest Queen said, stopping in the middle of the trail and pulling his face toward her own. "This is Memorial Day weekend, but you know what they ought to call it? Memorable Day. You know why? 'Cause being with you has made it the most memorable day of my life." They both excused the corn imbedded in the odd statement to enjoy the sheer pleasure of the truth it held. They kissed softly, then once again ardently.

"Isletta," whispered Eric, "will you marry me?"

"Of course," she answered the question as instantly and impulsively as he had asked it. Both of them knew that they had not really known each other all that long, but both of them felt instinctively that this was right. It was the trees that made it right. Or was it the sunshine?

"Well then, when?" asked Eric.

"What's wrong with right now?" Isletta teased and then amended her coquettish contract with judgment. "No, anytime after June 18."

"That's exactly what I was going to say," Eric laughed. "How can we both be thinking the same things? Is our love made in heaven or what?"

"It is made in heaven, but the marriage will only seem like it if we whip Callahan before we get around to the 'I do's.'" Isletta paused. "I just want my patch of trees to be a promise of that which was and will be again if people can learn to be good stewards of our Earth."

Eric nodded agreement. "Speaking of promises, I want to get to Renée's grave before dark to put a wreath on it. Let's head down the mountain."

Isletta was yanked out of her happy mood. "Must you . . . so suddenly?"

"I'm afraid I must," Eric said, hoping she'd understand his need to commemorate his friend.

Isletta frowned, then scowled, and finally grinned. She kissed him, and they started back down the trail. Somewhat infirm of purpose, Eric dawdled as they walked along. The blackberries were already forming blossoms, and the woods seemed to sing with the life they always contained. The song was composed of chirps and whistles and the hum of breezes brushing the boughs of the leafy sentinel. The symphony had never stopped day or night for thousands of years. Isletta was right. Her few trees needed to stay to remind the world that forests were the gift of God, just as felled forests represent houses and other gifts of God.

Whenever Eric thought like this, he felt himself the friend of God. He felt himself more than Isletta's attorney; he felt like God's attorney. He liked the idea of representing the biggest firm in the universe. God didn't pay as well as Pacific Woods, but he had a way of making a man far richer than the Fortune 500 celebrants could ever guess.

"Penny for your thoughts?" said Isletta, bringing Eric back to the world at hand.

"I love you," he said.

They walked together silently. When they arrived at his car, they exchanged farewells briefly. Eric held her close, and they both smiled.

"Wait until after June 18, Romeo," she grinned.

"Yes indeed," he raised an eyebrow and then scowled. "I can't believe that I've just agreed to take myself out of circulation so cheerfully and all so suddenly on such a wonderful day."

"Yes, me too!" she smiled. "But then, these are—"

"Strange days in Seattle," Eric finished her sentence. "You want to go with me to pick out your ring?"

"No, I want this to be your gift to me—all from you. I love you."

Eric wanted their conversation to end on that note, but she handed him the sheaf of legal papers, saying, "You really can whip Callahan, can't you?"

"Indubitably, my dear!" Getting into the car, he kissed her, shut the door, and sped away, quite possibly the happiest man in Seattle.

He could tell by the way the long shadows flew past the car that he had stayed too long and been too beguiled by his new Eve. It was very late, but he was determined to leave the wreath he had gotten for Renée's grave at the cemetery before he went home. He wanted to honor his friend. He knew people at Pacific Woods thought they were more than friends, though now that he'd resigned, he had no idea what they were saying about him. But he didn't really care.

He finally drove into the cemetery, removed the wreath from his trunk, and walked toward her grave. There, driven into the soft dirt, was a stake with a white placard stapled to it. It read: "Here lies Renée, the girl exec. Where went the feminazi wreck?" Underneath these charming lines were some filthy epithets. Eric could barely read the placard at all because the sprinkler system had caused some of the ink to run and the light of day was too far gone.

Angrily, he pulled the stake out of the earth, determined to throw it away, but then changed his mind. He laid the wreath on Renée's grave and stood over the earth, lost in thought for a good while. He thought of how Renée had given herself so wholeheartedly to building up Pacific Woods—a machine that now wiped her from its memory banks and moved on.

Then two ideas struck Eric. The first was that whoever was responsible for the killings might be the same person who had written the card staked over Renée's grave. This thought put his feet in motion. He headed back to the car, determined to call Inspector Jarvis and tell him about the cardboard sign that he still held in his hand. In fact, he would do better than that—he would give him the sign so Jarvis could check the handwriting for clues.

The second thought was that he was being watched. Fear rose in his throat, compounded by his being in a graveyard at the approach of night. He cast one last look at Renée's grave and hurried toward his car. Was there something moving in the bushes?

He quickened his pace. The bushes seemed to rustle more violently. He broke into a run, his athletic hobbies of running and hiking helping him outdistance who- or whatever was running in the bushes beside the car. He had to get to the car before the shadowy things in the shrubbery got there. Even as he ran, he fumbled in his pocket for the key pad that unlocked his car. He located it and pressed the Unlock button. The lock clicked open two strides before he reached the car. He lifted the latch and pulled the door open, vaulting into the car and locking the door behind him.

Just as he inserted the key in the ignition, a huge spheroid of fur flew over the front of the car and bolted into the windshield. The sheer terror of the moment might have caused Eric to fumble with the keys had they not already been inserted in the ignition. But they were in. He managed to twist the key, and the car's motor jumped to life, sending the avenging animal into a frenzy of scraping and clawing at the glass. The mouth of the animal seemed all engulfing to Eric. His terror was so great that he fumbled with the controls, inadvertently switching on the windshield wipers that pushed weakly at the demon on the hood of his car. It snarled and bit away the windshield wiper, throwing it aside with one toss of its ugly head. The giant feet of the brute were like talons. Eric finally fumbled for the headlight lever, switching it on so he could see in front of the car. The path was clear. He moved the shift lever to drive just as someone arrived at the side of his car. A huge man grabbed the handle of the door.

Suddenly the car rocked sideways. The man alongside his car was trying to pull the car door open. Eric knew the flimsy door lock would not last long. The next few seconds passed like hours. He heard a cracking sound as the door lock gave way. The door flew open, and the mammoth hand reached in to grab him. He released the hand brake and stomped down on the accelerator. He felt the car lurch forward and saw the hand retract. The sudden thrust of the moving auto spun the beast from the hood. The animal fell to one side of the car.

He glanced in the rearview mirror as he sped away. The man who had all but succeeded in breaking into his car had been thrown to the ground by the lurch of the car and was staggering to stand. Then Eric focused on the road and putting as much distance between himself and the man and his feral demon as he could. It was only after Eric realized that he was free that he saw he had somehow managed to get into the car with the white placard still in his hand. The stake had been dislodged in his furious dash to safety, but the card was still intact.

As he finally moved into the heavy holiday night traffic of the interstate, he cursed himself for not bringing his cell phone with him. *Why would I need my cell today?* he mocked himself. *I'm meeting Isletta in the woods where there's no signal, and she doesn't have a phone anyway. Stupid! Stupid!* He calmed his thoughts, realizing he needed to think of a spot where he could get to a pay phone and call Jarvis. He left the 405 in Bellevue and came off the exit ramp to a stop sign. The neon plastic sign of My Kind lounge greeted him. He remembered Renée had gone there often after work. It would definitely have a phone. He pulled into the parking lot.

Just inside the door of the lounge, he used the pay phone and called Information and then the Seattle police. Having obtained Jarvis's pager, he called him and hung up the receiver of the pay phone and waited. In less than a minute, the phone rang.

"Hello," Eric said. "This is Eric Compton."

"Jarvis, here," said Gary.

"Listen, Inspector, something has happened that you ought to know about. You said to call if anything came along that might help crack the case. Well, something has happened, and I think I might have a sample of what could be the handwriting of the murderer. Can I bring it to your office?"

"No, that might take too long. Where are you? Do you have it with you?"

"I'm at My Kind lounge off the 405 in Bellevue. And yes, I have it with me."

"Well, stay there and wait for me. And for Pete's sake, don't leave that lounge. Do you hear?"

"Well, yeah, I guess so, but what's the big deal?"

"Look, Mr. Compton, it was you who first told me of the lounge. That lounge is the one thing that all of the murder victims have in common. Every one of them was murdered after they left that lounge. Do not leave, and don't go outside till I get there." The inspector was insistent.

"OK," Eric said, "I'll just go out to the car and get the placard that has the handwriting on it, and I'll wait right here."

"No, please! Do not go out to your car! You wait right there. I'll be there in ten minutes, and we'll go out to the car together. I'm telling you, this guy acts fast, and it's all over quickly. Stay in the lounge. I'll be right there."

"Oh, all right!" Eric hung up. Initially resenting Jarvis's protective terms, Eric then thought of his near-brush with the killer and his huge dog. He decided that maybe the inspector's words were worth their counsel.

He took a chair at a lonely table and ordered a Mai Tai. He hadn't been there long when a stranger entered and walked to the bar to order a drink. The man looked his way, but the light was too scant to allow Eric to really get a good look at him. Somehow he seemed familiar, but Eric couldn't place him. After Eric nursed his Mai Tai for another five minutes, the man suddenly stood and left. Eric would have thought no more about it, except that his waiter, coming over to see if Eric wanted anything further, grumbled about the departing stranger.

"That man's a shrink! The last couple of times he's been in, he's left his business cards with his tip. Here, you can have it." The waiter flipped the business card to Eric. "You may need a psychiatrist someday. Though if he's as cheap with advice as he is with tips, I may not be doing you a favor."

Eric stared at the card then stuck it in his pocket, thanking the waiter and indicating he was fine with his drink. A few minutes later, Gary Jarvis arrived.

"Am I glad to see you," Eric sighed, then launched into an account of the attack at the cemetery and the placard. After awhile, they walked outside to Eric's car to retrieve the placard. Unfortunately, the window had been smashed on the passenger side, and the placard was gone. Shards of glass covered the inside of the car. Eric was suddenly overwhelmed with fear.

"If there is anywhere you can go tonight besides home," Gary said, "I suggest you do. Did you see anyone in the bar who might have done this?"

"No one. There was no one in the bar except me. Oh, and another man. He came in shortly after I did. He only stayed five or ten minutes and then walked out. The waiter said he comes in every once in awhile to ogle the merchandise. Says he's a psychiatrist. The last couple of times he's come in, he's left one of his business cards with his tip. For some reason the waiter gave me the shrink's card. Here." He passed the card to Gary.

Gary briefly examined it then stashed it in his pocket nonchalantly, though his face had lit up. He repeated his warning: "Do not go to your home tonight. Your life may be in danger."

Eric realized the hour was late. He had no regular job now, so there was no reason he had to go home. "All right," he replied. "I'll find a budget hotel and stay there for the night. But I can't afford to do this more than a few days. My bank statement looks like the national debt. Besides, tomorrow I'll have to get some personal things and a change of clothes or two if I keep moving around."

"That may be all it takes," said Gary. "I'm getting close to this guy. Even without the handwriting sample, I'm very close. I expect to crack it soon, but stay hidden until I do. Check in with me every time you change hotels and tell me where you are. You still have my phone number?"

Eric nodded. They shook hands. Jarvis watched Eric get in the car and brush some of the big shards of glass to one side. Fortunately, Isletta's sheaf of legal papers were still in the seat. He used them like a giant whisk to clear the glass from his seat.

They both drove off in their cars. Eric felt a chill caused by the damp night air. It was beginning to rain a little. The broken window would have to be covered with plastic. He would take care of that when he checked into the Royal Scot Motel; surely they would have an extra laundry bag to close the gap between the top of the car door and the metal jamb. He got a little jumpy when he noticed a pair of headlights in his rearview mirror, but when he turned onto the 405, they continued straight ahead. He felt better.

He thought of Isletta. In spite of his near miss with a killer and his brute, he still managed to smile. Somehow, inside the dull throb of his head, he managed to bless the day. It had been a long one, but its good fortune made him too rich to be impoverished by Seattle's night stalker. He only prayed that Jarvis was as close to cracking the case as he thought he was. Perhaps the city's long nightmare at last could come to an end.

CHAPTER 28

Early Memorial Day morning, the jangling of the telephone jarred Gary Jarvis awake. His hand fished around for the receiver on the nightstand, knocking over an empty soda can and his key ring before finding the telephone. "Hello!" he croaked into the ear-end before he got it turned rightside up.

"Hello, honey, I'm sorry to wake you up, but it was the only time that I had to call you."

His mind was groggy, so it took him awhile to realize who had just called him "honey."

"Melody?" he ventured.

"Yes, Gary."

"Melody . . . I . . . I . . ." Gary found himself stammering. It was partly the shock of hearing her voice after more than a year of no communication. "Honey," he said and then stopped. He couldn't believe that he had called her that, but somehow it seemed all right. "I mean, Melody, I—"

"Gary, I like the sound of it. Call me 'honey' whenever you wish. Not that I deserve it. I know I haven't treated you very nicely, and I'm sorry."

It was so early in the morning that Jarvis wondered if he could be imagining this. Surely he had not just heard his ex-wife call him "honey." He pushed some more words through the wires. "Melody, I got back your alimony check. I'll send it back, if . . ."

"No, please, Gary, you keep it. I don't need anything except you."

"Melody, this has to be a dream. It's a good dream! It's a dream that I have dreamed every night since the day I last saw you in court. Don't take it from me; I don't think I could stand it twice. Tell me you wanna come home, and I'll be unbelievably happy."

"I do want to come home, honey. Oh, Gary, if I do, I mean when I do, will you let me in? I need you. I want to come home!" She sounded as though she were about to break into tears.

"Melody, what has happened? What can have turned you so around? I've prayed for this for months now. I prayed that you would call me, and then when your note actually came, I knew there was a God in heaven. But what happened?"

"I met an old priest, Gary. He told me, in the kindest words that you can imagine, that I had broken my wedding promise to love you forever and to stick by you in the good times and the bad times. He told me that I have been too much in charge of my life and that I needed a new center. Even as he spoke to me, I realized that I have loved you too conditionally."

"Conditionally?"

"You know I promised that I would leave you if you didn't give up your job at the SPD. You don't have to quit the SPD."

"I don't? You'll come back even if I'm a cop?"

"Right. Oh, Gary, I have been the world's most stupid and demanding dope. I promised you for better or for worse, in sickness and in health, for richer or for poorer. Then the moment I got you, I tried putting some conditions on all that. But don't you see, this old priest opened my eyes and let me see my hypocrisy. He told me that I must give myself to you with no strings attached. I have done just that! I've quit tying myself all up in little definitions of what I once called the ideal marriage. I want to come home, my darling. I beg you to forgive me."

Gary Jarvis owned the world. All he really wanted was to grab Melody and hold her. He wanted to kiss her and hang on to her forever. He wanted to stand somewhere in a crowded square and bless the glorious circumstances that had befallen him. He wanted to shout praises to the wisdom of old priests.

"Melody, all is forgiven, but who am I to forgive? It is my own life and loving that's been so faulty."

"Gary, are you sure? Gary, Gary, are you there?"

"Yes, yes," he all but shouted. "Yes, I'm trying to take all of this in at once. It's nearly overwhelming. Yes, Melody, please come home . . . now? Today?"

"I want to come home to stay but only after the June 18 rally. But until then you can come up here, and we can be together as often as we like. Still, as for setting up a new home life, it must wait until after the rally. There's going to be thousands of people in these woods, Gary, and I can't help but feel that all of this will be some kind of celebration that none of us will ever forget. As soon as it's over, I'm coming home—do you mind the wait?"

"Of course I mind the wait, but I can stand it all now. Just knowing that we're going to be man and . . ." Gary paused. "We'll have to be remarried, won't we?"

"Yes, I guess we will. But this time I'm going to be a different person. You'll see."

"I'm going to be a different person, too, Melody." He paused a moment and then added, "Will I be able to see you? I've got to drive past the Callahan Grove on my way up the mountain as soon as they get the washout on the road repaired." The events of the previous trip some three weeks earlier came rushing back into his mind. He remembered getting home late from that awful experience of nearly driving off the mountain. He had thought of little on the way back home except for the dowdy old man and the wolf that had saved his life. "Melody, I was coming up the road to the Callahan Grove early in May in the driving rain—"

"That was some storm wasn't it?" she interrupted.

"It sure was, and there was a terrible washout in the road. I almost drove off into the gully. I would have been lost except that, when I came to that gully, I saw an old man and a wolf standing squarely in the middle of the road. At first I thought I'd hit them. I'd have sworn it to be true, Melody, except that, when I brought the car to a stop, I could find no trace of them. What I did find was a mountain washout that would have taken my life. I had to turn around without find-ing the person I was looking for."

"Well, who in the world were you looking for here in this wilderness?"

"Babe, I think I have a solid lead on the wolf killings. In fact, I may know who it is. I believe it's a Seattle psychia-trist named Shapiro. Further, I believe his wife may be his accomplice in this."

"Not Rhonda Shapiro?"

"Well, yes. Do you know her?"

"Yes, as a matter of fact, I do. She's a wonderful person." Melody told Gary of how the Gaians had brought them together. She went on to say how much Rhonda had come to mean to her. But Gary could not be turned from his need to warn his wife of Rhonda's treachery.

"Look, Melody, darling, stay away from her, do you hear? I believe that she's dangerous and may be harboring a very dangerous animal of some sort—a huge wolf."

"You mean Kinta?"

"Yes, Kinta. You sound as if you've seen him."

"Yes, of course I have. I met him up here too. Gary, dar-ling, Rhonda walks with that wolf every day. He's a beauti-ful animal. She brings him to the Gaian campsite regularly."

"Melody, please, I beg you. Don't go near that woman or that animal. They are vicious and dangerous."

"Nonsense, honey! I've petted him several times and fed him out of my hand. If you throw a stick for him, he'll fetch it."

Gary was horrified. "Please, Melody, he's fetched the throats out of four people now."

"No, Gary! Not possible." Melody sounded so sure of herself, and yet it made the hair on Gary's neck stand up just thinking about the danger to which she was likely subjecting herself.

"Melody, I tell you, I think the Shapiros have trained the wolf to do a lot more than fetch sticks. The evidence is stacked against them. Most of the murders have occurred in their area of the city, and we've found enough wolf hair among the victims that it leaves little doubt in my mind that Kinta, or whatever his name is, is the weapon. I say 'weapon' because Kinta has been guided to the scene of the murders by someone with a clear prejudice against businesswomen. There can be no other explanation."

Melody suddenly changed the topic. "You know the old man I told you about? I sat there pinching myself to believe that this thin old relic in clerical rags could actually be a priest."

Gary wasn't sure who Melody's old priest was, but he found the stranger's counsel coming to dwell at the heart of their marriage. But in his heart, he knew that Melody was wrong about the psychiatrist and his wife. He sounded forth the warning one more time. "Just the same, you travel a wide path around Mrs. Shapiro and . . ."

"Kinta?"

"Yes, Kinta."

"OK, honey, but I rode down here to use the pay phone with Rhonda Shapiro, and whether you're right about her husband or not, Rhonda is no killer. I tell you she's a very gentle, authentic person. Gary, there are a lot of people waiting in line behind me to use this phone, so I'll have to go for now."

"OK. Wait, how did you get down the road? It was still washed out when I inquired about it last week. The only reason I haven't been up to question your friend Rhonda is that the road has been impassable. I'm considering getting the police helicopter to bring me up if the road hasn't been fixed."

"They've repaired a bit of it now. They have cut out a new road in the soft bank with a bulldozer. By hugging the mountain side of the road, you can squeeze through the constriction one lane at a time."

"Well then, maybe I can see you when I come up to question Rhonda Shapiro."

"Oh, that would be wonderful! I want to see you so badly."

"Great! In the meantime watch yourself when you're around that woman. Do you hear me, Melody?"

"Yes, but I tell you I'm in no danger."

"Just the same—"

"OK, I promise."

They hung up. Gary Jarvis sprang out of bed. Cracking the case, as he had promised Eric Compton he would do, would mandate only two final interrogations. The first was Mrs. Shapiro. A plus for this interrogation would mean that he might be able to see Melody on his way back from the Shapiro cabin. It had rained almost all night, but from what Melody had told him, he felt sure that the washout in the road had been made passable.

Two hours later, he found himself at the same washout that had nearly taken his life earlier in the month. He edged his car around the orange-striped barrels that had been put up as a barricade. He hugged the inside of the mountain and squeezed by the horrible chasm that had been created when the asphalt had dissolved in the torrent of rushing water. In less than fifteen minutes he found himself at the Shapiro cabin.

The Cherokee was parked in the drive and wedged in between a tree and the side of the cabin. He knew it could not have been there more than two or three hours because Mrs. Shapiro and Melody had just been down to Carnation. This was all a kind of confirmation to the case his mind had constructed, for he felt sure that Mrs. Shapiro had often driven the wolf down to the city where her husband had taken it to call on those he had met at My Kind lounge.

He got out of his car and walked up to the cabin door. He could hear a radio playing inside. A golden oldie was playing. It was Johnny Mathis singing "Chances Are."

Jarvis knocked, and the door of the cabin finally opened.

"Yes," said Rhonda warily, holding the pistol behind her back. "Can I help you?"

"Are you Mrs. Shapiro?"

"I am. And you are?"

"I'm Gary Jarvis, Seattle Police Department."

Rhonda didn't relax, but she did put the pistol down on a side table behind her. "And you've come for Kinta, I suppose?" she asked, hoping he'd say no.

"Well . . . I . . . no . . . not exactly," Gary replied. To be truthful, the mild composure of the woman ate into his logic. All of a sudden, he wasn't sure why he had come.

"Mrs. Shapiro, when was the last time you saw your husband?"

"He came up here three weeks ago, I guess. Why?"

"Where's Kinta?"

"I don't know. He's out and about in the woods. He'll be back before long."

"And when was the last time that Kinta left this mountain? When was the last time he was in Seattle?"

"I've been up here for six weeks. I have talked nearly every day with Paul, but both of us believe that Kinta's innocence merits the pain we feel in not seeing each other very often. So I . . . no, we . . . chose for me to go on living up here. Kinta's been with me the whole time."

"He's not been back into the city a single time since then?"

"No, certainly not."

"If you don't mind me asking you, Mrs. Shapiro, why did you bring the wolf up here in the first place?"

Rhonda's lip quivered as she replied, "I knew you'd come and take him away. I knew that the animal rights people or the Humane Society or both would come and take him from me. I brought him up here because I couldn't stand the thought of them taking him away. I know that they would put him to sleep for crimes he has not committed. Mr. Jarvis, Kinta is not the killer you're looking for. You're not going to take him away, are you?"

"No, not at the moment, Mrs. Shapiro."

"Oh, thank the Lord, you believe me!"

"No, it's that I don't arrest and handcuff dogs. But, Mrs. Shapiro, I still think you have a problem—a very big problem. Sunday night, I believe your husband was in a cocktail lounge in Bellevue, and I believe that both your husband and Kinta tried to attack and kill a Seattle attorney just last night."

Rhonda looked at the policeman, incredulous.

"I've been on Paul's trail since Renée Thomkins' murder," he began. "All of the serial killings have occurred within a few miles of your home. Further, in the case of two of those murders, we have found wolf hair in the victim's wounds and wolf feces in the yard or near the scene of the crime. I'm sorry, Mrs. Shapiro, but Paul and Kinta are the only reasonable choices for these horrible crimes. To put it bluntly, Kinta kills where Paul says, 'Sic 'em, boy!' I believe Paul has some kind of anti-feminist complex. He is locating those female executives with his frequent visits to My Kind lounge. Then he follows them home and . . . well, you know the rest."

Rhonda was aghast at the precisely logical way Inspector Jarvis was arriving at perfectly illogical conclusions about her husband.

"Further, all of the victims have one thing in common. They all frequented and indeed spent some of their last night alive at the same bar in Bellevue. Now, I must ask you, Mrs. Shapiro, is this your husband's business card?" He extended to her the business card he had received from Eric Compton. Rhonda took it from him, gave it a hasty inspection, and handed it back.

"Of course, it's Paul's card," she said.

"Do you know that the last three times he has been in the Bellevue lounge where all of the victims spent some of their final moments, he has left one of these cards with his tip?"

Rhonda was thunderstruck.

They stood on the cabin's front deck, not speaking for a few minutes while Rhonda attempted to mentally sort out this preposterous situation. Finally, Rhonda broke the silence: "But why, if Paul is the killer, would he be so obvious as to leave his card?"

"I don't expect you to understand this, Mrs. Shapiro, but many serial killers, with each successive crime, become more and more proud of their covert success and increasingly want others to know how clever they have been—how wonderfully successful they have been in covering their tracks."

"Are you saying that they actually want to be discovered?"

"Yes, something like that. They want to be openly proud of themselves. They want to be able to hear people gasp at their villainy while they stick out their chests and acknowledge what they've done."

"No, no, no! Paul could never do that!"

"Now simmer down, Mrs. Shapiro. That's exactly what all of Jeffrey Dahmer's neighbors said. Remember, the Boston Strangler was just the 'nice man' next door. The truth is that Paul and Kinta are responsible for this. Paul is a psychiatrist, and psychiatrists are complex people."

"No, Kinta was locked up during the first two killings."

"Look, Mrs. Shapiro, I saw the broken window in the shed where you first kept Kinta. Paul himself told me that Kinta must have used the broken window as an escape. Besides, there were broken windows at all of the scenes of crime.

"In the meantime, Mrs. Shapiro, I would ask you not to contact your husband. I hope to question him further and perhaps get a warrant for his detainment. Right now, almost every piece of evidence that I have been able to dredge up increasingly makes your husband appear to be guilty of one of the worst strings of serial crimes ever in the Northwest."

Rhonda was gravely quiet now as she listened. It was odd that she had brought Kinta up to the cabin to hide him from the Humane Society. Now, in an odd reversal of fortunes, she wished that she could hide Paul from the Seattle police.

The detective interrupted her reverie with another question. "You don't know of a second wolf or dog that your husband might have been keeping?"

"No, of course not. He didn't even want me to have one. He was afraid of Kinta. He wanted me to turn him over to the authorities. We quarreled over that. I cannot believe that he could be keeping another animal anywhere."

"Where is Kinta now?" asked Jarvis insistently.

"I have no idea," admitted Rhonda.

"Then he could even now be with your husband!"

"No," insisted Rhonda, "he's roving in the woods nearby!"

The inspector knew that he was pushing her too hard. Jarvis had suddenly come to believe that Rhonda knew nothing. For the first time in his string of suspicions, he genuinely felt that she must be innocent of her husband's fearful undertakings. But he also knew that all the hard evidence of the case increasingly pointed to the Seattle psychiatrist—a man she had obviously trusted and even married but whose darker side she had never really known.

He felt sorry for her. "Mrs. Shapiro, if I were you, I would stay out of Seattle until the investigation is over. And above all, please make no attempt to call your husband. At this point I would consider it an obstruction of justice. Good-bye, Mrs. Shapiro."

"Yes, well, good-bye to you too," replied Rhonda.

Gary got into his car and drove away, suddenly realizing that in giving her the order not to contact her husband, he had really offered her a suggestion.

No sooner was Jarvis out of sight than she began to dress for her trip down to the telephone at the bottom of the mountain. She only hoped she could get to Paul in time.

CHAPTER 29

At the same time Inspector Jarvis was at the Shapiro cabin, Paul Shapiro was meeting Della at the clinic. Della had arrived first and made coffee. When Paul arrive, she was sitting at her desk and looked away from him as if to hide her face. When she finally faced him directly, Paul was horrified to see that the entire left side of her face was bruised yellow and blue. Further, the dark black stitches across her cheekbone told that she had spent some time in the emergency room. He was so moved by her injured face that he reached out instinctively and patted her hand.

"What happened, Della?" he asked.

She teared up and cradled her face in her hands. He waited for her to compose herself.

In the next few moments Della told him everything, only struggling to speak when she mentioned the name of Levi Twist. She told him of the erratic mood swings that now characterized her once predictable and gentle friend. She told him of the wedding date, the fake ring, and her inadvertent discovery of the dog Levi was keeping. She also told him of her visit to Levi's cabin and of the shed and the dog run behind it. She explained to him exactly the roads to take to get there. She told him of her night with Levi and of her hair-raising escape after he had gotten physical with her.

As she related her experiences, she seemed to calm down a bit. "Paul," she confessed with her head down as though she could barely stand the weight of her own folly, "I can't believe that he deceived me. I—"

"But, Della, how could you help that? Everyone in the office envied you. To them Levi was the ideal catch. He was attentive and kind and faithful, rich and powerful."

"Paul, believe me, he is none of those things. He was not attentive. You can look at my stitches and tell he wasn't kind. Not only that, but I don't believe he was faithful either. In his closet was a pink nightgown that wasn't mine. He's obviously had someone up to sleep with him. Here I am, pregnant with his child, and he's got someone else's nightgown hanging in his closet with his Halloween costume."

"His what?" asked the psychiatrist.

"His Halloween costume. He has this old Halloween outfit that he wore to a costume party last fall . . . I just don't know him anymore. Actually, I never knew him; I only thought I did. Paul, you specialize in crazy people. What's wrong with a woman who loves a man that on one day a year dresses up like Richard Nixon and the other 364 days has no idea who he is."

"Della, it's not your fault. You were taken in. Anybody can be deceived." Paul consoled Della while a niggling thought ate at him. *Richard Nixon . . . what about Nixon?*

"Excuse me, what's the ex-president got to do with all this?"

"Ex-president?" Della was confused.

"Nixon—why'd you bring him up?"

"I didn't, did I? Oh, you mean when I said Levi dressed up like Nixon—it's nothing. It was just his Halloween costume, that's all."

"You mean the mask in the closet with the pink nightgown?

"Yes," Della said. "It was one of those big rubber-head masks that you buy in specialty shops . . . and a black suit."

The color drained from Paul's face. "Oh no!" was all he said.

Della stared at him.

"Della," Paul began, noticing her bewilderment, "you could be in very grave danger. If indeed Levi and his dog, Daimon, are killers, this information must be turned over to the police."

"Paul, I can't do it. In the first place, I'm not sure that it is Levi. You know his reputation around Seattle. Everybody adores him. Nobody would believe him capable of those kinds of crimes. To accuse a man of his stature would invite lawsuits by a whole battery of his attorneys. No, Levi is many things, but he's not a serial killer. I just couldn't go to the police . . . at least not yet. I'm all mixed up." She paused again. "If the police got there and he wasn't there, he might try to come after me again. I . . . I can't think straight, Paul. I . . . ." She broke into tears once again but soon softly repeated the words, "I still don't think he's a serial killer."

"That's what everybody said about Albert DeSalvo."

"Who?"

"The Boston Strangler."

"Paul," Della was emotionally in tatters. "I want a few days off work. I've got a couple of weeks of unused vacation. I don't want to come back to work till my face gets somewhat back to normal. I may look for a new apartment today. I want to move somewhere else and start a new life. I want an apartment with two bedrooms, one of which I'll convert to a nursery when the time comes."

"It looks like you've made up your mind to keep the baby."

"Paul, I want this child. I'm going to be a mother. I may never be a wife, but I will definitely be a mother. I'm not going to let my sexual irresponsibility punish the child, born or unborn. I don't think I've ever really believed in abortion."

"Very well, Della. Have a much-needed vacation, but be careful. Levi will probably come around if only to hassle you."

"I've thought of that already. I'm going to change apartments in the next few days. Hopefully, Levi won't try to contact me before then. I'll call you when I get a new phone and address. I want to keep it all unlisted, so keep it to yourself."

They talked a bit more, then Della got up to leave. Through the clinic window, Paul watched her get in her car and drive away. He poured himself another cup of coffee. While it cooled, he thought about Levi and Richard Nixon. Levi Twist, his old patient—his antifeminist, Prozac-demanding neurotic—was a sociopath as well. He took a sip of his coffee and shuddered when he remembered that the president and CEO of Pacific Woods made house calls. He shuddered once again, realizing that Levi knew his wife's name at the time of their last appointment. Richard Nixon had come to their home! It had to be Levi! He couldn't bring himself to tell Della of the connection that she had inadvertently made him aware of. She was carrying enough.

While he turned the facts over in his mind, his pocket pager beeped. He pulled it out and clicked the response button. It was the number of the pay phone Rhonda used to call him. He rose quickly. Whenever she called, he promptly returned her calls, knowing she would not stay at the pay phone for long. He quickly pulled out his cell phone and dialed the number on his beeper. It rang only once then he heard Rhonda say, "Hello?"

"Hi, what's up?"

"Paul, were you in a gay lounge last night?"

"Yeah, sure. I had a few drinks with this big good-looking greaser named Harry. He had a bristly wart on his nose, but he was some dancer."

"Look, Pauly, this is serious."

"Well, what kind of question is that?"

"Paul, where are you?"

"I'm calling from the clinic. I just met with Della. I'll tell you all about it."

"The clinic? Great! Paul, don't go home. Jarvis was here, and he's got a case on you a mile long. He believes that you and Kinta were responsible for the wolf killings."

"What? Are you sure?"

"Paul, Inspector Jarvis just left here. In his mind he has built what he believes is an airtight case. He made it all sound so logical I'm convinced he means to arrest you for murder as soon as he picks up the warrant."

"Ronnie, if he just left there, he won't be back to the city for a couple of hours. I'm going to find someplace to hide out. I've got to check out a few things, but I think I know who your assailant is. And, Rhonda, dig this: the guy also is keeping a dog who may be responsible for the serial killings."

"Paul, go to the police with this. You're not a cop and shouldn't try to be a hero."

"Ronnie, you've already said that the police are laying for me. If I go to the police, they'll lock me up and the killer will still be free."

"Whatever you do, be careful," she said. "I love you, Pauly."

"I love you even more, Ronnie," he said.

"Impossible!" she said. They both hung up.

To support himself, he took all the money out of petty cash. He also made a mental note to withdraw several hundred dollars from three or four ATMs just to avoid leaving a trail to his whereabouts.

He happened to see a newspaper on the table outside his office. He picked it up, drawn by the photos and headline: "Wolf Killer." There were pictures of all the previous victims. The reporting included the mention of wolf hair and feces found in the vicinity of Renée Thomkins' house. The newspaper report included a statement by Gary Jarvis that the SPD believes that the wolf must belong to someone in the Seattle area who bears a deep complicity in the killings.

Paul picked up the paper and was walking toward the exit when he passed by the clinic cafeteria. He halted at the sound of two familiar voices.

"You know, Father Peter, I saw this priest in a *Phantom of the Opera* sweatshirt—only it was an old sweatshirt, the kind you buy in secondhand clothing stores. There's something else I need to tell you, but I can't think what. This medicine I'm on takes the mind right out of my head," said Emma Silone.

It was inevitable that Emma and Father Peter would meet. Paul knew that Father Peter had returned to the hospital and that Emma had been admitted, but he didn't know they were now friends. Paul hovered in the hallway, hidden by a partition that framed the nook where the old priest and his paranoid friend sat. Emma Silone and Father Peter talked, and Paul listened to their psychotic conversation. He felt a bit guilty eavesdropping on their conversation, but he found it immensely entertaining.

"Know what, Emma? I see old angels from time to time."

"You too? I've seen flocks of them at times, but I've never got to meet one personally. I would sure like to meet an angel personally."

"Why, Emma, you're such an angel, it would be redundant for you to meet an angel." Paul could hear her giggling at the priest's teasings.

"Oh, Father, I only wish my Harvey would say things like that. He's been trying to make an angel out of me by putting cyanide in my food." She lowered her voice and whispered so low that Paul could barely hear her, "You know he's been trying to kill me."

"Have you told anybody about this?"

"Just my psychiatrist, Dr. Shapiro. He thinks I'm crazy. That's why I'm here. When I told him I saw an old angel in a *Phantom of the Opera* sweatshirt, he instantly admitted me into this place. You know, these psychiatrists want you to tell them everything you believe, and when you do, they lock you up."

Paul felt rather ashamed to hear the case stated from her viewpoint. Still, he did not allow his remorse to interrupt his intrigue.

"You know, Father," Emma went on, "I think that's why more people turn first to priests for help. If you tell your priest you see an angel, he tells you to make a novena. If you tell a psychiatrist, he locks you up. Anyway, I know my Harvey wishes that the wolf murders could happen to me. Know what? I don't think the wolf murders are done by a wolf at all. At least the wolf isn't the whole story. I think that there is a very strong man who knocks down the door of some poor soul's apartment and then breaks the glass. This killer, who controls the dog, has got to be very strong. I think these murders are being done by a man with very strong hands—strong enough to rip and tear those doors and windows apart. I'll bet the dog owner is either an Arab terrorist or a Vietnam War veteran."

"What makes you say that, Emma?"

"Well . . ." she paused, "Did you ever see any of them Bette Davis horror movies, like *Whatever Happened to Baby Jane?*"

"No," answered the priest.

"Well, that's not important now. What is important is that Harvey is putting cyanide in my Big Macs. No, wait,

Harvey's not important—he's never been important. I can't find the end of the conversation. It's that awful medicine. It ruins a good mind." Emma started to cry, and the priest reached out to console her.

"Dear Emma, daughter of Jesus, take your time. Now, we were talking about the wolf murders, and you were asking me if I ever saw any old Bette Davis horror movies and I—"

"Oh yes, now that's where I went wrong. I meant Peter Lorre movies. Did you ever see any Peter Lorre movies?"

"No, never."

"Well, in this one called *The Beast with Five Fingers*, there was this hand that had been chopped off that kept running around just like Thing on *The Addams' Family*. It was a very strong hand, and it kept choking people. It would hop right on their pillow and choke them to death, while the poor things quivered and shook in their beds." Emma made a fairly authentic choking noise and continued. "And . . . oh, that's what Harvey would like to do to me." She started to cry again.

"Now, now, Emma, don't lose your way. What about the hand?"

"Well, everybody thought some strangler was going around choking people, but it wasn't a strangler at all, it was just a free hand."

"Well, it never hurts to have a free hand." The old priest laughed at his own, poor double entendre. It was the first time that Paul had ever heard him laugh. Emma, seeing nothing funny in his pun, ignored him.

"So here in this city is a someone with strong hands going around breaking in doors and windows with his dog."

"But what about the wolf hair and poo?"

"So he breaks down the doors, and then he sends in his dog to tear their throats out, and then he throws down a little glob of wolf doo-doo. Then everybody thinks it's a wolf, just like everybody thought it was a strangler and not a hand in *The Beast with Five Fingers*." Emma wasn't making a very sound comparison, and she knew it. "This doesn't make sense does it, Father?"

"Well, Emma, honey, if it doesn't, it's the medicine, I'm sure," the priest consoled.

"Well, on the body of that young accountant, they even found a few wolf hairs. But you know, Father, wolf hairs are all circumstantial. Any psycho could pull hairs out of a nice little poodle, and then we'd all be talking about the Eastside poodle killer."

"But Emma, where would a dog killer get wolf doo-doo? The State Wildlife Bureau says there are fewer than ten wolves in the whole state, so where would a killer get it?"

"You can always find it," Emma said, unconsciously oversimplifying the priest's very strategic question.

Still, when Emma Silone made her poodle observation, something inside Paul's mind clicked. If you wanted to incriminate an innocent wolf, where could you come up with the necessary wolf hair to plant as evidence? He thought of the Washington Wildlife Museum and made a mental note to check it out.

"Yes," Emma Silone went on, "on the last victim they found only wolf hairs but . . ."

"No wolf doo-doo?" asked Father Peter.

"The papers didn't say . . . or did they? Yes, I think maybe in the yard."

"How nice. The killer was housebroken," quipped the priest.

Emma neither laughed nor gave any indication that she thought the priest was funny. "Well now, don't you think that this is all a little odd?" she said.

"What?" asked the priest.

"Well, they've all been killed the same violent way, but only in the last two killings has there been anything that would link the murders to a wolf."

"You know, that's right," the priest responded. "You know, Emma, you have a very analytical mind. That was a good insight about the wolf droppings."

Paul, remembering that he didn't have much time to escape Inspector Jarvis, started down the hallway again, forgoing the rest of the interesting conversation. He had swiped Levi's home address from Della's files and intended to snoop around the Twist mansion while Levi was at work.

As he drove to Levi's, he thought about what Della had told him about Levi's dog. Maybe, though he hated admitting it, Emma was right about the killer being strong and deliberately planting wolf hair and excrement. As he thought of Emma's words, he smiled.

Within thirty minutes, Paul found himself at Levi's huge river estate. He decided to take a chance and try to find a way in. He went around to the rear of the house. The back door was locked. He tried unlocking the bolt with a credit card, but it didn't work. Frustrated, he decided on a more forceful entry. He kicked the door open, splintering the inside jamb. He was grateful there was no alarm on the door.

Apparently, no one was at home, so he walked in and pushed the door shut behind him. The inner rooms were huge and filled with big game. He had never seen such a large library with so many mirrors and so many animal heads sticking out all over the walls. He rifled through the bureau drawers and discovered stacks of pornography in each one. In a closet he found a hunting rifle and several boxes of shells. There was also an old military uniform, and hanging on the back side of the closet door was a picture of Levi in a military uniform, apparently taken somewhere in Vietnam. *Vietnam!* Emma Silone came to mind.

When he scoured the closet shelves, eventually opening a box that had been placed high on a shelf, eight newspapers were inside. Each of them had front-page pictures of the various victims of the recent murders.

In a short time he had put everything back in place and started for the door. For all her paranoia, he thought, Emma Silone had been right about two things. He was a Vietnam vet, and there was every possibility that Levi might be planting the clues to mislead the police. Clues! He should be looking for those clues. He turned back into the house. He went hastily through the closet again. Nothing. He looked under the bed. Nothing. Where would one keep fecal matter? Ah! He went to the refrigerator in the kitchen and opened the door. Nothing! Wine, whiskey, cold cuts. No, wait a minute. He pulled down the little blue celluloid door that snapped shut over the cheese compartment.

There he found one baggie filled with what appeared to be, in Emma Silone's words, doo-doo. *Merciful God,* thought Paul Shapiro, *Emma is right.* If Levi was responsible, he was deliberately planting clues that would point the guilt toward Kinta and the Shapiros. But why? He knew his former client did not like him, but would he take his personal revenge this far? Then Paul thought of Levi's abuse of Della. Of course, his revenge knew no limits. If Rhonda was right, it must have been Levi who had first shot Kinta in the Lee West Construction Camp. Levi Twist was a monster capable of anything.

He closed the refrigerator door and quickly fled. He pulled what was left of the shattered door closed on the way out.

He sped away from the scene as fast as possible. The only question that now remained in his mind was whether to contact Gary Jarvis. He knew that what he had stumbled on might seem purely circumstantial. The newspapers in Levi's apartment could have been collected by anybody interested in the killings. The feces, if it was that, might make the best part of a case. But how did he know it was feces, and if it was, how could he know for sure it was wolf feces? And if he reported what he knew, he would be forced to tell how he had found it out. He would have to confess his own breaking and entering. Once he owned up to that, the question of his own motives would arise. And if the feces turned out to be Kinta's, there would then be no chance of saving him. In such a distracted state of mind, he was struck by a horrible awareness.

He had handled the baggie.

His prints would therefore be on it. It would be easy for Levi to claim that Paul had planted the bag in his refrigerator and then insist that the psychiatrist was attempting to frame him. His fingerprints would also be on the newspapers in the closet and on nearly every other item of furniture in the house.

He stopped the car and determined to return to Levi's mansion and try to get rid of the evidence. It was an insane idea, for he had literally gone through and touched almost everything. But there might still be time before Levi got home from work.

When he turned into Levi's street, his heart nearly stopped. A familiar red Corvette sat in front of the huge mansion. Parked alongside the sports car was an SPD squad car. Standing in front of both cars were Levi Twist and Gary Jarvis. Paul stepped on the accelerator and drove on by the house, praying that he wouldn't be noticed.

Never had he felt more stupid in his entire life. He decided not to go home because the police might be watching it. He returned to the office. He knew it was risky, too, but safer than his house would be. He parked his car in the small parking garage that adjoined the clinic so that its presence would not be immediately obvious from the street. The office was empty. He picked up an old magazine and tried to read it to calm himself. "Stupid, stupid, stupid," he said to himself. He lay on the office couch and tried to watch the news. He left the office and walked down to a Wendy's on the corner and had a salad and a cup of coffee. He walked back to the office. He so wanted Rhonda to call. She didn't.

His mental fatigue got the best of him, and he fell asleep on the couch. He didn't know how long he was asleep before the telephone shattered his slumber with a jarring clatter. It took him a moment or two to find the phone and lift the receiver.

"Hello, Ronnie?"

"No, Gary Jarvis here. Dr. Shapiro, you have some explaining to do. If you have an attorney, may I suggest you call him."

Paul was stunned. He put the phone down and gathered his coat and tie. A little more money had collected in petty cash that afternoon. He took it along with the rest of the petty cash money he had already stuffed into his pockets earlier. He dashed out the door.

"Dr. Shapiro. Dr. Shapiro, are you there?" asked the voice on the phone.

He wasn't.

CHAPTER 30

The next morning Joanna Nickerson spent sleeping in, dreaming of the demanding duo of Isaiah and Spotty.

In her dream she heard the doorbell ring. "Go away!" she bellowed. "I preached twice on Sunday, and I didn't get no rest on Monday. I need sleep this morning."

"Arise and shine for thy light is come," said Spotty.

Refusing to be a poor hostess even in her dreams, she threw on her robe and went to the door. She unlocked the bolt and let the door swing open. Isaiah, with Spotty on his left shoulder, strode into the room.

"Come in, come in by all means," said Joanna, noting how they were already moving toward their favorite seat. Isaiah took the large chair that he had come to prefer when making his dream visits. Joanna seated herself in the smaller wingback chair and smiled as if to say, "Well, for pity's sake, get on with it."

He did.

"I've taken the trouble to ask Father Peter to order the porta-toilets."

"What porta-toilets?" asked Joanna, bewildered at Isaiah's conversation opener.

"What porta-toilets?" Spotty sneered sideways through his beak. "We've got a hundred thousand demonstrators soon to be moving up the mountain toward the Callahan Grove, and she asks, 'What porta-toilets?'"

Isaiah reached up and pinched the two yellow halves of Spotty's beak together to silence him.

"Well, Earth Day was back in April." Joanna seemed confused.

"Nope, the June 18 rally," Isaiah said. "We can't have all those people plodding around in the forest and not accommodate them."

Joanna wondered who would foot the bill for such an expense. "Ike," she began, "if you're sure Callahan will pay for them, then I'll sign the manifest."

"Oh, don't worry about that," Isaiah asserted. "He cares so much about his community image that he will sign."

The phone began ringing, interrupting the prophet.

"I'll get it, Ike. Just a moment." Joanna went to the phone. "Hello," she said. "Funny, there's no one there."

The phone rang again. Joanna dutifully answered it once more. "There's still no one there," she said.

"Joanna," said Isaiah, "it is the phone in your real world."

Isaiah and Spotty faded from view. Back in her bed, Joanna fumbled over the covers to the side table with her free hand until she found the phone.

"Hello," she said as her none-too-tidy bedroom came into view. She stared at the remains of the previous night's dinner—a grilled cheese sandwich. Half of the sandwich was still glued to the plate; its cold cheddar had mortared the old toast to the china.

"Yes," said Joanna. "You're who? I'm sorry, this connection must be bad. Could you speak a little louder?" She struggled to shake off her dream and gather in what was really happening.

"Callahan, here—CALLAHAN!" said the telephone.

He had called her a half-dozen times before to try to get her to abandon "her exodus." They were not friends, but they were used to debating the merits of Joanna's forthcoming rally in Callahan's grove.

"Oh, yes," Joanna went on. "Isaiah said you'd call."

"Who?"

"Oh, never mind. I guess you'll pay for the porta-toilets?"

"Yes—yes, I will. But this is only to protect my business interests and image. I won't have you church people in this area thinking I'm out to rape the wilderness. In fact, I'll not only pay for the toilets; I'll be sure there are plenty of water bottle dispensaries. I'm a friend of the wilderness, you know, Reverend Nickerson."

"'Rape' is a very strong word, Mr. Callahan," Joanna responded.

"Well, this is very serious business. I want those trees cut, but I don't want you sweet little gospel types gossiping that my kind are destroying future national parks before they're ever born. We're gonna cut those trees, Reverend Nickerson. But until we do, I'll treat all you religious folks to a free potty break on your way to the rally. I'm going to show the media a man who's concerned both about them and the logging industry."

"Well, Mr. Callahan, God loves the loggers even more than he loves the trees."

"That's good, Reverend Nickerson. The poor people of the Northwest can depend on people like me to protect the working man from tree-hugging kooks. Everyone will see who really are the noble ones in this conflict, and I am noble."

"And so utterly humble too," said Joanna. "Oh, never mind. Thanks for picking up the bill. Tell those porta people to have those potties in place by the fifteenth, do you hear?"

"Yes, and we will."

They hung up. Joanna could tell that Mr. Callahan was miffed, but she felt right about what she was doing.

CHAPTER 31

The following Friday Della Singleton left home to look for a new apartment in Seattle. The only thing she hated was that her face looked so beat up. She had pushed her makeup as far as it would go to help cover the scrapes and bruises. But makeup over new injuries has its limitations. She knew that everyone who saw her that day would still see her battered face, and a few would be impertinent enough to ask about it. Still, she would probably never see them again. And she had to find another place to live as soon as possible.

She didn't think Levi knew she suspected him of being the serial murderer. But she did think he would hunt her for reasons of personal animosity and further brutalize her. She looked at six condos during the day but found nothing that she really liked and could afford. She felt hopelessly frustrated by early afternoon and decided to get some lunch. She stopped by a small deli that she frequented and picked up a bit of macaroni salad and some sliced turkey, unaware that her pursuer also picked up some yogurt and a sandwich.

Back at her condominium, Della put her purchases in the refrigerator and took a nap. She then got up, put on her bathrobe, and watched the news while she ate a turkey sandwich on toast. She tried to get interested in a sitcom rerun but couldn't. Life was on stall, and she found nothing to make it move. Antsy, she decided to go for a brisk evening walk, hoping to tire herself out to enjoy a night of great sleep, which she so desperately needed. She methodically unplugged the phone and the answering machine so she wouldn't be bothered by any late-night callers. Last of all she put on some shorts and her running shoes, stuck her condo key in her pocket, and strode out into the fading light. In better times she would have considered this a splendid day.

Her legs pumped uphill and relaxed downhill. Still, a thousand images swam through Della's mind. She thought of all that she had once felt for Levi. She thought of how handsome she had once thought him to be. She found tears streaming down her face as she walked. One child in a park pointed at her and said to her mother, "Look, Mommy, that woman is crying."

The child's innocent statement produced a flood of tears. She thought of the baby she carried. She thought of the hope that she had held for June 17, her once-upon-a-time wedding date. She thought of all that she had lost—of her lovely Camelot that had perished in a single night. Last and most painfully, she thought of the time that she had lost. She thought of the cheap ring and of the pink nightgown in Levi's cabin that told her finally her dreams were dead.

In the forty minutes that she walked, her churning legs at last outpaced her churning mind. She found herself turning the corner toward her condo and slowing her stride. It was now dark except for the streetlight over her as she walked toward her house. She was glad that she had left the lights off in the front of her house. She felt dark inside and wanted to sit in the dark and fall asleep and never wake up. Tomorrow would be another day of apartment or condominium shopping. If she found one, she would have all the work of breaking her old lease and moving away and starting life over. The only thing that gave her much hope was the baby that she carried. Being a mother at least held a reason for her to go on living. She desperately needed that reason now.

She inserted the key in the lock and walked in. She pulled off her shoes and socks and tossed them in the floor and slumped back in a chair, exhausted. How long she rested there with her eyes closed she did not know, but when she opened her eyes, a strange apparition greeted her. A rubber-headed president stepped out of the shadows in the dark corner of the room. It was Nixon! He stooped down to unsnap a heavy steel chain. "Della," said a voice through the latex lips, "I brought Daimon."

Then out of the darkness hurtled the end of Della's pain.

CHAPTER 32

Eric, I've put all my money into defending my right to hold onto this piece of the forest. You are a godsend."

"It looks like all you need is a good lawyer, and you can finally hang onto what's yours," Eric said, pointing to himself with a broad grin.

Neither of them said much more. They were tired of talking business.

Eric had driven up to the mountain early on the first Saturday in June and walked to the Gaian camp. He and Isletta had lingered after the campfire to celebrate the day. It was turning out to be more of a celebration than he had imagined. He stood and set his coffee cup on a log and stretched out his hand. Isletta looked at the gesture with a cocked eyebrow then smiled and took his hand. They walked up the trail, holding hands. When the rest of the camp was out of sight, Isletta broke the silence.

"Pacific Woods isn't taking this lightly, are they? I can't figure out why they're so worked up. They get all the Callahan Grove. They're just greedy, I guess."

"They want to beat down all the tree huggers to make a clean sweep of it. When I told Callahan that the deal was off, he was furious."

"If I were you, I'd keep looking over my shoulder in dark alleys. You need to keep alert to safeguard your future, which does not look promising."

"Not only that, but I told him I'd be representing you, Isletta, in your right-of-refusal petition."

"What did he say to all this?"

"He said he'd eat my lunch—no, he said he'd eat me for lunch, or breakfast. I know he isn't going to take this lying down." He paused. "By the way, I met an old priest who was dressed in blue coveralls who—"

"You, too?" Isletta interrupted.

They were both dumbfounded. Each of them had failed to bring it up at their previous meeting out of the fear that the other would think them mad.

Now, at last, they did exchange stories. To Eric the most interesting aspect of Isletta's testimony was her account of Rhonda Shapiro and the wolf. Then Isletta sat stupefied while Eric told her of his near miss with the huge wolf or dog—he wasn't sure which—that had attacked him during his recent visit to Renée's grave. Then Isletta went back to Rhonda's story.

"According to her," Isletta went on, "the animal was apparently trapped by the deforestation of the Pacific Woods project. But a man has been trying to kill the wolf and has nearly succeeded. She fled up here because she wants to protect the animal's life."

"What part of the city do these Shapiros live in anyway?"

"I'm afraid they live on Snoqualmie River Road, the very area where most of the murders occurred."

"Isletta, there has to be a connection."

"I don't know, Eric. Before you jump to conclusions, you need to meet this woman and her wolf. Neither one seems like the type. They're in a cabin up above the Callahan Grove. Why don't we walk up there? You need to meet her anyway. Her property isn't directly in the wake of the project, but she made it very clear the other day that she didn't want to see the entire forest destroyed."

Eric conceded.

They began to walk up toward the Shapiro cabin. After they had crossed a stone fault, the steepness of the climb caused them both to sit down to catch their breath. The damp ground was sunlit and felt so warm that Eric lay back upon it. He was staring into the bluest sky he had ever seen. It was glorious, and he reached out his hand to Isletta and pulled her down in the grass beside him. She cradled her head on his shoulder, and they both rested quietly for a long, relaxing "skysoak." The earth and the trees all had a particular odor of their own.

They lay there a long time. They were nearly welded to the ground by the warmth of their love affair with the natural world. Eric looked up at the clouds, remembering his sophomore English class. He thought of their study of *Romeo and Juliet*. He remembered asking his teacher how

Romeo could know in such a short time that Juliet was the one for him. It seemed impossible to him that Romeo could know so quickly he was in love. Back then he thought it was so foolish, so instant, so impossibly immature. Now he felt a strange and glorious kinship with Romeo.

Isletta turned her head to the side and kissed him on the cheek. Eric felt suddenly overwhelmed at the thought of their love. He was glad they were to be married, for he knew that being only Isletta's attorney would never be enough for him.

———

Later, as they approached the Shapiro cabin, they could hear classical music coming from a stereo. It was beautiful but so loud that Eric found himself knocking extra hard to be sure that he would be heard. The knock instantly silenced the music. Isletta spoke to reassure Rhonda. "Rhonda, it's me, Isletta. I've brought a friend."

The door swung open.

"Come in, won't you?" invited Rhonda.

They entered. At her gesture Eric and Isletta took seats. It struck Eric that he was in the company of two of the most beautiful women he had ever seen.

"Where's Kinta?" Isletta asked.

"Out for his morning roam, no doubt," answered Rhonda. "Probably it's just as well; he's so protective of this place. I want him to live free, but at the moment his freedom is a bit of an inconvenience. Now that the SPD thinks he's suspect, I wish he'd stick closer. I worry that he might actually hurt someone sometime. Paul kept telling me that he wasn't tame, that he was a wolf and not a dog and that the vicious part of his nature would always be there."

Rhonda knew now that Jarvis was leaking everything to the press. She knew that there would now be heaps of evidence stacked against Kinta and Paul.

"Rhonda, you seem so deeply involved in thought," said Isletta.

Isletta's words were interrupted by a loud scratching at the door. It was Kinta. Rhonda stood and walked to the door to let him in. The proud and lanky animal walked directly to Eric and began sniffing at his clothes. Eric instinctively moved back into his chair. At length, however, he straightened a bit and reached out his hand and patted the wolf on the head.

"Why don't you scratch behind his ears. That's what he truly likes," suggested Rhonda.

"Is that what he'd truly like?" asked Eric hesitantly.

Rhonda laughed, and Eric scratched behind Kinta's ears. Isletta smiled. Somehow all seemed right with world. The three of them soon drifted into easy conversation, talking about everything from what they had done in grade school to the various kinds of music they had liked in high school.

After a long time Rhonda went to the refrigerator to get some cold drinks, and Isletta called after her, "Rhonda, Eric recently met the old priest too."

"Whoever he was," Eric interrupted, "he gave me a talk on the stewardship of Earth and then evaporated. You can bet it is the only 'save the world' speech given inside Pacific Woods."

"I'm so grateful Eric is my lawyer," said Isletta.

"He must have been quite a priest—an industrial-strength padre—for a lawyer to risk giving up his income."

Eric smiled and asked, "What did your angel have to say, Isletta?"

"He told me that God was not Gaia. I really didn't mind because I already had my suspicions that it was so. Still, the word would be most unwelcome to the other priestesses." She looked a bit concerned, but the conversation drifted back to Pacific Woods and the lawsuit it would likely take against those who would not sell. It wouldn't be only Pacific Woods; it would be supported by all of the laborers who made their living in the lumbering industry. The conflict could escalate from a cold war to a heated conflict.

"Paul will surely come up soon. If either of you have time, we would be glad to have your company." Inwardly, however, Rhonda lacked assurance that Paul would even be free on any weekend. She knew that Jarvis either had Paul in custody already or was trying to find him to make the arrest. She prayed that somehow Paul was still free. While she could not bring herself to confess those fears out loud, a single silent tear spilled from her right eye. She turned her face away from her guests lest they discover her needy state of heart.

CHAPTER 33

Once Joanna's Sunday night sermon ended, she launched into a persuasive altar call.

"Brothers and sisters, listen up! We're going to be joined by 100,000 men and women of faith for a massive march through the wilderness. We're gonna march from this church to the Callahan Grove. We're going to give birth to a future forest. Are you hearin' me, brothers?"

"Yes . . . Amen."

"We're gonna prove that there's life after chain saws. Amen?"

"Amen!"

"We Christians are gonna prove that when any of our people are out of work, we all hurt. Amen?"

"Amen!"

"And we're gonna prove that when God made humankind, he intended folks to honor his creation—to use it but never abuse it."

"Amen."

Joanna was through with the service when an odd occurrence took place. A whole crowd of people began coming in even as the crowd dispersed. It was clear they wanted to worship. So, right then and there Joanna decided to have a second service.

On that early June evening, an old priest in blue coveralls entered this second service of the Pathway of Light Cathedral and took a seat near the front of the auditorium, right beside Henry Demond. Henry had made no prophecies since Father Peter had first entered the clinic. In fact, it was rumored that the priest was well and would convalesce only a short time before being dismissed from the clinic.

By the time Joanna was ready to start her impromptu second service, the church was full of people. Still, before she spoke, she had to leave the little sanctuary and walk outside to take a breather. When she attempted to reenter the church, she was prevented from going directly into the small but tightly packed congregation by an old, homeless man with an empty shopping cart that he was trying to push up the three or four stairs into the crowded sanctuary.

"Sir," said Joanna, "you can't bring that in here. We're very crowded tonight."

"But if I leave it out here, the others will steal it," he protested.

Joanna knew he was right. Shopping carts were highly valued possessions among the homeless. As this poor homeless man protested, she could tell that he was a man who was trying to live a reformed life. She smelled no liquor on his breath, and he was clean-shaven. Still he wore the homeless uniform of the day—a soiled, soft-brim golf hat and a trench coat.

Even though she was already late, Joanna yielded. "All right, follow me."

He did, pushing his cart ahead of him. At the back of the church, Joanna unlocked a little shed she always reserved for these kinds of emergencies. The shed was full of cases of canned goods and old clothes that she distributed among the homeless. She moved some of the canned goods back further into the shed, grunting a little at their heaviness. When there was room for the shopping cart, she shoved it in, refastened the hasp, and replaced the padlock.

"What nice shoes you have, sir," Joanna said, suddenly noticing what appeared to be new wingtips. Usually the homeless wore very beat-up sneakers. "You didn't steal them, did you?" Joanna asked.

"No, ma'am," he said. "I found them behind the mortuary. Dead people throw away the nicest things."

It was not a great proverb but great enough to cause Joanna to wonder about him. He seemed far more refined than most of the homeless. Few of them came equipped with either proverbs or well-polished wingtips. But she had no the time to wonder long. She was already late, and she hurried into the sanctuary.

Because Joanna Nickerson was so very late, she quickly fixed her little Janie on the front row, giving her a coloring book and some crayons to occupy her while the adults around her worshipped. There were people standing in the back—mostly the homeless of Seattle—all awaiting her arrival and the beginning of the service.

Just as Joanna stood up, she saw the old priest. "Father Peter!" she exclaimed.

Father Peter smiled. It was terribly hard for Joanna not to be amused. He was sitting right beside a smiling Henry Demond. This rather formidable, grinning duo made her feel uncomfortable, but Joanna launched into a second sermon.

"I've never had two worship services on the same evening, but I just feel like startin' over." So saying, she sat down and began to play the piano.

In a few moments she had the whole place singing and clapping and swaying. When the fervor was at a peak, Joanna asked, "Does anyone have a word of prophecy?"

The ever-smiling Henry Demond raised his hand.

"Do you have another fireball in your pocket, Henry?" Joanna grinned. The congregation laughed.

"No, ma'am," replied the janitor. "I don't have a word of prophecy, but Father Peter here does."

Father Peter stood. "I do have a word of prophecy. I prophesy that every Christian man, woman, and child needs to join the Reverend Nickerson for the march to the Callahan Grove. I proclaim the march Joanna's Exodus!"

"Father Peter, this is the house of God," said Joanna sternly. "This exodus business is nonsense! Now you just go get yourself another word of prophecy or sit down, please."

"Sister Joanna, Jesus is the King, amen?" asked Father Peter.

"Amen!' said Joanna.

"Jesus is King of the whole world, amen?"

"A-a-a-men!" repeated the preacher, drawing her "amen" out extra long for emphasis.

"Jesus is King over all nature, amen?"

"A-a-a-a-men!"

"And he made everybody and everything, amen?"

"Amen!" She shortened her amen, wondering where this speech was heading.

"And he made the spotted owl, and he loved all that he made, amen?"

"Amen." She was barely audible.

"Brothers and sisters, the Bible says over in John 11:35 that 'Jesus wept'! I just want to remind you that there are still things that make Jesus weep. You remember that over in Matthew 23, Jesus wept over Jerusalem, crying, 'Oh, Jerusalem, Jerusalem, you who kill the prophets and stone those sent to you, how often I have longed to gather your children together, as a hen gathers her chicks under her wings, but you were not willing. Look, your house is left to you desolate.'

"Brothers and sisters, the whole world is his temple, and Jesus is even now at the right hand of the Father, weeping over the desolation of God's house. God made this beautiful world and filled it with beautiful things. He made the butterflies and the great whales and creatures of the deep. He made little soft-shelled crustaceans, eyeless in the vast depths. The world is myriad in its life-forms, and every creature exists to praise the glory of God.

"But these are the days when the Christ who once wept over Jerusalem cries over the desolation of planet Earth. You see, brothers and sisters, this is his world, and we are but trustees. Every time another species disappears from our Earth, we prove ourselves unfaithful in our stewardship, amen?"

"Amen, help him, Jesus," said one of the sisters.

"Praise the Lord, we're gonna be stewards, sweet Jesus!" shouted another.

"Well, who's God got but us to save the world?"

"But, preacher, I'm homeless," said a toothless old woman.

"But everybody can do something," said Father Peter. "We can make a difference. Today is June 4. We're gonna march on the wilderness. We're gonna march across the Snoqualmie like Joshua crossed the Jordan. We're going to stand before Mount Rainier just like Moses and the Israelites stood before Sinai. We're gonna walk and carry each other. We're gonna be the New Israel out to claim the land of milk and honey from the Moabites of misery. We're gonna confront Pharaoh Callahan! We're gonna plunder the Egyptians. We're gonna let the world know that God intends for us to honor his creation.

"We're gonna bless a small grove of forest sentinels owned by Isletta Borg. Why? So the world will know we are the stewards of Eden. We're gonna proclaim this world sacred to the God who loved us and died for us so that his great love would not perish from Earth. Now we're gonna march for him so that our Earth itself will not perish, amen?"

"Amen!" they cried.

"Now Sister Joanna will help you get organized and show you the way. We're gonna march all the way; it could take two weeks."

"But where we gonna sleep and what we gonna eat?"

"God once gave the manna, and you may be sure he will take care of all of those who trust in him. Sister Joanna will help you. She will lead you. She will show you the way to the mountain of God!"

Joanna was at first aghast; she really didn't feel much like Moses. She really didn't want to confront Callahan, who was so much like a modern Pharaoh that the very allegory made her afraid. She was beginning to understand the part she had somehow been designated to play in the old man's drama. She could see a kind of rapture glowing on each of the faces of her new band of Israelites. She prayed a brief prayer, and they were dismissed. A few of them wanted to go immediately to the mountain, so they lingered around her and waited for some further word, but she had nothing left to give. Gradually the crowded little church grew empty.

When Joanna took Janie's hand to go, she was confronted again by the homeless man whose shopping cart she had secured in the shed behind the church. "Could I talk to you a moment, Sister Joanna?" he asked.

"Of course," she replied.

The man looked all around him to be sure the church was empty except for them then took off his hat. The man's fringe of white hair was sewn inside his headgear and came off with his hat.

"Dr. Shapiro!" exclaimed Joanna. She was dumbfounded. "Have you hit the financial skids or something?"

"Joanna, we have to talk," he said.

He seemed desperate. Joanna had always thought he was a kind man, but now she saw a kind of emotional neediness about him.

"I need help, Joanna," he said plainly.

His desperation made her feel inadequate. She was used to helping desperate people—she was a minister of Christ—but Paul Shapiro was not the kind of person she usually helped. He was a doctor who got big bucks from Seattle's most important neurotics. She was only a minister to the poorer neurotics.

"I need help . . . please," Paul repeated.

"I can see that," she said. "But how can I help?"

"First, just hear me out," he replied.

She agreed to listen.

He told her the story of all that had been happening in his life since the day he had accidentally run over her little Janie. He completed the story with his discovery of the murderous crimes of Levi Twist. He told her how Twist had now reversed the truth, incriminating the psychiatrist. He told her how he was now wanted by the police.

"I had to leave my car at the office. I'm sure that by now the police are looking for it. I must try to get to our mountain hideaway somehow before I am apprehended by the police." The doctor paused. "Joanna, you do believe me, don't you?"

Joanna was not a person who could listen to anyone's troubles without taking them on herself. It wasn't her answer but the tears that Paul saw in her eyes that convinced him she cared. "Dr. Shapiro," she said, "I saw the kind of man you were when you began to care for my little Janie. I don't understand all that you are saying, but I know you are a man of real character. I believe you."

Shapiro was overcome. He somehow felt that in all his years of counseling he had never listened to anyone's troubles like the Reverend Nickerson did. She was listening in an entirely different dimension. He had listened out of the vortex of all the sciences he had learned, and when he had finished listening, he drew scientific conclusions, prescribed scientific therapies, and wrote up a bill.

He wasn't sure how a Christian pastor differed from a psychiatrist, but he knew that for Sister Joanna, it added a dimension of caring he had completely missed. He turned to Joanna. "A few weeks ago my life was under my control. Now my entire world is upside down. I've done nothing wrong, and yet I am wanted by the police on suspicion of murder. I am separated from my wife, who will be crushed if I am arrested. I can't drive my own car. I don't know how to get out of this mess, and yet, I've done nothing wrong."

"Doctor," Joanna said, "there are times when innocence finds no place. You're likely to be incriminated and suffer for the sins of someone else, just like my Lord."

"Joanna, can you help me? I have nowhere else to turn. You could get in serious trouble yourself for aiding and abetting a felon. My only hope is that, since we recently met, the police will make no immediate connection between us. Maybe you can help me, and no one will ever know. I can't be seen on the street. I can't drive my car, and yet, somehow, by God's good grace, I've got to get to Rhonda."

"Doctor, you gotta let Jesus help you carry this," she counseled. "He too was falsely accused, and yet he was completely innocent. So you see, Jesus can understand and help you."

She placed her hand on his shoulder, praying for Jesus' strength to flow into Paul Shapiro.

"Thank you!" he said, almost in the same way that Joanna would have said it in one of the services at the Pathway of Light Cathedral. None of his external circumstances had changed, yet it was as though his internal world had been renewed. He put back on his slouch hat with the white hair sewn inside. Janie had fallen asleep on the back pew. Paul Shapiro picked her up, and all three of them went out to the shed and got his old shopping cart.

Joanna filled the bottom of the cart with some nice warm blankets from the shed, and he laid Janie on the blankets to sleep. They walked in silence all the way back to the Nickerson flat. Paul carried the child inside, and Joanna took her to dress for bed.

When Janie was asleep, Paul and Joanna had a cup of coffee together. Paul gave her his wallets and explained how she could use his pin number and bank card. She promised to get him the cash and a bus ticket to Carnation, Washington. There Paul could walk up the road that connected with the cabin area. Joanna prayed for him, and he fell asleep on the couch.

When Joanna also had fallen asleep, Isaiah came into her dream as he often did. The owl was still on his shoulder. "No, not tonight, please," begged Joanna.

Isaiah said nothing, but Spotty did manage a few words. "You did real good, Joanna. Mind you, it doesn't look altogether good for a woman of God to have a strange man sleeping in the same house with her, but you did real good."

Isaiah smiled and patted Joanna on the arm and then vacated her dreams. She slept and thought how good it felt to serve an innocent man a generous helping of trust.

CHAPTER 34

Della Singleton's body went undiscovered until the apartment super noticed an odor and called the police. Levi Twist used the time to his advantage. When at last the crime was reported, Levi decided to leave Seattle in a hurry. He knew there was little use in trying to get rid of all the fingerprints he had left in Della's apartment, for he had been there so often and stayed so long that his prints were everywhere.

What is there to do but do what must be done? he asked himself. Daimon was asleep on the floor of Levi's Bronco. "What's there to do afterward?" he asked himself aloud. It was a question that he had asked himself after his dark dealings. He drove along old familiar streets with the light of the streetlights alternately lighting and darkening his face. Once north of the city, he drove faster back to the cabin where he knew he would have to put Daimon back in his run.

Once off I-5, he drove on up to his cabin. He fed Daimon after putting him in the dog run and went inside. He quickly undressed and looked at himself in a full-length mirror. He flexed in various poses. Obviously pleased with how he looked, he went into the small bathroom and stepped into the shower. He turned the hot water to a nearly scalding temperature and luxuriated in the steaming cleansing. He squeezed the thick shampoo directly into his hair and massaged the tangle brutally while the thick white foam washed away. He enjoyed his deviance. He had murdered, and yet he now stood in the scalding water, scrubbing his momentary guilt away.

With no regard for God at all, Levi Twist had long become accustomed to forgiving his own sin. The greater the sin, the better he felt about his own titanic self-forgiveness. The more he had gotten by with, the more he enjoyed his own homemade atonement. Now he had committed the ultimate crime. He adjusted the water to the hottest it could possibly go. It seemed it would burn his skin off. Oh, how he needed the scalding.

When the shower was over, he toweled himself dry and slipped under the covers in the buff.

The next day he found himself at work all the earlier. The Tuesday newspaper with a picture of Della on it lay beside the coffee pot in the executive lounge. Levi poured himself a cup of coffee and read the horrors of the account.

He was suddenly interrupted by Eric Compton, who had returned to Pacific Woods to gather up the last of his old office decorations and other things—paper weights, a stapler, and a box of old file folders. When Eric walked past the lounge, he saw Levi flipping through the paper. With a wave of his hand, Levi said, "Eric, did you read about this nurse over by Queen Anne Hill? You know, this is the woman I have been dating."

"This is the Della you talked about?" Eric was struck dumb. He poured himself a cup of coffee and pulled up a chair. "You must feel awful!"

Levi cradled his head in his big hands and stared downward at the glass tabletop. When he looked back up, he had coaxed a single tear out over the rim of his lower eyelid, and it coursed alone across his cheek. "Eric, we were real close."

Eric nodded sympathetically. "This is a real shock, I'm sure."

"I don't know what I'll do without . . . . How could this have happened?"

"It's part of a string of these sick murders . . . . And," Eric paused, "the police will probably be contacting you."

"It's inevitable," Levi said. "I'm sure when they talk with her boss, he'll tell them about me and then it will just be a matter of time before they come around to talk to me. I was all too recently a client of his, you know."

Eric was dumbfounded. "No, I had no idea."

"I don't think Della ever talked much about our relationship . . . at least, I asked her not to." Levi went on: "But I do know that she talked everything over with her boss. You can bet that someone from SPD will be around before long."

"It's inevitable, you were there so often. I'd bet a lot of people saw you coming and going."

Levi felt it was an expedient time to play the devastated lover card again. "Eric, it's hard to believe that my little Della . . ." he stopped, coaxed out one more tear, and went on, "is the latest of the wolf killings." Levi stopped for a moment and looked down at his own fingernails. "Eric, can you imagine being attacked by a wolf?"

Eric cringed. "The horror of it freezes the blood."

"I'm telling you, there is a big wolf out in the suburbs. I've been tracking him for the last year with my rifle. He was hanging around the Lee West Construction Camp. I mean, this brute is big. I got a shot at him and thought I had wounded him, but I only grazed his foreleg. He somehow made it across the river and was nursed back to health by—get this—the wife of the psychiatrist that Della worked for. This same doctor, mind you, was the one I so confided in to try and get over my wife's death. The woman, the wife of Paul Shapiro, has been keeping this killer as a house pet. Can you believe it? I tell you, I think the woman and her husband are demonic."

Eric thought of telling Levi that he had met the wolf and Rhonda, but he didn't fully trust Levi. He also thought of telling the CEO about his near attack by the huge wolf, but seeing Levi in such grief, he thought better of it. He still had not managed to see his boss as his Memorial weekend assailant.

Levi spoke again in a choked voice. "Oh, Della, Della . . . Della." This time he coaxed out a whole barrage of tears and sobbed. Eric reached around his broad shoulders and consoled him.

"Eric, you have no idea how I really felt about this woman. I had begged her to marry me, but she just kept refusing. I know we would have been so happy together."

"Look, Levi, I'm going to call the police. So help me, God, I'm going to help you get to the bottom of this."

"No! No! Please, Eric! I'm not up to answering their questions just yet. They'll come soon enough. Please! I don't want to be implicated before it's absolutely necessary. I want to remember Della as she was the last time I saw her. I can't bear to think about that animal—that horrible wolf—the savagery of her final moments . . . ." Again Levi buried his head in his hands and stared at the glass table. Eric again held his convulsing shoulders.

"Eric, you've always been a good friend to me," said Levi. Gradually Levi seemed to get control of himself.

He reached for Eric's hand. "Thanks . . . thanks for letting me talk." He gave Eric's hand an appreciative squeeze and warmly patted him on the shoulder. Then Levi waved good-bye with one of his heavy, meaty hands and walked out.

The huge hand stirred a memory in Eric. Though still recovering from witnessing Levi's breakdown, he couldn't help focusing on Levi's hand. Pictures of hands flashed through his mind like a furious slideshow. Where had a hand played a role in his life lately? Where had he seen a huge . . . the hand . . . the grasping hand . . . . The murder it intended. Yes, the hand!

It was you and your dog that night, wasn't it? At the cemetery? It was you who stuck the horrible graffiti on her grave. No, God! No! Tell me that what I think I just discovered is a lie!

Levi was gone. Eric doubted, and yet he knew the truth.

———

In a few minutes, Levi was sitting in his Bronco looking over his Day-Timer. He closed his book and headed in the

direction of the Shapiro home. Levi drove out of the corporate parking lot and through the employee parking lot. He
drove past his red Corvette, stopped, went to the Corvette,
unlocked it, and removed his pistol. It was strictly forbidden
to bring firearms onto the company grounds, but Levi had
long ago quit caring about corporate rules.

Within thirty minutes he was driving up the river valley
toward the Shapiro home. He parked in a street a half mile
from their home and threaded his way through the trees
until he came to the old toolshed. He could see that most of
the traps he had set for Kinta had been intentionally sprung
some weeks earlier. He had kept a constant surveillance
on the Shapiro home over the weeks, hoping that Rhonda
would return with Kinta. He was determined to avenge himself, and Rhonda still had not made the connection between
Seattle's leading CEO and the assailant, from whom Kinta
had delivered her.

As far as Levi knew, Paul Shapiro also was ignorant.
Indeed, when Della died, Levi remained unaware that in her
final conversation with her boss she had clued him in to the
one vital connection that allowed everything to gel for the
psychiatrist. Paul now knew that Levi was the killer. But
what Levi didn't know was that Paul Shapiro, still hiding out
at Joanna's flat, had taken on an investigation of his own.

Levi walked to the house, which was empty. He decided
to use the same small deck window to enter the house that
he had used before. It had been repaired, but he managed
to throw a huge rock through it and break it. He slipped on
a pair of gauze gloves to be sure he left no telltale fingerprints. It was all but impossible for him to brace himself on

the deck rail and turn his torso sideways and squeeze in. He managed to do it only with extreme effort. But any other entrance would have set off the alarm. And the difficulty of entering over the sink certainly added to the problem. He did at last manage to stand upright inside the empty house.

He was fairly sure that the motion detectors would be in the front part of the house. There the large windows and commodious front door allowed for the greatest chance of intrusion. Avoiding that area of the home, he moved to the bedroom area upstairs. The second-story windows were so high off the ground that they needed no alarm system.

From a pile of laundry, Levi extricated one of Rhonda's blouses. It had been worn but not washed. He knew it would carry enough traces of her scent that Daimon would use it for the last job Levi needed him to accomplish.

He stuck the blouse in his pocket and continued looking for any piece of paper that would give him a clue as to where the Shapiro cabin was located. More than once, Della had told him the Shapiros had a cabin two hours from the city; he just didn't know where. But in nearly an hour of checking through every drawer, calendar, and file folder, he found nothing that would indicate Rhonda might be at the cabin.

He was about to give up when he heard the front door of the house open downstairs. He swung into the linen closet and pulled the door shut. He heard footsteps bypass the stairs. Apparently whoever had entered went to the front hall closet and punched in the code to disarm the alarm system. Whoever it was must also have noticed that the kitchen window was broken, for Levi heard him pronounce a mild oath. He then heard the sound of a whisk broom brushing at the broken glass over the scratchy enamel of the kitchen sink. Then he heard the psychiatrist say, "Hello!" as though calling someone on the phone.

"Reverend Joanna," he went on, "I've stopped by the house to pick up a few things. This place is under near-constant surveillance. I mustn't stay here but a minute. The police are looking everywhere for me. I'm driving up to join Rhonda at the cabin. I appreciate your letting me borrow your late husband's old car. Again, I can't tell you how much it meant to me to have been given a place to stay. When this is all over, as God is my helper, I'll find some more tangible way to say thank you. Until then, however, I want you to do me a favor. I want you to call Detective Jarvis of the Seattle Police Department and tell him that if he will look off I-5 at Farm Market Road 607, and go six miles east, he will find the rustic cabin belonging to Levi Twist, president and CEO of Pacific Woods. Behind the cabin is the 'wolf' that has been the cause of all of these serial killings . . . What? . . . Yes, the FM 607 . . . Yes, the man who's behind all of these killings is a one-time client of mine, Levi Twist. Are you sure that you can remember all of this? Tell the inspector I've done a little homework on Levi and the wolf. Tell him that if he does a check on the wolf hairs that have been found on the victims, the hairs will compare very favorably with those on the taxidermied wolf in the front of the Washington Wildlife Museum. The feces are Kinta's—they have been intentionally planted from those samples taken from around our home, I'm afraid.

"Have you written this all down? Thanks so much, Joanna. I'll probably see you when you're at the June 18 rally. Good-bye."

Levi's hopes began to sink. Paul Shapiro would soon be on his way to join Rhonda. He didn't know who Joanna was, and there was no time to identify her before she called the police. He wanted to kill Paul Shapiro, but if he did, there would be little hope of locating and settling his final grudge. He must follow Paul Shapiro. It was the only way now of finding and avenging himself on Kinta and Rhonda. He waited while Paul came up the stairs. He came toward the door of the linen closet while Levi shrunk back against the wall. Paul opened the door and methodically removed some clothing without really looking. If he had looked, he would have seen Levi flattened against the wall. He closed the door. Levi breathed ever so shallowly until he heard Paul packing up some things before he walked down the stairs. Paul seemed to be in the kitchen and then the pantry, boxing up foodstuffs and groceries.

After a few trips from the house to the car, he reset the alarm and left the house, locking the door behind him. Levi knew he had only forty-five seconds before the alarm would click in and pick him up as an intruder. He rushed down the stairs and flew at the back door, crashing through it and leaving it splintered in its jamb. He closed it to secure the alarm connection. He hurried toward his old black Bronco, worried that too much time would pass and he would lose the psychiatrist in the Taurus. It was most imperative that he catch up, or he would not know which way he had gone and he would have to take a fifty-fifty guess that he was turning the right way.

Driving at a furious speed, he at last caught sight of a pale blue Ford Taurus. Once he was sure the doctor was driving, he dropped back on the road. When Paul at last entered the I-5, Levi followed at quite a distance, never losing sight of him. He cursed his luck for being in the black Bronco, which would be all too obvious when he hit the lonelier roads he was sure the psychiatrist would eventually take.

When Paul Shapiro pulled off for gas at a convenience store, Levi wheeled his vehicle in behind a group of trees on a side road and watched. He suddenly remembered an electronic monitoring device he once rigged to keep track of Victoria Billingsley. It was still in the Bronco. Paul bought some grocery items at the store and then slipped into the outside restroom, giving his stalker just the time he needed. Levi approached Joanna's old car and inserted the magnetic device under the rear bumper.

As Paul pulled away from the station, Levi rustled through a large black case at the back of his car. Finally he found what he was looking for—a small black receiver. He pulled out the telescoping antenna and pushed a small black button. A red light on the top of the gadget began to blink off and on. With each blink it beeped with an odd electronic chirp.

"Yes!" exulted Levi, clenching his fist triumphantly.

The homing device was working, and the signal was so loud that Levi knew that the battery on the sending unit was still strong. It would continue working well. He was, therefore, in no immediate hurry to follow the doctor. He got into the Bronco and for the moment reversed himself on the I-5. He probably had just enough time to rescue Daimon before Reverend Joanna, whoever she was, sent the Seattle police to the discovery that would at last disclose the hideout of the Seattle killer.

Levi knew he had to leave his Corvette forever and depend entirely on his old black four-wheel drive. More than that, he knew they would impound his Corvette and put out the paperwork for his arrest. He didn't have much time. They would quickly surmise he was driving the Bronco. They also would know the license plate for the truck and would, therefore, be waiting for him at a half-dozen blockades. He knew he would need both his guns and his faithful accomplice, Daimon. He had no choice but to risk arrest on the assumption that he had time to get them both before retracing his journey through Seattle and turning east toward the town of Carnation, following the homing device that would end his long-standing grudge against a wolf and a woman. Risk seemed to innervate his whole being.

He actually whistled in his Bronco. "It's great to be alive!"

But Levi's exultant mood and deviant plan were destined to end shortly.

———

Paul Shapiro found himself in bumper-to-bumper traffic as he neared his exit. He was impatient to get off the crowded freeway and be with Rhonda. He was locked in a sluggish traffic jam. A heavyset, red-faced woman behind him was most impatient and bumped Joanna's old Taurus after following too closely. It was not a hard bump but hard enough to dislodge the electronic device. The noise the homing device made as it dropped off the car was barely audible. Paul heard it fall from the car, but not really knowing what it was, dismissed it as unimportant. The third vehicle back was a semi-truck whose giant wheels crushed the device to silence.

CHAPTER 35

Late in the afternoon, Gary Jarvis reached the small, rustic cabin of Levi Twist. Levi had cleared out all of the most incriminating evidence, but what he hadn't taken was quite enough to implicate him beyond all reasonable doubt. The dog run was there. In his haste to clear out, Levi had neglected to take the hideous flog he had used on the animal and had accidentally left some photos of himself and his dog among the pictures of himself and Della.

Two items left in the cabin brought Jarvis the most discomfort. One was a separate stack of the six newspaper accounts of the murders. Seeing this special file of newspapers gave Gary a kind of quick shame. He had been wrong. He was a thorough investigator, and it bothered him that he had wrongly applied several of the major clues.

There were also a couple of Dr. Shapiro's business cards lying on the cheap credenza. Gary suddenly understood that these must have come from Della Singleton or that Levi had taken them from her purse. Then he realized that

Levi could have easily picked them off the psychiatrist's desk when he went for his therapy. Then, of course, Levi had left the cards at My Kind, falsely incriminating the psychiatrist.

Further, Gary found a full box of thirty-ought-six rounds. He knew that this kind of ammunition designated Levi either a big hunter or a sniper, or both. He did not find the rifle that fired the rounds and could only assume that Levi had that in his possession. One thing was sure: Levi was armed and extremely dangerous.

Gary wasn't sure exactly what Levi Twist intended to do with the shells but knew that the killer had unfinished business with Rhonda Shapiro and Kinta. And Gary knew where the Shapiros' hideaway was. He wasn't sure whether Levi knew, but he dared not presume in the matter. He had no time to lose. He quickly removed the telltale items he had found in Levi's cabin. He put them in the trunk of his car and headed back down the interstate. He found it hard to evaluate the items he had recovered. The newspapers were a kind of circumstantial evidence. Still, it seemed right to have them as prosecution exhibits.

Once on the interstate, headed for the Shapiro cabin, he called in to the lab to see how the second part of Joanna's revelation had checked out.

The lab chief picked up on the first ring. "Hello, John here."

"John, this is Gary Jarvis. What about the wolf hair?"

"Well, Joanna Nickerson was right. I don't know what to make of this. This wolf couldn't have killed anybody for the last twenty-five years."

"And why not?" asked Jarvis.

"He's been too dead. The wolf died at least two decades ago—probably longer. The question is, how did a long-dead wolf leave his hairs in the lesions of his victims?"

"Joanna Nickerson said that Paul Shapiro found Ziploc bags of wolf feces in Twist's refrigerator. I want you to send a squad car over to check this out. If there are bags of fresh wolf feces in his refrigerator, he must have picked those feces up at the Shapiros' backyard when they kept Kinta in their toolshed. Check the hair we have against those of the taxidermied wolf in the front of the Washington Wildlife Museum. If this all checks out, Paul Shapiro has done a hefty piece of forensic work."

"How does that make you feel, Gary?"

"Like I should have gone into psychiatry," said Gary.

"There is one other thing you ought to know: I went back and checked the hair samples under the fingernails of Della Singleton, the last victim."

"And?"

"And that is dog hair. Obviously from a German shepherd. If you could find this animal, I think we might bring the curtain down on the president of Pacific Woods. You know, your incrimination of the shrink might have been helpful, in a way."

"Yeah, when a man is fighting for his life, he obviously does better police work than the police. There's really only one piece of evidence that I have to check out in Bellevue at My Kind lounge."

"And that is?"

"I'll let you know later. 'Bye, John." Gary hung up.

He eventually pulled out of the sluggish flow of traffic onto the 405 toward Bellevue. He was sure My Kind would already be opened for the day. Gary grabbed a picture of Levi and Della from the trunk and took it in to the bartender.

"Excuse me, do you know this man and woman?" Gary showed him a picture of Della and Levi, adding, "I'm a policeman."

"So where's your badge?" the bartender asked.

Gary pulled out his leather wallet and displayed his silver credentials and picture.

"Well, OK," drawled the bartender. "I don't know the chick. But the man with her is Dr. Paul Shapiro. He came in here quite a bit. The last couple of times he left his card with his tip. He was probably trying to drum up business."

"You're absolutely sure this is the psychiatrist?" asked Gary, pointing to Levi's picture. "Is this Paul Shapiro?"

"No doubt about it," offered the bartender. "He came here so often in his black Bronco that all of us who work here would instantly recognize him."

"Is this the business card he left?" Gary handed over one of the two cards taken from Twist's place.

"That's it."

The detective turned to leave. At the door, Gary turned back and half shouted, "Thanks for your help!"

With his questioning of the bartender, his picture was complete. My Kind was where Levi Twist had located and trailed businesswomen. Everything was falling into place. What was not complete was his understanding of what Levi was about to do now that he was on the lam. Gary felt that he had two jobs to do as soon as possible. First, he had to get to the Shapiros and warn them that they might be in danger. Second, he knew that he owed Paul Shapiro a huge apology for his unjust incrimination.

———

It was almost 8:30 that evening when Gary Jarvis knocked on the door of the Shapiro hideaway. For a moment he thought he saw someone peek out from behind the rustic curtains and heard a hasty shuffling inside the house as though someone might be trying to hide. He stood pondering the whole scenario when two yellow eyes approached him on the porch, striking fear into his soul.

"Kinta . . . Kinta," he spoke the words as kindly and loudly as he possibly could.

The wolf crawled toward him, whimpering as though he wanted to be stroked. Wondering if he would draw back more than a bloody stub, Gary reached down and stroked the wolf. He was amazed at how the powerful animal yielded to his touch. He found himself stooping down and petting the beast, who generously rewarded him with a sandpapery lick. While he thus exercised his hand in the animal's fur, the door swung open. It was Rhonda Shapiro.

"Hello, Mrs. Shapiro. Are you surprised to see me again?"

"Rather so," said Rhonda.

"Well, I'm a little surprised to be here."

Rhonda said nothing. Gary broke the awkward silence.

"Is your husband here?"

"No," Rhonda lied so unconvincingly that the both of them knew it instantly.

"Well, tell him I'm very sorry. I wrongly accused him. His detective work was a piece of genius. He was right. We haven't caught the real criminal yet, but we know who it is. We followed your husband's lead. Joanna Nickerson called it in. We will catch the real killer soon, and when we do, I want to take both you and your husband out to dinner for simplifying my case."

"Wo . . . won't you come in, Mr. Jarvis?" asked a dumbfounded Rhonda.

As he did, Paul Shapiro stepped out of the front closet.

"Oh, so you are home, Dr. Shapiro. I'm afraid I owe you an apology."

"I . . . I . . . ," stammered the psychiatrist.

"I know all this had to be hard on you, sir. I do apologize for all my wrong assumptions. My work was shoddy, Dr. Shapiro. You cracked the case, and all of us at the SPD are grateful."

Rhonda burst into tears of relief.

The Shapiros' broken world was beginning to mend.

Jarvis jolted the euphoria by saying, "There's only one problem. The suspect is still very much at large, and you and Rhonda and Kinta may be in a great deal of danger. I believe that Levi Twist is armed with a thirty-ought-six rifle, and it could have a scope on it. Do not go out of the house by the front door during the day. Keep Kinta as close to the cabin as you can."

CHAPTER 36

By the end of the first full week in June, the area around the Callahan Grove was becoming congested with the arrival of hundreds of backpackers and campers. By the middle of the month, the number had risen to the thousands. George Callahan, true to his word, had seen to it that there were plenty of toilet and water facilities. But even he was overwhelmed by the sheer number of protesters. And the media were awed by the masses demonstrating their interest in the primal grove of great trees.

The date of the rally had been printed in papers far and near by every environmentalist group in the western United States. Still, the support the rally engendered could never have been guessed. Within the last mile of the road that led to the grove, several No Vehicles Beyond This Point signs had been posted. All drivers seemed to obey. An uncanny sense of law and order prevailed.

Fortunately for Paul and Rhonda Shapiro, they had stocked up on groceries and other necessaries. They had seen the crisis coming their way. People flowed into the area but not out of it. The human swarm blocked all roads. Even the small private lane that led to their cabin was blocked where it split from the old reservoir road that led to the Callahan Grove. Fields of tents stretched down and away from the main grove. The media began begging people not to join the impossible congestion that had become a scourge in the wilderness, but the pleas were futile. There was some question in the media that what demonstrators were trying to preserve was being undone by the effects of their numbers.

By twisting and turning through swarms of parked cars into the no-car area, the water trucks made their way to the protestors. Callahan made sure that his name was stenciled on the side of each truck. But those who attended the rally understood that politics had brought the water and politics never served merely water. The water was part of a much larger deal that Callahan hoped to sell, but no one seemed to buy.

By Thursday, June 15, the crowd was expectant. Something wonderful was about to be unveiled. Everyone waited to behold the revealing of whatever this something might be. This was to be an experience, a memory, a vaulting change that would touch the world. Seattle was the happy point on the map where this incarnation of human spirit would occur.

Gary Jarvis managed not to let the occasion dull his duty. He still had major fears for the Shapiros and their wolf. He knew that wherever Levi Twist was he still bore a killing grudge.

Following Joanna Nickerson's call to inform the SPD, Levi Twist had become a hunted man. The Bronco that he had driven successfully through, or more likely around, the numerous roadblocks had been found deserted on a country road in northwest Oregon. The keys were missing, as were the suspect's personal effects. If Levi Twist was alive, he had become a master of stealth. His picture had been printed multiple times in the newspapers of the Northwest and had been shown repeatedly on television. Pacific Woods stock had plummeted. Until the board of directors could come up with a good cover and a new leader, stock values were likely to remain low. Scores of supposed identifications were reported, but none of them checked out. Levi seemed to have disappeared into thin air.

Gary, like all of Seattle, wondered if the killer had retained his dog. Like Levi, Daimon was nowhere to be found. And yet, just the presence of the animal would have made it hard for the killer to move out in the open without being noticed. Jarvis was almost sure that wherever Levi was he must be moving by night. He might have fled across some lonely border area into Canada or taken flight to another remote corner of the United States. But Gary felt that the nature of his psychotic vengeance would sooner or later bring him back to the area where he still had grudges to settle.

Romance, however, had dulled the edge of the inspector's investigation.

Gary had found Melody once more. Their reunion was wonderful. He met her for the first time since their divorce at the Shapiros' cabin. Paul and Rhonda told them of the wonderful way that their own ailing marriage had mysteriously begun to repair itself, for some odd reason, on the day that Kinta came into their lives. For Melody, the entrance of Kinta or the old priest—and she wasn't sure which had the most to do with it—into her life had prefaced a sense of guilt over the divorce that she had forced upon Gary.

While these two couples regrouped their shattered marriages, Eric Compton and Isletta Borg were finding love for the first time. Eric had known from the first that he was not merely Isletta's attorney in the *Borg v. Callahan* suit. He was in love. It seemed the whole chaotic world had become mystically organized around one of two poles. It had come together around either Kinta or the old priest. And yet behind these odd explanations lay no sensible notion of anything terribly mysterious. It was just that life—which had never worked very well for any of the three couples—was suddenly working well for all of them. There are times when it is good to be alive, and both life and the goodness it gives are to be enjoyed rather than reasoned through.

On Friday, Joanna Nickerson and Janie finally led her foot-weary band of pilgrims up to the grove. "Joanna's Exodus," as the press were calling it, wound its final way up the high hill that led to the grove with a sense of conquest. But many others from Joanna's church were there too. This crowd of ex-derelicts and homeless city people seemed enervated by the mountains and the smell of damp pine needles. Each of these happy pilgrims sang praises around their evening rally fires.

Joanna had challenged her disciples into making five or six miles per day. Her happy, if weary, band had come out of Egypt where they were powerless pariahs. Joanna's Exodus had given front-page status to the thousands who had followed her from Seattle to the wilderness. Further, the United Way and other relief organizations brought loads of food to care for her "Exodus." There was indeed manna every morning and honey in the rocks, just as the cheeky Isaiah of her dreams had promised her.

It was Henry Demond who had suggested that Father Peter come along, and thus the old priest found himself in the company of the congregation of the Pathway of Light Cathedral. The name of the church amused Father Peter. The storefront worship building was quite unlike anything that most pictured when they used the word *cathedral*. Still, he found their worship so wonderful and free that he felt a genuine admiration for their simplistic piety.

As Henry Demond had brought Father Peter along, so the priest had brought Emma Silone to the mass gathering. Emma was still convinced that her Harvey was trying to poison her. It had done Paul Shapiro little good to try to convince her otherwise. But Emma and the priest, blessed by their odd psychologies, had become good friends.

Here and there throughout the throng gathered lone singers who wailed out various ballads about saving Earth. The event was being called the "Envirowoodstock." There was also a New Age piper or two, saffron-robed Hare Krishnas, and the white-robed Gaians. There were several other Earth-worshipping groups as well. But the Christians massively outnumbered the others, their praise and worship giving the rally a tenor of splendor.

From their cabin, the Shapiros could see everything. In the evenings, Paul and Rhonda and Kinta often walked from their cabin down to the remote perimeter of the throng of 200,000 or more. The anticipation of June 18 was so magnetic that it filled the senses and hung in the air.

The Shapiros, still uncertain of Levi Twist's whereabouts, were glad they had decided to stay at the cabin rather than return to their home on Snoqualmie River Road. The huge crowd at the Callahan Grove had unwittingly afforded the Shapiros better police protection. Paul felt there was safety in numbers.

It was on the Saturday afternoon just before the rally was to begin that it occurred to Rhonda that she had not seen Kinta since Friday. She would have thought nothing of it except that it was so unlike him. She suspected that Kinta was moving far and away from the huge crowds. He—as befit his nature—was a loner. The crowds seemed to make him edgy and afraid. Rhonda still had a trembling concern that the euphoria that filled the Callahan Grove might be destroyed by the fugitive Levi Twist, who had so recently made all Seattle tremble. It was this remembrance that caused her to be afraid for Kinta as well. She convinced Paul that they should venture away from the crowd to look for Kinta.

Paul stuck his pistol in his pocket as they moved from the backside of the cabin and through the thinner woods toward the upper slope. They picked a well-worn trail that became quite overgrown as they moved upward. When they were more than a mile from the cabin, the paucity of trees gave way to dense thickets.

As they rose higher, Rhonda repeatedly called Kinta's name aloud, always without response. Finally they reached a clearing and stopped to rest on a sun-warmed flat boulder.

The Callahan Grove protestors were only a distant hum, but it was that distant hum that caused Rhonda a sense of disorientation. She thought she could hear a whimpering over and above the faraway din. She tried to dismiss the notion, but the feeling persisted. "Paul," she said, "do you hear that?"

"Yes . . . yes, I do," he responded.

They both rose from the warm boulder and began slowly walking toward the odd sound, stopping every now and then to listen. Repeatedly, Rhonda called Kinta's name and waited again. It seemed that each time she said it the whimpering was instantly on the air, as though Kinta was responding as best he could, although he could not respond well. Gradually, they closed in upon Kinta's weak signal. Then from a berry thicket they glimpsed shadowy sunlight falling on silver fur.

It was Kinta.

They could see that he was weakly thrashing in a trap. Paul pulled back the heavy foliage of the concealing shrubs. Kinta's forepaw had been nearly severed by the closing jaws of a steel trap, exposing the bones and tendons beneath the bloody pelt of his foreleg. Paul took the pistol he carried and emptied it of its bullets, sticking the ammunition in his pockets. He then wedged the barrel into the metal teeth of the trap.

Using the unloaded weapon as a pry bar, he sprang the device open far enough for Rhonda to extricate the animal's foot. The teeth closed again on the barrel of the gun. The prying motion severely scratched the barrel of the weapon, but Paul managed at last to pull the pistol out of the steel teeth.

"Let's get Kinta to a vet," said Rhonda.

Paul carried Kinta to an opening in the thick foliage and stopped for a moment to rest. They had worked so long under the cramped thicket, it felt good just to stand up. Paul immediately realized how big Kinta was. He carried him fifty feet or so down the path they had taken coming up the mountain. Now the burden of the huge animal was too much for him. He set the animal down and patted him on the rump. Kinta walked, limping in such a way as to favor his crippled foot.

They had not gone another fifty feet when they heard the remote crack of rifle fire, and at the very same moment Paul felt the impact of a bullet strike his shoulder. He spun sideways, falling helplessly forward across the animal he was trying to save.

"Paul!" screamed Rhonda.

They heard a second crack of rifle fire. It was probably intended for Rhonda, but her sudden movement to save Paul put her momentarily out of harm's way. At that moment the errant bullet missed her and smashed into the hard ground in the clearing just beyond her. The worst part of their predicament was that the wide clearing offered them no place to hide. They expected that at any moment they would hear a third shot, but while they waited for it and feared it, it didn't happen. Why?

Rhonda saw through the blurring of tears that Father Peter was coming through the tall trees. He was still dressed in blue coveralls. She breathed a sigh of relief. He came rapidly up the trail, temporarily stopping the sniper from firing anymore shots. The gunman, expecting more people to come up the trail, fled for fear of discovery. For the moment, no rifle fire came from the small clump of scrub-oak trees near the trail several hundred yards above them.

"Oh, Father Peter, thank God, it's you! Please, Paul's hurt!" sobbed Rhonda. "Please, help us!"

"Not to worry, Mrs. Shapiro, he's going to be all right!"

"No, no! Please, he's been shot!"

"Please, Mrs. Shapiro, trust me; he'll be all right."

At his words, Rhonda stopped crying and watched as the old man bent over her husband. Ordinarily she would have wondered what he was doing, but deep in her heart, she knew he had a right to be there, doing whatever he wanted to do.

"Oh, please do something," urged Rhonda, returning to her former despair. "He's bleeding. See if you can get it stopped."

"What's that supposed to mean?" said the priest. "Of course I can get it stopped."

He took Paul's face in his hands, turning the doctor's eyes to face his own. When he had Paul's undivided attention, he said very simply, "Dr. Shapiro, in the name of Jesus!" he shouted, "I must insist that you stop this pointless bleeding right now! NOW STAND UP AND GIVE GOD THE GLORY!"

"Is that how you intend to stop the bleeding?" asked Rhonda. "What makes you think that it will work?"

"I watched Sister Joanna do it over at the Pathway of Light Cathedral," beamed Father Peter.

"And did it work?" asked Rhonda.

"It appeared to! It's a little hard to tell if these things really work as well outdoors as they do in Sister Joanna's church. I think the key may be that others respond to her words with a hearty 'amen!' Would you two mind saying 'amen'?"

"Amen!" said Rhonda.

"Amen!" said Paul, though very weakly.

"Paul, the bleeding has stopped," said Father Peter.

"Proving that you are a great faith healer," said Rhonda.

"Proving that this was just a surface wound," said Father Peter. "We better get on down the mountain. I'm not as good at healing head wounds."

Paul shook his head to clear it and felt his shoulder. "It's OK," he said.

Rhonda was ecstatic. She collided with Paul and hugged him so hard she nearly toppled him back over again.

"Easy, miss," said Father Peter. "It won't do us much good to heal him if you insist on crippling him again. Besides, it makes my healing look ineffective. I just love being a faith healer! I want to get as good as Reverend Nickerson."

It was only after Paul and Rhonda were embracing that Father Peter turned to look at Kinta. "In the name of Jesus, Kinta, be healed and stand up and walk! RIGHT NOW. I COMMAND YOU!"

Kinta still walked with a limp. The old priest looked confused.

"I guess I need a few more lessons," the confused cleric lamented.

The priest settled down and tried again. This time he merely walked over and touched Kinta, saying nothing. But abruptly, at his touch, the animal looked at him and stood up. He was still a little shaky, but it was clear to all he was on the mend, even if he required a long rest to make the healing happen. Paul and Rhonda were amazed. But not Father Peter. He did not regard Kinta's healing as unusual, neither did he pay any serious attention to the Shapiros' amazement.

"We must get back down the mountain before there is anymore trouble," the cleric repeated. At his word they all began walking back down the mountain and soon were well hidden within the security of the trees. Paul felt the wetness in his shirt and jacket, still a deep-red from his loss of blood, but there were no other indicators that he had been shot. He smiled when he thought of the comic way the old priest had ended this near-disaster. He knew deep down that there was more to all this than the priest's hasty lessons in the Pathway of Light Cathedral.

Kinta, as always, now trotted along behind them. Rhonda, in watching him, thought it was unfair to call this odd enchantment magic, for it was more than that. But it seemed equally odd to call it miraculous in the kind of culture Seattle had become. Still, looking at Kinta walk along, Rhonda was convinced that it was just that: miraculous.

One thing for sure had happened: God had come to be a short word of immense content to both of the Shapiros. Paul gave Joanna Nickerson the credit for having blessed his life with an example of real faith. He had a vibrancy about him that he had never had before. It was impossible for Paul Shapiro not to bless the hard times in his recent life. He was even thankful for those few days that he had been a fugitive. It was those brief days in flight from the law that had reduced the psychiatrist to needing God. The crisis of his fugitive life had brought him ever so gradually to feel his need and to be open to admitting it. But all his crises were not yet passed.

The rifle fire on the mountain told both of the Shapiros that their worries were not over. They were still in need. Indeed, they were still very much in danger. They would need God and Gary Jarvis to help them if they were to survive. As much as they feared for themselves, the trap that nearly destroyed Kinta for a second time was a clear indication that they must continue to watch over the wolf as well.

They both knew that Levi Twist was alive. While he was free, neither of the Shapiros would be safe. They were both sure that following the rally on the morrow, they would return to their home on Seattle's River Road. They liked the idea of going home. They knew that they would be safer in the city than in the wilderness. The police could offer them closer surveillance once they were back in Seattle. They prayed that God would somehow watch over them until Levi Twist was safely behind bars.

CHAPTER 37

Once the Shapiros disappeared into the forest across the clearing, Levi Twist emerged from his concealing clump of trees. He was carrying his rifle strapped diagonally across his back.

Daimon, closely leashed, followed along at his side. His powerful head was muzzled as usual. They both looked thin and worn. It was easy to tell that both man and beast were fugitives. Levi's once handsome appearance was mottled by an unkempt beard. His clothes looked dowdy and worn. His Fortune 500, Pacific Woods CEO appearance had become wild and monstrous. Neither of them looked like they had eaten in a long time. Daimon's fur was always mottled with scars, but weeks of hunger made his coat especially ugly.

Levi Twist—fugitive and sniper—was a man driven by deep grudges. In the weeks since he had ditched his black four-wheel drive, he had moved covertly through the backcountry under cover of darkness until he came to the Cascade Highlands. He and Daimon had hitched rides on freight trains in open boxcars or walked deserted roads and over creekbanks, always traveling at night. A couple of times Levi had broken into isolated mountain cabins and stolen enough food to survive. But for most of the trip both had been sometimes hungry and often cold.

Levi had set the few traps he had been able to carry with him in the vicinity of what he had come to discover was the Shapiro cabin. He had not come upon the cabin entirely by accident. He knew that Della's boss had a cabin directly east of the city. He had prospected cabins in that vicinity until by trial and error he had eliminated all but the Shapiro home. When he at last caught sight of Kinta, he knew he'd found them. What he didn't know was that the Shapiro cabin was close to the Callahan Grove. Then the rally came and complicated his plans.

He had watched for Kinta and, after a couple of days of observation, set his trap near the particular trail Kinta always took in his running about the countryside. He wasn't sure that the wolf had actually stepped into the trap until he saw the Shapiros coming up the trail. It was at that time that he decided to use the rifle to stop all three of them.

His former grudge against Rhonda had now expanded to Paul as well. It was Paul, through Joanna, who had first set the SPD on him. Now Levi had no place to go. There was no doubt about his guilt. But before he was taken in, he would deal with the Shapiros once and for all.

When Daimon and Levi reached the berry thicket, Daimon got a scent of the blood that Kinta's injured leg had left on the jaws of the trap. This scent of blood caused Daimon to grow agitated. He strained at his leash, trying to sniff the trap much closer than the heavy leather mesh of his muzzle would allow him to do.

Levi began to flog him with the short chain he kept in his pocket. Daimon lurched toward the end of the leash to avoid the blows but was unable to escape. Blow after blow fell across Daimon's back and chest until the great dog was again bleeding profusely. When it was clear to Levi that he was no longer lurching to be free but had begun to lunge at his master, Levi knew what to do. He thrust Rhonda's blouse under Daimon's broad nose, and the suffering animal sniffed the blouse and seemed even more agitated.

Then Levi bent down and removed the muzzle. The large dog eyed his cruel master. It was that same look of hate that Levi Twist always redirected from himself to all of those he wanted Daimon to destroy. Now that Daimon had Rhonda's scent on his broad nose, Levi unsnapped the leash.

"KILL!" Levi commanded.

With the scent of Rhonda so recently on the trail, Daimon leapt away from Levi and sniffed in half reversals of his trip, making sure that all he smelled of Rhonda's blouse still lingered on the trail. Levi stuck the leash in one of his large coat pockets and tied the muzzle to the rifle strap that angled across his chest. Daimon was off once again to do his master's work, only this time Levi could not accompany him.

It was nearly dark when Rhonda and Paul decided to walk down to the evening festivities in the broad lea before the

Callahan Grove. The green meadow had now soaked up the fleeting light of day, but no matter. There were bonfires burning and a portable speaker system amplifying the poetry and songs of the celebration.

The Shapiros took a seat in the grass at the distant side of the meadow just as someone began to read an Emily Dickinson poem. Next, there was a reading of Sara Teasdale's "There Will Come Soft Rain." Rhonda didn't recognize several other selections that were beautiful. A quartet from a state university sang the choral version of Joyce Kilmer's "Trees." While this was not one of Rhonda's favorite poems, musically it set the tone for all that was going to be happening in the Callahan Grove on the morrow. Some of the Christians read passages from the Bible on the Creation and sang hymns like "Morning Has Broken" and "Fairest Lord Jesus, Ruler of All Nature."

But something sinister was happening. It was now dark, and the amber light of the bonfires provided only flickering suggestions of what was causing the disturbance. People seemed to be backing away from the center of some encroaching uproar as if they were afraid. Then, before they were quite able to absorb what was going on, the spectators shrunk away from the path of the animal that had left them so afraid. Daimon advanced steadily through the crowd as people fearfully scattered.

Rhonda stood up as quickly as she could. Paul followed her lead. Kinta, who had been lying beside them, stretched and stood up. He seemed to hold his injured forepaw for a few seconds, but no longer. All too soon the dog that had caused the uproar on the far side of the crowd was racing half crazed toward the Shapiros. The blood that Levi had earlier cut into his fur was now scabbed and scaly. The dog's eyes were slits in the scarce light of the bonfires. Far before the Shapiros were ready for the horrible confrontation, Daimon landed only a few feet away from them, his ears flattened against his head. He snarled, and his fangs sank down under his broad nose that wrinkled away from his yellowed teeth. Paul watched in horror and for the first time really understood what it was that Della must have faced in her final moments of life.

He felt his own flesh crawl as Daimon circled them. The only member of the trio that wasn't afraid was Kinta. It was a moment or so before Rhonda noticed that Kinta looked at Daimon with a determined intensity. The wolf began to paw the ground and snarl as he began his own circling ritual. A part of the dispersed crowd began to gather at a safe distance to watch this odd dance of brutish enemies.

Kinta and Daimon at last stopped their distant circling and moved closer and closer to each other. Bit by bit they picked up the pace of the odd ritual, snarling louder as their hateful circle tightened. Then they struck. Black and silver fur swirled in a roaring dervish of hate and tearing flesh. There seemed to be no way to stop the settling of their murderous grudge. Even if it had been possible, no one was possessed of the courage to try to interrupt the fray of these snarling enemies.

When the sound of their death lock was at unbelievable intensity, an old man in blue coveralls stepped out of the fearful crowd.

"No, Father!" cried Rhonda.

The old man turned to the amazed crowd and cried, "Perceive where hate always ends . . . in claw and fang. Hating is of no use to God. It maims and destroys. It makes beautiful things ugly and ends God's greatest gift—life. Violence begets violence . . . always."

Now Kinta was pulling at the throat of Daimon, and blood was spurting all over the fur of both animals. The war would soon end, and it looked as though Daimon would be dead. The old man stepped between the snarling, twisting tornado of feral struggle. He stuck his hand between their flashing claws and fangs. He pulled Kinta's head up and sharply rebuked him. "Kinta, Kinta, Kinta. Is this how God made you? Don't you think you would better serve your Maker by letting go of hate?" It was an odd thing to say to a wolf, but hardly were the words out of his mouth, when Kinta unhooked his bloody teeth from Daimon's throat. "There, there. Now that's much better, my friend. Quit acting so much like people!"

No sooner had Kinta released the German shepherd than the huge dog lunged at him, trying to grab his throat. But Father Peter caught his lunge mid-air and pulled him down to his knee. "Now, now, Daimon, it was an evil man who trained you to kill. It's time to master some better lessons."

He paused a moment and then said, "Kinta, this is Daimon. Daimon, Kinta. Kinta, I order you to give up your prejudice against dogs. Daimon, I order you to surrender your antipathy for wolves. Now! Now! That's better, isn't it? Exercise a little restraint in your grudges. Maybe we can sell your new self-control in places like Los Angeles and Seattle?"

The old enemies looked at each other a moment. They moved together and began to rub their necks against each other. Like whelps discovering their world, they began to play at each other's ears with their paws.

The crowd broke into cheers and applause.

Had Eden come again? It seemed as though the beasts were dancing on a new planet born within a gracious solar system. Before an awestruck crowd, Daimon and Kinta had established a peaceable kingdom where a lion might indeed lay down with a lamb.

Gary and Melody Jarvis were among those who beheld this odd taming of savagery. They walked up to Paul and Rhonda just as the priest walked away. Kinta and Daimon lay down in the grass beside Rhonda and Paul. Melody reached out and stroked the derelict German shepherd, as she had stroked Kinta several times at the Shapiro cabin. This was not an act of courage. The world was somehow new, and fear was prohibited. Dog petting was now a deliberate calling in life—a ritual of initiation into Eden reborn. Indeed, the whole scene seemed so ordinary that no one took notice of it. Melody looked at Rhonda and said, "Ronnie, you'll never guess what Gary brought with him."

The riddle invited no guess. Melody followed it up with an immediate answer before Rhonda had a chance to reply: "A marriage license!"

"Whose marriage license?" asked Rhonda.

"Ours!" said Gary as he extended Melody's hand. She had her old engagement ring on once again. "We're going to be married tonight by the Reverend Joanna Nickerson."

"Tonight!" gasped Rhonda. "Isn't all of this a little sudden? I mean, not that you haven't been married before but—"

"Rhonda, there is something wonderful going on here. I don't want to go down from this mountain with our marriage still in disrepair. This is a night for everything that's broken to be mended."

In other times an environmental rally would have seemed an odd place for a wedding, but given the enchantment that throbbed in the air, nothing good seemed inappropriate.

"Congratulations, old man!" said Paul Shapiro, roughly clapping Gary on the back.

"Thanks," Gary replied, almost shyly. It seemed impossible to Paul that only two weeks ago the blushing bridegroom was his all-consuming foe. Just as Rhonda and Melody stood up to hug, Joanna and Janie Nickerson came out of the crowd.

Gary walked up to Joanna and introduced himself. "I'm the officer you talked to on the phone about the clues at Levi's. And I'm the officer Father Peter told you about. I believe he mentioned that Melody and I would like to be married tonight."

"Did you bring the paperwork, Inspector?" asked the Reverend Joanna.

"I'm off duty now. . . . It's OK if you call me Gary."

"Well, Gary?"

"Yes, yes I did; it's all right here." Gary drew a document out of his jacket pocket and handed it to the Reverend Nickerson. She took it.

"Shall we meet back here in an hour or so, after you've all put on your tuxedos and bridal gowns?" asked Joanna.

"No, we had that kind of wedding last time. We'll do it now in Levis and windbreakers," said Melody.

In the distance, they could hear an a capella group singing a choral version of Bach's "Jesu, Joy of Man's Desiring." In the flickering of amber fires, Melody and Gary Jarvis performed a magic kind of therapy on their old and broken vows. Joanna said the simple words, and they replied with simple promises. And Rhonda, whose own marriage had made a dramatic return to life, found tears streaming down her face in the firelight.

When Joanna had pronounced the Jarvises husband and wife, Paul gave them a gift that he had been given from an old passage in the book of Ruth. "Gary and Melody," he said, "this is from the Bible. It's been my companion since God began to heal my own broken marriage."

The four took turns embracing one another, and in the smiles and tears, Paul spoke the ancient words of Ruth: "Entreat me not to leave thee, nor to return from following after thee. For whither thou goest, I will go and wither thou lodgest I will lodge, and thy people shall be my people and thy God my God."

"Pauly, your struggles have made you wise," Rhonda beamed.

"Maybe," he said, "but after all Gary and Melody have gone through, maybe what the king said to his lover in the Song of Solomon would be the best benediction."

"And what is that?" Melody asked.

"Mighty waters cannot extinguish love, rivers cannot sweep it away."

"Paul," said Gary, "I want you to help us understand all of this God business when we're back down the mountain. As for right now, folks, this is my wedding night, and we have our own tent over in the east grove. I think we'll excuse ourselves for now."

They all laughed.

"It was a lovely wedding," said Rhonda.

"Thanks," said the newlyweds, laughing and then running off toward their tent.

The Shapiros signed as witnesses on the marriage certificate, which Joanna stuck in her purse. Then the Shapiros walked back to the cabin with both the wolf and the dog following behind.

Instinctively, Paul felt that Levi would not venture so close to the mass of people to inflict any harm on them. He even smiled a bit as he held the door and the two huge animals went inside. He and Rhonda prepared for bed as they listened to the singing down in the heart of the Callahan Grove.

Somewhere Daimon's master waited in the darkness, and the night needed light to see what insanity his desperate grudge yet bore. But tomorrow was the rally day, and good is rarely so glorious that single demons can't squeeze their way into throngs of angels.

Rhonda looked at Kinta and feared the coming of the day.

CHAPTER 38

"A re you the Virgin of Stockholm?" Father Peter asked,
extending his hand to Isletta Borg.

"Well, so far, Father," replied Isletta. "But what an impertinent question."

"If you don't mind my saying so, you're the woman of
my dreams," said Father Peter.

Isletta, considering him to be some kind of crank, turned
on her heel to walk away.

Father Peter became very agitated.

"Please, don't leave me," he said. "I've been waiting a
very long time to meet you. You may not believe this, but I
am a poor priest, and I've spent quite awhile now in a mental institution."

That was not hard for Isletta Borg to believe. Still, his
utter honesty caused her to turn back toward him.

"Please, sit a moment with me," he said.

She looked afraid to do it. Her first impression—that he
was mad—passed into the oddest sensation that he was not

mad but holy. Isletta remembered seeing *Agnes of God* on the stage and was now utterly possessed by feelings of déjà vu.

"I know what you're thinking," said Father Peter. "You're trying to decide whether I am a fiend or an angel. Whether I am hopelessly mad or marvelously divine."

Isletta decided to at least spend the time with him to hear him out.

"Though this be madness, yet there is method in it," mumbled Isletta, almost to herself, though it was quickly evident that the old priest had heard her.

"Hamlet," said the old priest. "Act 2, scene 2." She was amazed and sat down in the grass. It was near eleven o'clock, but the splendor of the June night—the lights of the fires, circled by singing and conversation—was wonderful. No one wanted to sleep; the world was too full of wonder. The music and the voices served as a background to Isletta's chance meeting with the old priest.

"Isletta, it is so good to finally meet you. It is so good to know that you are the Virgin of Stockholm."

"Stop it. Stop saying that!" demanded Isletta. "It sounds stupid. Stop it!"

"You do have the deed to this meadow, don't you?"

"Yes," she said, a faint flickering of understanding breaking across her darkened mind. Then suddenly she understood it all.

The priest reached up and unsnapped his clerical collar. He pulled his shirt and coat away. Under his black suit, he was wearing blue coveralls.

"Have you ever thought of surrendering your Eden to become a practical reminder that the good Lord is quite a conservationist? This would be a good place for the world to recognize that the world is in need of such a reminder."

Suddenly the Virgin of Stockholm knew what she would do with her piece of the forest, for it was indeed her piece of the world.

CHAPTER 39

The magic of Saturday's campfire vigil evaporated into a bright new day. But the morning sun did nothing to lift Emma Silone out of her depression. She felt truly alone and confused. She had heard that her psychiatrist had a cabin somewhere uphill from the grove, but she was too old to walk very far. Besides, this rally was an odd gathering of souls that seemed as odd as she seemed to herself. Everyone was reading books of one kind or another. The daylight sun seemed somehow glaring. Those who were not busy gathering firewood for the final vigil seemed to have moved further into the forest to enjoy the shade-patterned forest floor that was far cooler. Emma took an aluminum folding chair that she had brought along and moved off into the trees. She had almost disappeared in the trees when she heard someone call to her from the far side of the meadow.

"Yoo hoo! Emma, honey, it's me!"

Emma's blood froze. She knew without even looking around that it was Harvey. At first, she decided not to wait for him. She tried to hurry into the trees and give Harvey the slip. She failed in this attempt. When she did look around, she could see that he was carrying a sack from McDonald's; no doubt he had stopped on his way to the rally site and bought her a Big Mac. Somewhere in the interim she knew he had laced the hamburger with strychnine or whatever it would take to do her in.

She was just at the edge of the tall trees and had determined to hurry on in when she met Father Peter. He gently wagged his long, bony index finger in her face and asked, "Now, now, Emma, should you be so unkind to your life mate?"

"Some life mate!" insisted Emma obstinately. "I'm only alive because I keep away from this mate!"

"Now, Emma," said the priest, "you've been a little sick. You're suffering from what your psychiatrist calls paranoid delusions."

"Well, I don't know about all that," said Emma. "I'm just afraid of Harvey."

"There's nothing wrong with Harvey, Emma; it's you who has a problem. Harvey hasn't been bringing you Big Macs to 'do you in,' as you say; he's bringing you Big Macs because he genuinely loves you."

"You're sure?"

"No foolin'!" said the priest.

"Honey! I brought us some lunch," said Harvey, who had finally caught up to the priest and his poor Emma.

"Big Macs again, Harvey?" asked Emma.

"Yes, indeed!" Harvey grinned broadly. Two of Harvey's gold teeth glinted in the sun. "Emma, remember how you used to love Big Macs?"

"You know I do, Harvey, but I won't eat anything with you unless you take the first bite." She paused a moment and said, "Harvey, this is Father Peter. I think he's a real angel."

"Oh, Emma, you're sweet, but you get so mixed up. Remember when you thought the mail lady was Shirley MacLaine? Bless your heart, Emma, it doesn't matter." Harvey paused, turning to the priest, "I'm so glad to meet you, sir. Don't worry about what my Emma just called you. She's always been an angel herself; it was a natural mistake for her to make." He turned back to Emma and said, "Hey, Emma, angel, come on. Let's go into the shade, and you can eat your Big Mac."

Emma resisted Harvey's tug on her sleeve, but in a moment all three walked under the shade of one of the huge trees of the Callahan Grove. Emma unfolded her aluminum chair and sat down. Harvey leaned back against a tree and opened the sack from McDonald's. He pulled out a large beverage cup. "Here Emma, here's a Diet Coke, and I had them put a slice of lemon in it just like you always order."

Emma refused to reach out.

Father Peter took the drink for her and had a sip. "Emma, it is a hot day," said the old priest. "Why don't you take a sip? It's good and cold, and it won't hurt you." To prove that the drink was harmless, the priest took an even bigger sip and said, "See there, it's harmless!"

"That's easy for you to say, Father; you're religious. I'm more poisonable than you are." She was finding it hard to pick good words, and serious conversations usually gave her a headache.

Then the priest did a wonderful thing. He reached out and took the top of her head in his long, bony fingers. He held her head for a moment and twisted his fingers in a rotating method around her head and then twisted them back again. "Hmm," he said, staring at her head as though he were looking inside it. "I detect a small throb of low, electric density pulsating from your right occipital lobe. I know the problem. Let me check to be sure. I never like to heal things that aren't broken. It's not a good use of my time."

He paused, stared fixedly once again, and rotated his hand and then waited fully a minute. The empty gaze on his face broke to a broad smile. "Yes, I was right. Hold very still, Emma. You had a slight stroke on February the second that burned out three of your synapse plexi. That allowed a hyperelectrical impulse to short across three cells and burn them up, impairing the phobic-prone area of your brain. You know, it's those strokes. You've got to watch your cholesterol. I might not always be around," said the priest.

His fingers suddenly snapped into pencils of white light, and he looked at the side of her head where the light entered. "You know, of course, brain cells never replace themselves. There," he said, the light pencils from his fingers concentrated downward. "Hold on, Emma!"

Emma Silone shuddered under his grasp of her cranium. She made a little outcry as some unspeakable but short-lived pain passed. She fell limp for a moment and then blinked.

"Look, Emma, here are the trouble makers," he said, extending his hand toward her. "Can you see them? They're awfully small."

Emma stared into his hand, "I'm sorry. I can't see a thing!" she said.

"That's the trouble with you mortals. Your eyes are weak, and you have absolutely no power to see the little things that ought to be clearly visible," said the priest, admitting to Emma's delusions. "You should all be allowed to park in handicapped stalls as far as I'm concerned."

Harvey laughed so loud at the comment that Emma turned to see him. "Oh Harvey, you're here," Emma exulted. "Oh, honey, I'm so glad you've come." She then looked at the sack in his hand, "And you picked up something at McDonald's! Great, I've been dying for a Big Mac. I'm starving. Let's eat."

"Sounds good to me," said Harvey. "You want me to take a bite first, so you can be sure?"

"Sure of what?" she asked. Then she became pointed, "You take a bite of my hamburger, and you'll lose a hand. Get your own hamburger, Harvey."

Emma reached for the sack. Harvey held onto it and pulled her face close to his and they kissed. She noticed that Harvey was crying. Emma seemed a bit baffled as to why anyone would cry over a sack of Big Macs, but then Harvey always got sentimental at fast-food places. She started to offer the priest some fries, but when she looked up, he was gone.

Father Peter had gone to pay a call on Eric Compton. He had to be made to understand the import of Father Peter's midnight call on Isletta. They would both be key in the matter. Actually, Eric Compton thought he had only fallen in love with Isletta Borg; he had no idea he was about to marry the Virgin of Stockholm. It was a concept that the priest knew he would need a little help with. When he came upon Eric, he was with Isletta.

"How are you lovebirds?" he asked.

"Great!" Eric replied.

"Terrific," Isletta chimed in.

"Well," said the priest, "if you think you're having trouble understanding me, think of the adjustment I am having to make here in Washington. I'll never understand people. So many here seem unsettled unless they're doing something evil or immoral. How does anybody ever trust anybody in this perverse world?" He was getting preachy.

"Hey! Back off!" objected Eric. "We're not all that bad."

"It's not the exterior that counts; it's what's in the heart of men that really counts. And human hearts are so perverse. You constantly fudge on speed-limit signs and complain of injustice when you get caught cheating. You tell any white lie that will speed your own agenda. You all cheat on income taxes and shade expense vouchers in your favor. You tell lies and call in sick when you don't want to go to work. You make foul excuses when you're late. Day in, day out. Lie! Lie! Lie! You lie even when it would be easier to tell the truth."

"Well, I'll be a monkey's uncle!" said Eric, interrupting his sermon.

"Nonsense! Monkeys have honest uncles!" the priest protested the metaphor.

"Well, Isletta and I are not dishonest."

"Of course you are. She's not as dishonest as you, but your whole planet is infected with wrongs. The odd thing is that no one believes much in sin anymore. You all run around saying, 'I'm OK, you're OK,' and absolutely nobody's OK. I find this is the first and worst dishonesty of all. No wonder guilt has died out on the planet. You've all sold yourselves a wonderful bill of goods on your perfectly rotten, moral condition."

"Gosh, Eric," said Isletta. "He sounds like Jerry Falwell."

It suddenly became clear to the priest that while he was telling an important truth they were clearly not into it. So he reluctantly pulled back. "Isletta, do you have the deed to this meadow that has for so long blocked the Callahan deal?"

"Yes, yes, I have it with me. How did you know that?"

"I make it my business to keep fully in touch with whatever might become the upcoming will of God for the planet," offered the priest.

There was a bit of silence before the priest spoke again. "Well?"

"Well what?" asked Isletta, suddenly baffled at the direction the conversation was taking.

"Well, you are the Virgin of Stockholm! Didn't I make that clear to you?"

Eric burst out laughing. "You're the what?"

Isletta was now fully annoyed by both the priest's irritating arrogance and Eric's snide laughter.

"I am a virgin."

"Yeah, but from Stockholm!"

"I have Scandinavian roots. My ancestors were all from Stockholm."

Eric laughed again, this time doubling over.

Isletta spoke. "It's the Stockholm part that baffles me, not the virgin part. But I am. Tell him, Father."

Turning to Eric, he said, "Yes, she is. But she is more than that; she holds the deed to this meadow, which she is shortly to donate to the National Park Service."

"Do I have to?" she asked.

"You do indeed. You will bless your age with an understanding that God is the steward of all this world and that his children who worship him have taken too long to press their stewardship of Earth as far as they need to. Do you realize there are more than six billion people living on this planet and that there may be twelve billion in the next forty years? We must realize that all must live and let live. Do you realize that every year another twenty-four significant species of living things disappear from the face of the planet? All those lost plants and animals are nonrenewable. We are not talking about losing some species; we are talking about losing Earth itself. The Virgin of Stockholm can give us the proper answer. May I have the deed now, Isletta?"

Isletta rummaged through her rucksack until she drew it out. She looked at it a moment. "It belonged to my grandfather. He bought it when he first came to this country. Here," she said, extending the folded deed to him.

"No, Isletta, it's yours!" protested Eric.

"No, Eric, it's everybody's. It belongs to the planet. Father Peter is right! I've been out here in this meadow, camping out and holding on to this property. I've been holding out and leading all these Gaians in their worship. But I'm through with Gaia; the world belongs to all of us. It is God's gift to those who treasure it. Keeping Eden, preserving the world—that is a dimension of our faith that recognizes that God really does love the whole natural world."

Father Peter took the deed from her.

"I'm going to give this to Joanna Nickerson, Isletta," he offered. "She is going to announce the purpose of this grove to the whole world."

"It's all right with me. Everything is all right with me except for one thing. This Virgin of Stockholm thing—could you please just call me Isletta Borg? Drop the virgin bit, OK?"

"Okeydokey!" agreed the priest. It sounded so corny to both Isletta and Eric that they burst out laughing.

"One other thing," said Isletta when she had managed to get control of herself. "I won't be able to give the land anonymously since my name has been in the papers and the land itself has been publicized well as the thorn in Callahan's side. Still, I don't want any credit for the gift, so I'd like as little mention of it as possible."

"That's good. The other donor felt the same way," said the priest.

Isletta pondered what her bit of land and all of her life had meant. She knew that, somehow, her former religious confusion had just become organized around a strange new worldview.

"Don't be late for the rally tonight!" Father Peter instructed.

"I won't," she agreed.

CHAPTER 40

Late on Sunday afternoon the Shapiros set out to take a short hike. They huffed and puffed their way along the same uphill path they had taken the day before when Kinta got caught in the trap. Even though they feared more of the sniper fire they had encountered already, they believed that on Sunday afternoon there were so many people camping in the environs of the grove that they would be safe. Everywhere they walked, they were greeted by scores of other walkers.

It was because the Shapiros felt so nonchalant about their hike that Gary Jarvis took it so seriously. He felt a driven need to watch over the Shapiros. But his concern was more than a mere fixation. In spite of all that had happened, Gary believed that Rhonda underestimated the force of Levi's grudge—that Levi would stop at nothing until Rhonda and Kinta were dead. Because Gary had no idea where to look for Levi, he was following the Shapiros on their walk.

On this particular outing, Gary traveled far afield, watching the Shapiros quite closely from the perimeter of the meadow. He shuddered every time they moved over a stretch of bald, unprotected trail. He, on the other hand, took the more rigorous, slower route through the trees.

His Saturday-night marriage had delivered him into a blissful Sunday, but he would not risk the Shapiros' safety further. Melody would have liked him to stay home, but she had grown quite fond of Rhonda Shapiro, and Rhonda's safety was as important to her as it was to Gary. So on the first afternoon of their marriage, she kissed Gary good-bye at the flap of their tent and encouraged him to be as careful as he could be.

As the Shapiros moved higher up the trail, they were greeted by fewer hikers. The exercise and the sun warmed them. Both of them took off their jackets.

When they first started up the trail, Kinta and Daimon had played along at a comfortable distance ahead. But both of the big animals liked to run, and soon they were well ahead of the Shapiros. In fact, the two animals were out of view.

Over the past few weeks, Rhonda had noticed that with each successive day Kinta traveled further from the cabin. Each day seemed to lure the silver wolf to stay out longer than he had the day before. Daimon's entrance into his world only seemed to whet Kinta's wanderlust. Rhonda could see that Kinta, the beautiful animal that she had saved, was increasingly torn between his love for her and his love of freedom. She and Paul had talked about whether they should take him back to the suburbs of Seattle. They had both agreed that Kinta should make that choice himself. Day by day it was becoming clearer to them that Kinta, in his own way, was telling them what his choice was.

They were oddly pleased with his choice. He belonged to the wilderness. Freedom for Kinta could never be a can of Alpo or a veterinary tag jangling from a studded collar.

What baffled them as they walked along was how Kinta and Daimon had quickly arrived at a natural brotherhood of sorts. It was only the day before that Daimon had tried to kill Kinta. Now their hostile grudges had acquired a strange civility. Now they ran together in the sunlight. Levi Twist would have scarcely recognized the dog's demeanor. The renegade fugitive would want to get rid of Daimon. Just as he had always hunted Kinta, he might soon stalk Daimon with his scope and rifle.

Gary had dressed himself in greens and browns to avoid detection. He studied not only the Shapiros but also their animals. He was sure that if Levi Twist could be sniffed out ahead of time, the two animals were far more likely to accomplish that than he was. The question that still dogged Jarvis was if Daimon had happened into the rally site on his own or been sent by Levi. It was an important question. If Levi Twist had actually brought the dog to the camp, then he was bold enough to work near to the crowd. This would indicate he might actually seek some closer, unsuspected spot for a sniper's surveillance. The detective had turned those possibilities over and over in his mind. Still, he could see no logical place on the downhill side of the meadow where Twist could gain a sniper's advantage. The upper trees beyond the meadow were so full of campers that Levi, without a good disguise, would find no good place to hide. All of these things preoccupied Gary as he watched the unsuspecting Shapiros. They were totally unaware of his benevolent surveillance. He, like the God that the Shapiros had come to believe in, watched over them, eager to protect them from harm.

Gary used the binoculars at his waist to search every clump of trees that existed in the wake of their climb. Nowhere did he see any significant stand of natural cover that could hide a sniper. But he had worked for the SPD long enough to know that snipers were the hardest killers of all to spot. They camouflaged their clothes and faces with paint, so that their whereabouts were all but impossible to discover. Gary knew how to look for Levi; he just did not know where. After a half hour of scrutiny, he started to relax a bit, lulled by the beautiful day.

As he walked along, looking through binoculars at the area near the Shapiros, he nearly tripped over a tuft of weeds. In looking down at the tawny clump of weeds, he noticed that it was covered with flies. When he pulled the weeds back, he saw that the flies were after a large piece of meat that was rotting on the tongue of a steel trap. It was just like the trap that had caught Kinta the day before. The discovery caused him once again to remember how very close to danger the Shapiros really were. He jabbed a stick into the trap, and the steel jaws exploded upon the stick. The trap settled down into the dust it had stirred up. The flies once again settled down upon the stinking meat. Jarvis continued walking.

A new seriousness occupied him. He spotted Kinta and Daimon. Maybe they weren't just sniffing old game trails. They seemed to be moving faster, even running as they sniffed the earth. Jarvis found himself running, panicked. Suddenly he could find neither Kinta or Daimon.

He mentally noted where the Shapiros were: they were still highly visible—too highly visible. They laughed as they walked the well-worn trail to the higher meadows. They were too exposed. For the moment, however, his mind was on the strange behavior of the animals. He struggled to run through the trees while staying concealed. Finally, he ran out of trees. He had to cross the clearing that would bring him where he had last seen the two huge animals. Kinta and Daimon had entered a smaller cluster of large trees attended by some dense thickets of scrub oak. There the animals found the traveling much easier than he did.

Once he had regained the security of this natural cover, he again felt more concealed but was still unnerved by the rapid travel of the dogs. He had to stop for a moment—his lungs were bursting from his wild running and dodging through the brambles that cut at him and tore his ungloved hands. He could feel the comfort of his pistol under his arm, and yet he hoped there would be no need to use it.

He took out the binoculars again as he moved through yet another thicket. Again he stopped and studied the distant trees. They were not very tall but tall enough to conceal a sniper who would have the advantage of looking down on the trail up which the carefree Shapiros were advancing. He glanced at Paul and Rhonda for a moment. They still seemed oblivious.

He turned the binoculars on a smaller clump of trees to the right. He noticed a quail burst upward into flight and then saw Kinta and Daimon. They were crouching in the tall grass and had spooked the quail.

Suddenly a whole covey of quail burst into the sky, the collective rumble of their little wings sudden and loud. It would have jangled some hunters at that range, but Kinta and Daimon never flinched. Neither rose from their crouched positions. Suddenly Gary realized it was not the quail that had brought the animals into their crouched positions; they were tracking something else. And they were crawling—actually inching toward a small clump of trees not thirty yards in front of them. What was there? Not deer at this time of afternoon.

Onward the crouching animals moved. A sparrow darted across the indistinct darkness in a clutch of foliage. Gary's heart shot into his throat. There in the indistinct shadows was something geometric—a stick—a limb—no! It was the steel-blue barrel of a rifle almost parallel to the tree, almost not there. A portion of a shaded face was parallel to both the tree and the gun barrel. There was an eye also. It had to be Twist, hiding and waiting. He tried to imagine what Levi was seeing but could not. Was he watching the animals? Had the quail brought him to an alertness? Did he even know what he was watching?

Then the barrel leveled itself. Now Gary could see the rifle scope too. He tried to calculate the angle of the gun barrel. It was hard from his concealed viewing position. To get to Twist, Gary would have to cross the opening where the quail had emerged. In the dash he would be visible to both the Shapiros and the rifleman. He was in a quandary over whether to run in a serpentine flight to Twist's stakeout position. Scopes were usually not good for getting off shots at uncertain fields. So Gary's erratic running would likely bring him safely to the grove. He would, however, spook Levi, who also might run. He cautiously worked himself to a position behind a tree to the very edge of the grove. He drew his pistol and waited.

Apparently, Levi Twist had still not seen the animals. They were now within a few yards of Seattle's stalker. Jarvis watched, mesmerized as the animals drew closer and closer to the rifleman. When they were only a few feet from him, Levi's focus on the Shapiros was shattered. The gun barrel pivoted dramatically. Levi had obviously heard the rustling of the animals and wheeled in their direction.

When Gary saw that Levi was preoccupied with the animals, he began his mad dash toward the thicket. In thirty seconds, Gary entered the grove with his pistol extended, but he never had a chance to fire at the rifleman. As he leveled his pistol to pull the trigger, the animals attacked. Although both of the animals had their reasons to hate Levi Twist, it was Daimon who launched first.

The huge dog had not forgotten a single lesson he had learned from his abusive master. Levi got off but a single shot. The shot caught Daimon in midair, jolting him a bit to one side. But the bullet did not stop him. With full force, the German shepherd's huge jaws caught Levi's own throat. In an instant the serial killer was sprawled on his back as Daimon's jaws closed on the jugular side of Levi's neck. The flesh gave way as the dog's huge, drooling jaws whipped sideways, ripping off most of the flesh on that side of his neck. The exposed jugular was spurting blood like a crimson Vesuvius. Levi tried first to reach his hunting knife to stab at his wild assassin. Then he dropped the knife to use his bloody hands to compress the pumping veins. But even as he moved his hands to his throat, Daimon's savage jaws tore at his hands. Levi tried to stand and push the dog away but failed. He staggered upward, trying to stop the blood, but Daimon was on him at once. Again Levi sprawled in the dust, flat on his back. The savage teeth tore at his face and ripped through his scraggly beard, tearing off nearly half of Levi's face.

He tried a final time to rise, but he sunk down into the grass and finally lay still. Daimon looked at him. He circled him, snarling and growling. The Seattle killer was dead. His well-trained accomplice had rendered a kind of justice for the whole city of Seattle.

Gary could see that the one shot Levi had leveled at Daimon had caught the dog in the neck and upper chest. Daimon was bleeding badly. He could not last long. He circled his master's body, still snarling, until his own strength at last began to fail. The creeping darkness that Daimon had brought to five others now began to camp behind his own eyes. The dog could not see. He stumbled and fell. He tried to get up again and swaggered first against the tree, and then he fell crossways over Levi's silent body.

By this time the Shapiros, having heard the rifle shot and snarling, had dashed toward the thicket. They seemingly felt little fear. Had they known that the bullet that hit Daimon was really intended for them, they would have been more cautious as they entered the grove. They saw Daimon lay his head on the broad chest of his faithless master. He looked at them with his sad eyes and whimpered for help. He was dying. Kinta now moved up to Daimon and muzzled his body with his silver-black snout, but the wolf could not nudge the dog back to life.

"How horrible!" said Rhonda, seeing the ripped neck and face of Levi Twist. "How utterly horrible!" She grimaced and turned her face away.

"Seattle's reign of terror is over," Gary offered.

Suddenly Paul Shapiro looked at Gary Jarvis, reached out his hand, and said, simply, "Thanks for looking out for us!"

"It's what I do," Jarvis replied. "Don't mention it."

Rhonda knelt in the grass and pulled Kinta away from his attempt to raise Daimon back to life. Rhonda knew they were both dead: her one-time assailant and his malevolent brute.

When they had all three stared overlong at the corpse and the dog, Paul Shapiro finally asked, "Shall I go back to the cabin and get the shovel to bury Daimon?"

"Better not," Gary said. "He'll need to be autopsied. I'll call the SPD chopper and have them pick up both Levi and the animal. I'll ask the police to approach this site from the top of the mountain. I doubt if the people gathering for tonight's rally will know they've been on this mountain. Paul, can I use your jacket to mark this tree?"

Paul quickly relinquished his red jacket, handing it to Gary, who tied it to a tree. "The chopper should be here within the hour," Gary said.

On their way down the mountain, Kinta seemed reluctant to follow them. "Come on, Kinta. Come on, boy!" Rhonda tried in vain to get him to follow. He would not.

She approached him on the trail and held his great head in her hands. She knew what he wanted her to say. She caressed his head for a final time. He was a fugitive from a wild and beautiful world. He wanted to return. He had once saved her from Levi Twist. For the oddest of reasons, her own marriage had begun to heal the very day that the wolf had come into her life. But now she saw the truth. Her marriage had not healed because Kinta had come into their lives but because God, who created Kinta and all things wonderful, had come into her life.

She looked into those steel-gray eyes. "Who are you, Kinta?" she asked.

He stared back blindly, blinking into her stare with a powerful innocence. She had often experienced such innocence in Kinta.

"Who are you?" she stopped. "For that matter, who am I; who are any of us? We are all creatures of a loving Maker who has made a world where we are free to be either saints or villains, worshippers of life or empty souls, lovers of good or pointless strugglers. Kinta, you taught me how to see again."

By this time, Paul had come up to the pair. Paul knelt down by Kinta and Rhonda. He reached his hand out to pet Kinta. He noticed the hair rise on Kinta's neck. The brute's eyes that had been so kind to Rhonda seemed to stare savagely at him. There was just a hint of a gurgle in the beast's throat.

Paul withdrew his hand.

"He's not a pet, you know," said Rhonda.

Paul had first told Rhonda that she was too playful with this animal who might destroy her. More than that, they had always known that Kinta was Rhonda's friend more than Paul's. For the moment, he was glad that it was so. He withdrew his hand.

"Go, Kinta!" said Rhonda, feeling a bit foolish that she had tried to hold on to him for so long. It was all the permission that the wolf needed. He stood and circled Rhonda. She patted him on the head. He whimpered as though he was open to being talked out of leaving. Still, he was really begging for his freedom. He needed only a single syllable of permission.

"Go!" she repeated.

He circled her one more time and then took off up the hill, running with such giant strides that he seemed to fly in the air above his long shadow cast by the afternoon sun. Was he running or flying? His exultation seemed to take wing, and the sky at the bottom of the horizon swallowed him whole.

He was gone.

Rhonda was sure they would never see him again. But Kinta's brief sojourn in their lives was not a final chapter for either of them.

Paul Shapiro studied the distant purple mountains as they engulfed his friend. It was to Kinta and the hills that Paul whispered his benediction: "I will lift up my eyes unto the hills from whence cometh my help."

Kinta, like themselves, had come from the Maker of all things bright and beautiful, all things wise and wonderful.

Kinta was the untamable symbol of power and peace sent to touch their lives with grace that saved everything about to be cast away.

"Maybe," said Rhonda, "here and there, heaven touches Earth with miracles that are so ordinary that we might miss them unless our eyes are hungry to see how things really are. Do you know that out here I have actually awakened on nights, thinking I heard anthems being sung by the stars? It was all an illusion, I know, but sometimes illusions border on majesty."

They were quiet for a moment, and in the distance, they heard the clarion notes of a howl, not threatening but subtly floating on the wind. "It's Kinta," Rhonda offered.

Paul took Rhonda's hand and kissed her. They weren't sure, but they thought that they heard the wolf howl once again, even as they kissed. But if so, it was the last time.

It was enough.

CHAPTER 41

Just before dusk, two helicopters approached the Callahan Grove. The one that came over the hill from the upper meadows settled unseen. It was met by Gary Jarvis, who watched as its crew loaded the carcasses of a man and a dog. Gary scratched some final notes on a clipboard and gave it to a fellow officer. The rotor revved, and the helicopter vibrated upward into a pale blue sky with yellow-tipped cirrus clouds that promised a beautiful sunset. Gary watched the helicopter pass back over the brink of the hill and disappear over the dark horizon to the east. The darkening skies made the helicopter's lights shine like stars in some new constellation. When he could no longer see the helicopter, Gary began walking back to the meadow on the front side of the mountain where the rally fires were already beginning to blaze.

The second helicopter landed on the front side of the mountain in the Borg meadow. The craft was marked with the seal of the vice president of the United States. His sudden appearance caused a rallying shout of exultant support.

He was met under the dust-swirling rotors by none other than George Callahan. The two of them stood only an instant under the rotor before the helicopter lifted off.

Most people wondered just what Callahan and the vice president were talking about. What they couldn't hear them saying was this: "Now Bert, just because you've written a best-seller on ecology, I'm not going to stand still while you proclaim my trees some kind of wilderness memorial or national park, boy!"

"You know, Callahan," said the vice president, "I don't want to play hardball with you, but we're not going to let Isletta Borg's 10,000 acres get away from all they've come to symbolize. Her acres are nothing compared to your 40,000 acres, except that hers stand for all that's most beautiful in a chain-saw world. Reverend Nickerson just wants you to know that we're going to honor Isletta's desire to give the trees to the National Park Service. Giving another 10,000 acres of your own to the state would be the best way for you to come out smelling like a rose."

"Well, what about Pacific Woods?" asked Callahan. "They're not going to take this lying down. You can't expect the lumbering industry to get busted in the chops and come up smiling."

"They'll get over it. Besides, what's 10,000 measly acres of timber when you consider the 30,000 acres of timber they're still getting?"

"Unacceptable—my trees are all my trees!" shouted Callahan. "I can dispose of them anyway I want to!"

"That may be," said the vice president, "but Eric Compton, this fancy-pants lawyer, has you over a barrel. Isletta Borg didn't budge on this, and Seattle loves her for her generosity. You know it, George. Eric Compton made a powerful case for Pacific Woods and still spoke to the delight of all but the most radical of the environmental groups. I can tell you, he'll win again, and it won't be a Callahan victory this time. Go ahead and match Isletta Borg's gift. It'll warm the cockles of your black, stingy heart.

"Isletta Borg is seen all across the nation as the poor little woman whose inheritance you guys wanted to turn into sawdust. It's not going to sell here, and it won't sell in D.C. The chief thinks that you ought to march up to that microphone tonight and give some of your own trees to become a part of the Callahan National Refuge. Actually, Callahan, I'd like to introduce you to the group tonight, so that when those cameras start popping, you will come off decent enough to win the next election. And if you don't, you're in deep."

Callahan had known from the moment he ordered the portable toilets and the water trucks that nothing so simple was going to appease the environmentalists. He knew that anything he did do to make money would be conceived as greed. "These environmental bloodsuckers are stealing millions of dollars from me and all for the sake of a few acres of trees."

"Possibly, George," said the vice president. "But if you come across as someone who doesn't care, you will find your reputation so worthless that you'll face a string of boycotts on all your operations. I think the Callahan Grove is about to become a national monument, given by the hero of the Northwest, that great lover of nature—that whole-earth, man-of-the-year George Callahan.

"You're the man of the hour, Mr. Callahan," laughed the vice president. "You know, Georgie, if God loves a cheerful giver, I can only guess what he must think of you right now."

Callahan didn't even smile.

"Well, George, when I introduce you tonight, what are you going to say?"

"I'm gonna tell these sorry tree huggers how wonderful they are and that because they mean so much to ecology and the state, I'm going to give them 10,000 acres of my good board timber."

"And they are going to love you for it," said the vice president. "In fact, they will probably erect a statue of you feeding Bambi and Thumper. You'll make us all real proud. Maybe you'll get to star in your own Disney movie. They may soon forget what a corrupt politician you really are."

The clouds were turning purple when a band got on stage and began playing "Happy Days Are Here Again." Tom Dallas, a Seattle folk singer and the emcee for the evening, then introduced the vice president.

"Ladies and gentlemen," the VP began. The crowd broke into applause. The huge speaker boxes, powered by a distant gasoline generator, heaved official Washington greetings at the crowd. "As your vice president, it's an honor to see such massive support in favor of both using and saving this wonderful wilderness. The lumber industry is moving once again. Many of you are going back to work." The crowd cheered. "But thanks to Isletta Borg, 10,000 acres of the most beautiful timber will be forever preserved by the National Park Service."

The crowd broke into wild cheers.

"Ladies and gentlemen, I've just been given the most wonderful piece of news by George Callahan. But then, you know George; he's all heart. But he's also one of the shyest men you'll ever meet. George, come on up here. I want you to tell all these beautiful people what you've just told me."

Callahan's feet were like lead as he approached the makeshift platform. He almost stumbled as he mounted the crude wooden steps.

"Here he is, ladies and gentlemen, George Callahan—the most generous benefactor this state and this great country have ever had."

The vice president's exuberance stood out in sharp contradiction to things as they really were. Callahan was pale and quiet. "Well," he stammered, "I've always loved the good God of nature, and it richly pleases me to be able to say to you that I want to see that 10,000 acres of my own trees are also safe . . . forever, safe. I want to donate 10,000 acres of the Callahan Grove to the State of Washington to be used as a national preserve, forever protecting the national resources of America. Like Isletta Borg, I want some of my trees to both serve humankind and inspire them."

The entire crowd cheered once again. The amber light of the fires was now briskly visible in the darkening night. The purple sky had run out of blue, and the ultraviolet colors were lacing themselves among the stars.

The emcee took the microphone, and Callahan walked away from his victorious presentation in a very unvictorious manner. "Ladies and gentlemen, the gracious woman who owns this very meadow and some of the trees that join the main grove also has a little presentation to make. Let's all say a big Washington howdy to Ms. Isletta Borg."

Once again there was applause and cheering as Isletta took the microphone. "Hello," said Isletta, amazed at the power her voice had picked up just by talking through the microphone. "This meadow where we are standing right now was an inheritance I received from my Swedish grandfather. I want to give these trees for the very same reasons Mr. Callahan has so eloquently stated."

She spoke briefly, calling for a new wave of concern about the world's resources. To model this concern, a small church would stand in front of the titan trees of the Callahan Grove. She told the vast multicultural crowd that she was a Christian, and she wanted to live to see that the environmental sins of all humankind did not make moonscapes out of God's beautiful world.

Isletta then turned the microphone over to Reverend Joanna Nickerson.

"Hello, brothers and sisters," said Joanna. "It's taken the good Lord a long time to get it through this thick head of mine, but he does love the world of nature. One day, God just spun me around and told me, 'Now you listen to me, Sister Nickerson. I love this beautiful world I made, and I got nobody to care for it if folks like you don't.' Well, I knew that I'd lived for more than forty years, and I just keep taking all the good things that the earth gave me, and I never give much back to it.

"We take a lot from God's world. When God created Eden, he placed man and woman in that garden to tend and to keep it. He asked us to take care of his Earth, not to take from it continually and never give anything back to it. There are thousands of us here tonight, and we have brought with us, on our backs, 20,000 miniature Douglas firs—little trees eager to grow to become the forest of 2050, which will one day stand as tall as the forest of 2006, which must soon fall to provide the much-needed lumber for the world at hand.

"Tonight I want all of us—environmentalists and businessmen alike—to realize just how much God has to say in the Good Book about his world," she said.

Joanna paused. "Tonight we're going to cut the first of the trees to fall. When the tree lies horizontal, it will point to the world of men whom God loves. Do not grieve the fall of this one great tree. Out of its fall will grow homes and a living for many of you here. But we're also going to celebrate the trees that continue pointing upward to God. Their vertical witness shall point to him from whom all the world came."

The Reverend Joanna paused and closed her eyes. "Why the great Lord God says he made it all—that in the beginning, God created the heaven and the earth. And that in this great universe, 'He spreads out the northern skies over empty space; he suspends the earth over nothing' (Job 26:7). Look up into those night skies. How true it is that the heavens declare the glory of God! But folks, his thunder roars loudest not over galaxies; his greatest celebrations are for the wee little things that he made. How sinful it is for us to abuse the little creatures that God made and stalk them until they pass out of existence forever. You see, brothers and sisters, God sings in the cries of hawks and the wails of owls. He cries even in the great monsters of the deep, the whales that sing in the fogbound seas of this world. He cries out in the great Leviathans whom he has made so the oceans will never be lonely. Consider his vastness and unspeakable splendor.

"And into this unspeakable splendor is born God's love for all that he has made—the big things, the little things, the unspeakably glorious creatures that make this poor world rich. 'Are not two sparrows sold for a penny? Yet not one of them will fall to the ground apart from the will of your Father. And even the very hairs of your head are all numbered. So don't be afraid; you are worth more than many sparrows' (Matthew 10:29–31). Why, he's got the little bitty sparrow in his hand."

Suddenly Joanna's rich voice broke into singing: "He's got the whole world in his hand. He's got the whole world in his hand. He's got the whole world in his hand. He's got the whole world in his hand."

Joanna closed her eyes and lifted her arms toward heaven. Someone began to accompany her on guitar. It was gently theatrical and beautiful, and she once again began to sing.

"He's got the little, tiny sparrow in his hand. He's got the little, tiny sparrow in his hand. He's got the little, tiny sparrow in his hand. He's got the whole world in his hand."

Joanna stopped. The guitarist played only a moment or two before he quit. The fires crackled. The gasoline-generated spotlight was etched with silvery white night vapors.

Gradually the spotlight died. As it did, a brighter and more powerful beam settled down in a column that held Joanna Nickerson at its core. She was visible through the transparent column of light. Her beautiful bronze face looked metallic. The odd, blue shaft of illumination bore a gorgeous contrast to the amber bonfires that ringed the campsite. The enveloping column of light was so bright some actually shielded their eyes against it.

A photographer was standing near the rim of the camp and focused on the amber fire and the blue column. There seemed to be an army of old men in blue coveralls. The flashless camera clicked. What the photographer did not notice until the film developed was that all about the old ones, standing in and out of the shadows, were animals. It was unthinkable that they would be there, but they were there. Some were so small as to be unrecognizable in the rather large and distant photograph. One animal that was easy to see was a huge silver wolf, standing in the center of the photograph near the front of the circle.

All who beheld the breathtaking spectacle now heard only one voice issue from the center of the light column. The single cry of Joanna Nickerson moved from that great light into the darkness: "Inherit the Earth!"

The crowd began to move away.

Two things survived their leaving: a better world and a photograph. The message from the column of light over a dramatic photograph covered most of the front page of the paper in Seattle and, for that matter, every paper in the nation.

There were other pictures of Callahan as well as three more of Isletta and Joanna. There were pictures of the vice president and various crowd shots.

What did not get much space in the paper was the good news that Levi Twist, the vicious serial killer of the Northwest, was dead and that the city could once again sleep in peace. Perhaps only the best part of truly great news is all that can be absorbed in a short time. Perhaps at the end of the celebration there was only one great message that could hold a real place in humanity's hope. It was the voice of the pilgrims who formed the core of Joanna's Exodus crying, "INHERIT THE EARTH!"

EPILOGUE

A group of old friends were gathered in the Shapiros' rustic cabin.

"Human visions come and go, and we are rarely sure of what it was that we saw in the darkness," said Isletta, being more dramatic than she really needed to be. "Was it really a year ago?" she asked.

"A year, indeed, Isletta," said Rhonda, looking down at the baby who had fallen asleep on her lap. Rhonda smiled. So did Paul and Eric, and so did Gary and Melody Jarvis. The only one who didn't smile was Joanna Nickerson. She was serious.

"You know," offered Joanna, "I haven't had any of those weird dreams I used to have. I'm sleeping soundly, but sometimes I wonder just how much of the glory of those days was real and how much we manufactured. But isn't it odd that for one wonderful season of our lives we came together and our souls were somehow healed in their presence?"

"It was wonderful!" said Melody Jarvis.

They all agreed.

"You know," said Paul Shapiro, "I think we will all look back on Joanna's Exodus as the beginning of the day that all people began to deal with the survival of the planet. I think it will be little people like us who make it happen, if it happens. What was born last summer was an understanding that Earth is the final address of every last person. It's not like we can move somewhere else if our current galactic address doesn't work out."

"You know what I can't put together?" asked Gary Jarvis, completely changing the subject. "Was how Kinta and Levi Twist got mixed into this Exodus business. How odd that some in Seattle had to be stalked by the night fiend and were destined to die. Why did all this evil have to tarnish all the wonderful things that were happening in our world?"

Nobody answered his question. Finally, Gary's eyes met Joanna's eyes and locked onto them. She knew that she had to try and answer.

"Well, Mr. Jarvis," she began, "in the book of Job it says that when the 'sons of God came into his presence, that evil came in with them.' Levi Twist was no accidental player in this drama of things. He corrupted, killed, and laid waste the world with hate and death. But God is always redeeming things, making all things new."

People were beginning to comment on Joanna's remark when Melody Jarvis broke into the conversation: "Shh, Gary! Listen, everyone," she counseled. She heard something that the rest of them had not.

They all grew quiet at her rebuke. Even the Shapiro baby seemed to be very quiet. Then they all heard what Melody had heard. They heard the baying of a wolf. It sounded far away at first, but the more they listened, the closer it seemed. Finally it sounded like it was right at hand, perhaps only a few yards from the house.

"Maybe if we're all very quiet . . ." Isletta said, moving toward the door.

Everyone shuffled to the door as Paul turned off the lights and opened it. They stared out into the darkness, finally spying a pair of steely blue eyes. "It is Kinta!" breathed Rhonda. It was the first time she had seen him since the day of the rally one year before.

The woods seemed suddenly filled with old ghosts of past glory. The great trees of the Callahan Grove seemed alive with voices. They felt the force and power of all living things.

"Kinta!" called Rhonda into the darkness.

The great wolf looked at her, but he did not come.

"Kinta!" Rhonda said one final time. The wolf looked away. A tall man stepped out of the trees. He was gracefully angular and quite tall.

"Father Peter?"

The man did not reply.

He walked to the wolf, squatted down before him, and looked into his eyes for a long time. Then the wolf rose from his haunches as the old man stood. They walked into the trees and were gone.

"Kinta!" Rhonda Shapiro shouted into the darkness. Her eyes glistened with the mystery of a curtain falling on the haunting pageant. There was a long silence. "KINTA!" she called one final time, "INHERIT THE EARTH!"